The Awakening
of
Claudia Faraday

Patsy Trench

A Roaring Twenties novel

Prefab Publications

Published in 2019
by Prefab Publications, London

ISBN 978-0-9934537-3-1

'She had the oddest sense of being herself
invisible . . . there being no more marrying, no
more having of children now, but . . . this being
Mrs. Dalloway, not even Clarissa any more; this
being Mrs. Richard Dalloway.'

Virginia Woolf, *Mrs Dalloway*

§

'I never travel without my diary. One
should always have something sensational
to read in the train.'

Oscar Wilde, *The Importance of Being Earnest*

Claudia's diary

Author's note

It began with a visit from Claudia's great granddaughter. She'd heard from a mutual friend that I was a writer and there was this diary she'd come across in the attic of the family home she was clearing. She wondered, would I mind giving it a quick look and telling her if I thought it might be publishable? It would mean changing all the names of course, she explained breathlessly as she thrust the linen bag into my hands, including hers, because there were reputations to be protected, and well, you know.

I was intrigued enough to start reading the diary right away, and I have to say that once I'd got used to the quirky handwriting and the opaque references to things inexpressible I became so absorbed I could barely put it down. It took some editing to create a proper narrative and to clarify episodes that were, shall we say, hinted at rather than openly described. The 'inciting incident' that set off the chain of Claudia's adventures is a case in point. There is no way of knowing exactly what happened that night in Claudia's bedroom, so I have made a guess, however unlikely it may seem, based on what happened subsequently.

So here it is: all names changed as promised to Claudia's great granddaughter, who remains anonymous of course. I have done my best to stay true to the Claudia who emerged from the diary, and to the accompanying photograph of her as a mature woman: elegant, beautiful, a little remote, smiling shyly at the camera.

Here and there, for fun, and by way of adding an extra touch of period flavour to the piece I have embedded references to books, films, plays and people from the 1920s. Kudos to you if you can spot them. (Answers on my website at patsytrench.com)

Patsy Trench
London 2019

1

England, the Home Counties, 1920s

It was strange how enormous the house seemed now there was no one in it.

When the girls were around the place felt like an overstuffed cubby hole. It was impossible to move from one room to another without tripping over something – an object, a human being, someone's dog – and there never seemed to be the smallest corner where a person could be quietly on her own. But now, as Claudia wandered from room to room, several times within the last hour, all she could hear was the sound of her heels clacking on the floorboards and bouncing back at her off the walls as if to remind her, as her friend Prudence had put it, 'How clever you are, managing to get rid of three girls in less than a year.'

The other day she had spent the best part of an hour walking up and down the wooden staircase. It had occurred to her, the second time she had made the journey, that despite placing the same feet on the precise same spot on each step – setting off on her left foot because, as she had only recently discovered, she was left-footed – the boards creaked differently each time, and sometimes not at all. And it seemed to make no difference whether she stepped lightly or heavily, the nature and volume of the creak, if there was one, was never quite the same. This harmless, if pointless experiment had absorbed her to such a degree it was only the sound of the clock striking noon that had restored her to her senses.

Only this afternoon she had gone upstairs to fetch something from her bedroom and, having forgotten what it was, had sat down on her bed for a moment and drifted right off to sleep. The next thing she knew it was an hour and a half later and Lily was tapping at her door.

'There's a gentleman to see you, madam,' said she.

'A gentleman? What kind of gentleman? Am I expecting someone?'

'A young gentleman,' said Lily. 'He says he's a friend of your husband's.'

'Oh. Then tell him I'll be down directly.'

This was, needless to say, unexpected, not to say unprecedented. In normal circumstances there was no reason why a woman like Claudia should feel in the least obliged to interrupt her daily routine in order to entertain a total stranger who, for whatever reason, lacked the grace to wait to be invited, or indeed to have written to announce his intended visit beforehand. But, she reminded herself, normal circumstances were not what they were; and so she rose quickly from her bed, slipped on her shoes and checked her appearance briefly in the mirror of her dressing table, before presenting herself to the young man in the drawing room on the ground floor.

'Mrs Faraday.' He turned from the window out of which he had been gazing and stretched out a hand. 'Apologies for the lack of protocol, but I found myself with an unexpected afternoon free, so I thought – Why not jump on a train and pay a call on Mrs Faraday, as promised.'

'Do you have a name?' asked Claudia, receiving the hand, tentatively.

'Gabriel Carter.'

He was an odd-looking young man and he did not sound in the least apologetic. He was tall and thin and had a mop of unruly light brown hair that had constantly to be pushed, or tossed, out of the way of his eyes; which were, Claudia observed, an unusual light green and remarkably penetrating.

'As promised to whom?' she enquired.

'To your husband, of course.' He tilted his head at her in a way that was almost coquettish, and Claudia smiled despite herself.

'Well, now that you're here, perhaps some tea?'

'Splendid.'

So Claudia rang for tea, and as they sat together, the young man and the middle-aged woman, in the fading light of an early autumn day, she asked the stranger how he came to be acquainted with her husband.

'I was working with him,' he said. 'In Africa. A great privilege.'

'And what part of Africa would that be?'

'Tanganyika, the Olduvai Gorge, you may have heard of it.'

Claudia nodded vaguely. 'How is he?'

'Excellent. Yes. You've not heard from him recently? No, he did confess as much. He gets very caught up with his work, very dedicated. Single-minded, you could say.'

'He only made it to one of the three weddings,' said Claudia.

'Three weddings?'

'Three daughters, three weddings, within a few months of each other. He made it to one but was unable to stay for the others.'

'I see.'

'And what exactly did he confess?' said Claudia, trying to keep the archness from her voice.

'Confess?'

'"He did confess as much." Your words.'

'Ah. He confessed he had a family.'

'"Confessed he had a family"?' Claudia's eyebrows lifted imperceptibly. 'And did he talk much about his family?'

'I believe he said he'd been over, yes, he'd been over for a wedding earlier in the year, though he didn't mention a daughter. A family wedding I gather, I didn't really ask.' He flashed her a disarming smile. 'But I did promise to call in on you,' he went on. 'To give you news of him.'

'Ah, not to see how I was.'

'I beg your pardon?'

'Never mind,' said Claudia. She gave a small sigh.

'I'm tiring you. Would you like me to go?'

'You might as well stay for supper,' she found herself saying.

'That's very kind of you,' said the young man. 'I accept.'

So he stayed for supper, and they spent the evening talking about Africa, and what it was like living in the wilds, far from civilisation. He described to Claudia in vivid detail the process and the aims of working on an archaeological dig and the excitement of new discoveries – or revelations, as he called them – that stood to alter one's entire perceptions and understanding of ancient history; and above all to be working alongside a man of such inspirational spirit, such *insight*. He told the story of the day they came across a piece of blackened rock, no bigger than a child's fist, which no one but the master thought to be of significance. So while the rest of the party slept, the master worked through the night, by the light of a failing torch, until his fingers were bleeding, and by dawn he had uncovered a portion of the skull of what some time later proved to be *Homo Habilis.* And while to some extent Claudia had heard it all before – indeed she had herself many years ago witnessed what it was like living under canvas, in the middle of nowhere – such was the young man's passion and eloquence she felt she was hearing it for the first time.

'So,' he said finally, and fell silent. A moment passed and then he added, 'And what about you?'

'Me? What about me?'

'It can't be a lot of fun, here at home, a woman on her own, no husband.'

He was watching her out of the corner of his eye. She was not disposed to rise to the comment so she said something to the effect that she managed quite well, thank you, as did many other women with absentee husbands.

She wondered what her husband Gerald had made of this forthright, enthusiastic and forward young man, at which point a startling thought came into her head and she said, 'Did my husband send you on a mission perhaps? To spy on me? See what I get up to while the cat's away?'

'Spy on you? Gracious.' He pretended to look shocked for a moment. 'What an intriguing thought. So I must unearth your secrets.'

She was about to tell him that would take no time at all, but deciding a little mystery would do no harm she gave him her best Giaconda smile before realising, to her simultaneous alarm and amusement, that he might think she was flirting with him. So by way of a change of subject she asked her visitor where his adventures were to take him next, at which point the conversation took an unexpected turn.

'India,' was his instant and emphatic reply, and in particular a temple in a place whose name Claudia could not quite catch; where, he explained, were to be found sculptures representing the Hindu 'Four Truths', among which is Kama, or Desire. He had a specific interest in a set of erotic sculptures which were believed to date back to the eleventh century and which contained, in addition to representations of homosexuality and hermaphroditism, images of self-pleasuring, both male and female.

'Self . . . ? Oh!' said Claudia, in such a way, she later realised, that might have given the (mistaken) impression she wanted to hear more. So the young man hurtled on, relating what he knew of the culture of sexual congress through history and at what point it was believed that women, as well as men, had discovered the delights of self-pleasuring. It was his view that the ancients, in this respect at least, were ahead of their time – you only had to look at the Romans and the Greeks – indeed, ahead of *our* time. Imagine attempting to display such artefacts in modern society!

Quite what all this had to do with archaeology was unclear, and so Claudia sat, silent and perfectly still, until the clock struck ten; at which point the young man at last drew breath and said, 'It's ten o'clock, I must be on my way.'

'Where do you have to get to?' Claudia asked.

'London.'

'Well, you've missed the last train.'

'Really?' he exclaimed.

'You will have to stay the night.'

'Ah,' he said. Then, 'How kind.'

'Not at all.' Claudia rang for Lily and asked her to prepare Flora's room, because her guest was compelled to stay overnight.

'This was not intended,' he said, unnecessarily.

'It's been a most interesting evening,' said Claudia. 'And enlightening too. This Mr Faraday you have been describing, he sounds fascinating, I would so love to meet him.' She smiled. 'Sometimes one discovers more about one's nearest and dearest through – well, in this case through a total stranger.'

'Indeed.'

'Lily will show you where to go,' said Claudia, as she rose to her feet. 'I hope you sleep well.'

'I always sleep well,' said the confident young man, and gave her a little bow.

~

What happened later on that same night is a matter on which Claudia would ponder for some time to come.

It's true she was glad to have Flora's room occupied again, albeit by a stranger. It had been a month since her youngest daughter had married her Spanish husband, and brought to an end the ceaseless bustle of preparation and panic that inevitably accompanies the planning of weddings. But later, Claudia would wonder whether she had appeared a little too eager, too ready to invite a stranger to stay the night, especially in mind of the evening's conversation. Had the young visitor misinterpreted her intentions? A man and a woman alone in a house together, why, what would her friends have made of that? What would Gerald have said? It was not like Claudia, not at all, to show unnecessary encouragement. Was it?

Yet how else to explain why the young man felt he had the right – or more to the point, *permission* – to enter her bedroom, late at night, for the purposes of . . . For the purposes of something she couldn't quite bring herself to articulate, even to herself. That it had to do with their previous conversation, that much she acknowledged, but had her unfamiliarity with the notion of 'self-pleasuring' been quite so obvious? And even if it were, had she given the *slightest* indication that she had wished him to come to her bedroom for the purpose of what one might term a tutorial on 'Nature's miracle', as he had described it?

At the same time she had to admit there had been plenty of opportunity for *dis*couragement; not for one moment did she feel she had been, shall we say, taken advantage of. On the contrary one could argue she had colluded in the whole business.

It was a big puzzle. All Claudia knew for certain was that life would never be quite the same after the young man came to visit.

She only had herself to blame.

2

'How did you sleep?'

It was breakfast-time the following morning and he was up before her.

'Extremely well,' she replied. 'You?'

'Like a log.'

She had delayed coming down out of embarrassment, and uncertainty. Nothing in her experience had offered any hint as to how one should behave in such circumstances. Should she appear aloof, or friendly? As if nothing had happened?

In the event it was he who set the tone.

'I'm helping myself, I hope you don't mind. Lily told me I might.'

'Of course.'

In the event it seemed he was more interested in the breakfast than . . .

'Are these your eggs?' His left hand held aloft the lid of the porcelain dish and his concentration seemed to be focused wholly upon the contents.

'No, I don't keep hens,' she said. 'But they are fresh.'

'They look delicious,' said the young man, digging in. 'What a treat.'

And so breakfast took place, as it might well have been taking place in a thousand dining rooms in a thousand homes throughout the country: quietly, politely, with minimal conversation – at least he had the wit not to try to engage her in small talk, or any other talk for that matter – with little sound other than the clink of cup upon saucer, the scrape of knife upon plate, and a 'Do you take sugar, Mr Carter?' and 'Just the one, thank you Mrs Faraday', as if nothing at all unusual had taken place.

If it had been a dream, which was the most likely explanation, why then did everything appear so vivid? The folds on the curtain pelmet, the twirls on the ceiling cornice, the shadow on the edges of the leaves of the Virginia creeper that framed the window. It was as if she had suddenly been granted perfect vision. Enhanced vision even.

Every tiny movement, of her knife and fork, the lifting of her cup, things she did every day, several times every day, why did it suddenly feel as if she'd never done these things before? As she gently pushed her empty plate away from her and folded her hands beneath her chin, she felt like an actress in a play, observed by a hundred hidden eyes, which was nonsensical as the young man's attention was still upon his plate (which he had piled high). Then when he was done, his plate wiped clean, his coffee drunk, not till then did he look up at her and smile genially and say, 'That was delicious. I don't remember when I last tasted such a splendid scrambled egg.'

But then how could she have dreamt about something of which she had no previous knowledge?

She cleared her throat delicately. 'Have you had enough?'

Suddenly the world was full of *doubles entendres*, and the hot flushes she thought were in the past came flooding over her again.

'I should say so,' he said, tapping his stomach. 'I thought I might catch the 11.15. Lily tells me there is a train at that time.'

'There is, yes.' Claudia blinked, startled. Should she ask him to stay on? Whatever for? 'You don't have to rush off,' she said.

'I've encroached upon you enough as it is.' Then he looked at her quizzically and added, 'I trust I did not offend.'

She wanted to laugh at the word but instead she replied, truthfully, 'Not in the least.'

'Good,' he said. And he gave her a cock-eyed wink that made her laugh.

It had not been a dream.

~

Earlier that morning, before she had made her cautious appearance at the breakfast table, she had done something she'd never done before. As she'd completed her *toilette* she had caught sight of herself, naked, in the bathroom mirror. Normally she would have shied away in embarrassment, as if the mirror itself were a Peeping Tom, but this time she allowed herself to linger and to look – not quite head on but obliquely. Her breasts were not large but they were quite firm and had not yet begun what all ladies of a certain age are led to believe is that unavoidable voyage downwards. She gazed at herself quite dispassionately, and as she did so she was conscious of the fact that the only naked human bodies she had ever seen had been in a museum – the Victoria & Albert or the British – petrified in stone or marble. And that even the most accomplished sculptor could not begin to replicate the texture of human flesh.

She marvelled at the symmetry of the two perfect orbs (were they perfect, what did she have to compare them with?), and she was tempted to touch them; and so she did, tentatively, as if they were not quite her property, and was surprised to find them soft, and pliable, and she was even more surprised as she ran her hands gently over her nipples to see them rise in response. What could that mean?

~

He left just before eleven, on foot, with a jaunty tilt of his hat and a playful salute. Claudia stood on the doorstep to see him off and then remained outside for some time.

The thought of the empty house oppressed her. As she wandered across the all so familiar lawn, down the few steps to the fountain and round it to the wood beyond she realised, to her shame, she did not know the names of the trees. Apart from the willow, and the monkey puzzle, they'd all seemed rather alike to her: some small, some large, with indeterminate leaves, some of which dropped off in winter and some of which did not. Gracious me she'd lived here for – how many years? – so long she no longer saw things. She made a mental note to have a word with the gardener, Sellors, next time she came across him.

As for the young visitor, he had left without so much as a 'See you again'. She'd watched him saunter off down the drive, whistling, hands in pockets, eyes fixed to the ground – typical of an archaeologist, just like Gerald, always on the lookout for treasures beneath his feet – glancing back and waving cheerily as he turned the corner. She wondered if Gerald remembered him and whether or not she should tell her husband his protégé had paid a surprise visit. Perhaps not. Especially not, it occurred to her, as try as she might she could not recall the young protégé's name.

3

It was a day or two later that Claudia embarked upon her fact-finding mission into the wonders of the natural world.

She had never properly explored the wood before. Yes, she had taken the occasional stroll through parts of it, particularly on a warm day. But like so much of the rest of her life it was a fixture, as was the garden itself, something she gave very little thought to and rarely truly looked at. Now as she stood in the heart of it, the gardener Sellors by her side, she wondered at the size of it, and the density.

'This'd be one of the oldest woods in this part of the country,' said Sellors.

'Truly?' said Claudia. 'How old, do you suppose?'

'Parts of her over five hundred years old, at a guess.'

'How can you tell?'

'By the size of the tree. The bark, the shape of her. This one for instance.'

He went to stand beneath the largest tree of all and gazed up into its branches. Then he leant forwards and rested the palms of his hands flat against its trunk. 'Here.' He beckoned her over with a jerk of his head. 'Place your hands here.'

With some hesitation Claudia moved towards the great tree and placed her gloved hands upon it.

'Can you feel it? Can you feel her pulse?'

'Her pulse?'

'Take your gloves off, you'll not feel her properly through them.'

Well, that was a bit abrupt. But it would be churlish to refuse, so with careful deliberation Claudia peeled off her gloves and tucked them into her pocket, before extending both hands again and placing them against the trunk of the great tree.

'How does she feel?'

'She feels . . .' In all honesty she – it – felt like what it was, the gnarled trunk of an ancient tree, no more no less. So Claudia closed her eyes and tried to imagine a pulse.

'She's a fertile one, this one,' Sellors said. 'I'd reckon she's responsible for most of the oaks in this wood, and no doubt still is.'

Claudia opened her eyes. She saw him step back from the tree and stand gazing upwards again.

'Not bad, eh? Five hundred years old and still fecund.'

Claudia started slightly at the word.

'Not like us,' he said.

He continued to stand there, hands on hips, the sleeves of his shirt rolled up to the elbow. He had good, strong arms, Claudia observed, and his body was perfectly straight, not an uneven line in it. His limbs moved in perfect synchronicity and when he stood still he did so with his weight on both feet, firmly, four square.

'Why do you call it "she"?' she enquired.

'Because that's how I think of her,' he said. 'Though strictly speaking she's bisexual.'

'I beg your pardon?'

'She can propagate on her own or she can propagate by fertilisation. Clever, eh? She has male flowers and female flowers and she can keep right on going until the moment she dies. And the older she gets the more you love her.'

'Unlike us,' she found herself saying.

He didn't seem to hear her. His remarks were directed more to the old lady-oak with the trunk, and the apparent pulse, than to the old lady who stood next to him.

'I see her as the mother and the grandmother and the great-grandmother and so on down the centuries, spreading her seed as far as the eye can see, and further.'

'Isn't it the male who spreads the seed?'

Did she really say that?

He laughed. 'She's got both sexes so she spreads her seed and she fertilises it all in one. If human beings could do that we'd be . . . '

'I think,' said Claudia quickly, 'that's probably enough, thank you Sellors.'

'I didn't mean to offend, madam. I was just going to say if human beings could do what the great oak does we might be a happier species all round.'

'And there would be no need for men,' said Claudia.

'Do you suppose so?'

'Well, in one sense perhaps.'

How had it come to this? Where had this extraordinary conversation sprung from?

'But there'd always be a place for women,' he said, tipping his hat back from his face and looking right at her.

She tried not to stare back at him but there was something about his face: something noble, like the great oak, even though he was only a gardener – perhaps *because* he was a gardener. Noble yet earthy, of the land, as if he too had sprung from the seed of the great oak. There was a purity about him, as there was about the tree, a purity that, to Claudia, was distinctly romantic.

She envied him. So at one with the earth, so in tune with the great tree, this live, fecund organism whose heart, she believed it, he could physically feel pulsating through its massive body. How wonderful to be so immersed in Mother Nature that the outside world could not touch you.

'Forgive me for mentioning it but you are younger than I remember you,' she said.

He laughed at this. 'I'd like to think I'm getting younger year by year but I fancy that's not the case.'

'I remember you with grey hair.'

'Then you're probably thinking of my father.'

'Your father? Did he used to work for us?'

'For thirty years, madam, till he retired and I took over.'

'And when was that?'

'Three years ago, Mrs Faraday.' He chuckled.

'Good gracious.'

How could she have been so – so vague, so distant? How could she not know her own staff?

~

That evening, as she lay in her bath, the scented water lapping around her, her mind drifted to this conversation and to the tender young man with the noble face and the passion for the ancient oak. How was it that a tree could command such veneration, such love, as the years went by and her trunk, which was really her skin, grew more and more wrinkled and twisted the longer she stood there: grand, majestic, continuously fertile. Was it that that made a woman suddenly become invisible? she wondered. Not so much the wrinkles and the grey hair as the end of fertility. Did the death of fertility signal the beginning of futility?

Claudia moved her body slightly and as she did so she became aware of the warm water shifting and breaking with gentle ripples against her skin. She found herself moving her knees apart so the water could lap closer, so it could, in a sense, enter her, and as she did so she felt her body begin to respond. It was extraordinary. She wondered, if something as innocent and inanimate as water could thrill her so then . . . Thus it was that, almost without her willing them, the tips of her fingers set off on their tentative journey of exploration, across her belly and over her *mons veneris* where, after some hesitation, they rested, before moving on to the spot between her legs; there, bolder than its companions, the middle finger separated from the others and gently, and just as young Gabriel had taught her, it began to press down, leading Claudia to gasp, and to try to shake it off; but the trespassing finger held its ground and even began to move in a circular fashion, just as the young man's had done. Then had it not been that the stirring of her body was beginning to cause the water to slop right over the rim of her bath and onto the floor, shocking Claudia back into her senses, there is no knowing what might have happened next.

4

The following morning Claudia made an impromptu decision.

'I'm going into town, Lily,' she said.

Her maid gave her a quizzical look, as if to ask, 'For what purpose, madam?' But instead she said, 'Very well madam. Shall I ask Sellors to run you in?'

'There's a bus, isn't there?'

'There is madam, yes.'

'Then that should do me.'

There came a pause, as Lily continued to stand there.

When, thought Claudia, does one's personal maid, companion, comfort and source of dependency become one's mother? Or worse, one's keeper? Am I expected to explain my every move? That thought alone alarmed her. There is nothing, or virtually nothing, that I do in my life that someone else does not know about.

'I will be back this afternoon.'

'So you won't be needing lunch, madam?'

'I'll find somewhere in town, thank you Lily.'

The local town of S was hardly, then or since, the hub of the universe so far as fashion or industry were concerned. Yet for Claudia it was a rare venture into a world from which, she realised with consternation, she had become almost unnaturally detached in recent times, so much so that she found the bustle of people quite overwhelming. Anxious, and then excited, it took her a while to decide where she might go and, indeed, why she had decided to go into town in the first place.

She wandered without purpose for a while and the more she wandered the less she worried about purpose. So this is the world, thought she, this is what goes on every day while I cocoon myself in my home. The expressions on the faces of the people around her were surprisingly matter of fact, but then why shouldn't they be? It was a day like any other day for them. This was not, for them, the Day They Chose to Go Into Town. This was the world ordinary people inhabited and she was the odd one out.

No one took much interest in her. She thought from time to time she might have spotted a familiar face but she made no effort to approach its owner. On the contrary, the more alone she felt the more she was able to relax. Nobody (except Lily) has any idea where I am or what time I will be back, she said to herself. I am accountable to no one.

The town had become busier since her last visit, whenever that had been. She stopped to window shop and more than once, mere seconds later, an eager woman sprang through the doorway asking if madam would like some help? Or better still, would she care to come inside and peruse the merchandise at her leisure?

She might have been tempted had it not been for the eager women. Had she been allowed to do so in peace she might have wanted to take a closer look at the latest fashions which, now she came to study them closely, through the window, had changed almost out of recognition. There was even a brand new department store, T & M (& Son), of which she had heard some interesting things. She was accosted the moment she stepped through the door, which of course caused her to turn on her heel and exit immediately, and against her will, and annoyingly because all she wanted to do was to stroll through the building and take it all in without feeling any compulsion to buy.

Soon it was lunchtime and she found a restaurant quite by chance. It was small, and modest, with unthreatening flowered curtains, and she asked for a table by the window so she could continue to watch the passers-by. The pavements were filling up with workers on their lunch breaks – secretaries and labourers, clerks and hairdressers – let loose from their cages for an hour for a breath of air and a quick bite.

The next-door table was occupied by a pair of young women, perhaps in their twenties; they could almost have been her daughters. They sat opposite one another, heads bent closely together as they exchanged – what? – gossip, most likely, about their fellow workers, and no doubt the nuances and minor irritations of office life. These women have a purpose, thought Claudia. They get up in the morning and go to work, and at the end of the month, or the week, they get paid for their labours, and life was that simple. After a few years they would meet a man and marry him and cease working and become a producer of children, and in time those children would grow up and leave home and they would be . . . what exactly would they be then?

Claudia had never been one of those young women. The nearest she had come to working had been a brief spell helping out a friend whose aunt owned a hat shop, and that was more for something to do. But for the women of today, perhaps there would come a time when there would be a further life for them beyond child-bearing. Perhaps they would be still young enough, and energetic enough, to take up a hobby once the children had fled the nest, possibly painting – that was all the rage these days, so she had been led to believe. Prudence went on painting holidays to Italy, and another friend, Lucy, had taken up writing poetry, but Claudia did not believe she had a creative bone in her body. She had no aptitude for needlework. There wasn't really anything she had a particular aptitude for, except reading, and that only lightly, not for long stretches of time. As for travel, she had done a fair bit of that, with Gerald, BC (before children), but if venturing into S was daunting, the idea of journeying further afield, to foreign climes, without her husband, was frankly too alarming for words.

The two young women let out a sudden shriek of laughter, and immediately covered their mouths with their hands and glanced furtively around the room in giggling embarrassment. The topic of conversation was obvious, for what else would make a young woman shriek so? Claudia wondered if they had lovers, if any young people had lovers these days, before they were married that is. She was fairly sure her daughters were *intacta* on their wedding day, although she was never quite sure about Harriet. Things were so different now.

The clothes, for a start. As the young women got up to leave she noticed their skirts reached only to their knees, exposing a length of leg that in Claudia's youth could only be viewed on a female person on stage in pantomime. Moreover they were virtually flat in the bosom area, which meant they had eschewed the corset for . . . for what? Why, for nothing at all!

But then these were the young, like her own young – loose, carefree, unshackled in every sense, enjoying a freedom that to Claudia was both exciting and rather terrifying. At their age she had been corseted and supported to within an inch of her life, and scarcely a bare patch of flesh showing. In her day a woman did not sleep with a man until her wedding night, unless she was no better than she should be, and lovemaking was for one purpose only: procreation. Why else would a woman tolerate such bestial behaviour? Not, she hastened to correct herself, that Gerald was bestial, not at all. But the whole practice of sexual congress was, quite frankly, if you were to stand outside it and observe the act, clumsy and ridiculous. The idea that it might be done for *pleasure* was not something that had ever occurred to someone who, like Claudia, was as yet unfamiliar with the writings of Marie Stopes. But the very existence of . . . the name of it escaped her momentarily . . . meant there was more to the conjugal act than she had been previously aware of. It was a startling thought, especially for a woman of beyond child-bearing age.

All of a sudden Claudia realised she was being stared at. Reflected in the glass of the window she was gazing out of was the face of a man, and he was looking directly at her. Slowly and casually she turned and glanced around the room, as if to attract the attention of the waitress. He was sitting a couple of tables away: about the same age as herself, on his own, a newspaper on the table in front of him, and as her glance rested fleetingly on him he smiled, and gave her a little wave.

Do I know him? she thought, in some panic. If so then not to return the greeting would be rude; but if she didn't, it would be forward. In the end she pretended not to have seen him at all, and when the waitress arrived at her table she dropped some coins on the table without even looking at the bill, and left.

She realised immediately that he was following her as she headed, again without purpose, along the pavement towards the park. She did not hasten her footsteps, nor did she change direction away from the emptiness of the open space toward the more crowded areas of town. Once in the park she stopped dead. She could feel his breath on the back of her neck, he was standing that close.

Without speaking he laid a gentle hand on her

shoulder. She turned and looked straight at him and, of course, he was a total stranger. Still without a word he took her arm and led her away from the path and across the grass towards the trees where, the moment they were out of sight, he slowly and deliberately removed first her coat, and then his, and laid both garments carefully on the branch of a nearby tree. Then he took hold of her hand and held it, before gently guiding it towards him. Feeling her resistance he stopped and looked at her until she was forced to look back at him, in the eye, at which point he smiled and, squeezing her hand by way of reassurance, encouraged it on its continued journey in the direction of his crotch, where for a moment it rested. Then, seeing she was in need of further prompting he helped her to spread her fingers and to place them on his bulge. Claudia gave a sharp inward breath of surprise, but she did not attempt to pull back when he pressed her hand against him and she felt a distinct movement and swelling beneath her gloved fingers which, to her astonishment, she found to be a not unpleasant sensation. She hesitated for a moment and then, without any renewed prompting on his part, she removed her hand in order to rid it of its glove and took hold of him again, through the fabric of his trousers and rather more firmly than before; which gesture seemed to delight him as much as it astounded her, for not only had she never done such a thing before, the item she found herself holding was that which she had hitherto regarded as the single most absurd, and obnoxious, part of a man's anatomy. Yet she felt no revulsion, no absurdity, she even began to . . .

'Will that be all, madam, or would you care for some dessert?'

Claudia blinked, looked down at her plate, up at the enquiring waitress and then over the waitress' shoulder at where the stranger, so she thought, had been sitting.

'I'll just have the bill, thank you.'

The table was there, and the newspaper, but of its recent occupant there was no sign.

She reached in her handbag and pulled out a small mirror. To her dismay she saw her cheeks were flushed, but other than that everything appeared in its place. She dabbed delicately at her lips with her handkerchief, smiled at the returning waitress, paid the bill, and headed for the ladies' room, where she stayed so long that the attendant, having asked her three times if she was all right and having received the answer, 'Yes, I just had a bit of a dizzy spell,' was threatening to call a doctor. At which point she pulled herself together and left.

5

The experience had left Claudia profoundly shaken. It was if she'd dreamt, in minute detail, of travelling to some exotic place she knew nothing about, like Zanzibar. She felt she'd been taken over, possessed even, by someone else's fantasy.

Lily sensed there was something up, especially when her mistress asked for a cold supper to be sent to her room, but she put it down to what she saw as unnecessary, and unexplained, exertions.

The telephone rang just as Claudia was preparing for bed. At this late hour it could only be Harriet, her middle daughter, whose evenings began when most people's were ending. But no, it was a male voice.

'Claudia, how are you?'

'Who is this?'

'It's Douglas. Dougie.'

Claudia went momentarily blank.

'Dougie?'

'Yes, sorry to call you at this late hour. I hope I didn't wake you or anything.' He laughed, in a braying kind of a way.

'*Dougie?* Do you mean . . .?'

'Yes, it's been a long time. How are you?'

'I'm – very well, thank you. Goodness me.' Dougie. She hadn't seen him for, what . . .

31

'I'm in Town, and I thought, I simply must get hold of Claudia. I'm so glad to have caught you.'

'You're in Town?'

'Yes, London.'

'From where?'

'Oh, all over the place. Couldn't begin to tell you, though I'd like to. Wondered if you were free for lunch some day. Or better still, dinner.'

'I don't live in London you know, Dougie.'

'I do know, of course. I don't forget things that easily.'

He gave that odd horsey laugh again and Claudia wondered if he hadn't perhaps had a tot or two, as she remembered he liked to do.

'Well I suppose I could come up. I could stay with Jessica.'

'Jess! My goodness, how is she? Enjoying married life?'

'How did you know she was married?'

'One hears these things. So what do you think? One day next week perhaps? We have quite a lot to catch up on.'

'I suppose so. Yes. I'll have to check with Jess.'

'I'll ring you again in a few days, how's that?'

'That would be fine.'

There was a pause. Was there anything left to say? Or was there so much they were both pitched into silence?

'You know that, er, Gerald isn't here.' She wasn't sure why she said it but she felt she had to.

'I do. He's in Tanganyika. I know all about you.'

'That sounds ominous.'

'Not meant to, not at all,' he chuckled gently.

There was another brief silence. She could hear his breathing.

'I've been thinking about you quite a lot recently,' he said at last.

'Oh?'

'Yes. Wondering about you. You know.'

'Well, I'm fine. The girls have all left home now. But you know that already I suppose.'

'I do.'

'You have been keeping tabs on me.'

'It must seem strange, in that great big house of yours, alone.'

She laughed. 'It's quite nice really, the quiet. I'm enjoying it.' What a liar.

'I'm so looking forward to seeing you again.'

'Me too, Dougie. And now if you'll excuse me, I am on my way to bed. I've had rather an exhausting day.'

'Oh, I am sorry. Yes of course. Well. Goodnight then.'

'Goodnight Dougie.'

'Wonderful to hear your voice.'

'Yes. You too.'

'Till next week then.'

'Till next week.'

~

Douglas McAvoy. Dougie. The one that got away. That was her night's sleep gone then.

She felt unaccountably excited. It was not so much the prospect of seeing Dougie again – that held its own challenges and pitfalls – but the notion of going up to Town and having dinner with a friend, and a male one at that.

With Gerald absent for nine-tenths of the year, or more accurately these days eleven-twelfths, Claudia was unsure of her status. During the war all the men were away and one just got on with things, looking after families or helping with the war effort, and a woman on her own was not an unusual thing. But now that was, thankfully, over and the surviving men had returned Claudia felt rather out on a limb. Neither a wife nor a widow but something indeterminately in between.

Prudence for instance, whose husband had been killed in the war – no one quite knew how – had, after a brief moment of shock and grieving, launched into her new life with vigour. She travelled, took up, and abandoned, hobbies, and lunched and dined with different people, male and female, almost every day of the week, in a way she had never done before in her married life. It was as if she had found a freedom not accessible to the married woman, and of course Claudia admired and, to some extent, envied her.

But with Gerald some thousands of miles away Claudia felt neither the comfort and security of the married woman nor the freedom of the widow. The idea of an independent life suggested a kind of disloyalty, which made no logical sense, as what was Gerald doing other than leading a life that was not only independent but largely foreign to her as well? Who could tell what he got up to over there? (Not much, she suspected, he was always wedded to his work. But who was to know?)

So what was a woman in such a situation supposed to do? Twiddle her thumbs until her husband decided to return to the family home for good? How many years might that be? Follow the example of Prudence and act like a widow? (Prudence boasted of her dalliances, although you never quite knew whether the adventures she hinted at were wishful rather than real.) Take up a cause, do good works for charity, yes, that is what might be expected. But one was not getting any younger, and in ten years' time one would be old, and no longer interested, or able, to do very much at all, and then soon after one would die and be remembered for – what?

So, Dougie. The thought of his reacquaintance filled Claudia with trepidation. Nothing was ever straightforward with Dougie. If one did want a simple life one did not fraternise with the Dougies of this world.

But then maybe the simple life was not all it was cracked up to be.

She had not seen him for over twenty years, so his memory of her would be of a young woman, the mother of three small daughters. Claudia had been at her most beautiful then because being a mother had brought her such joy and fulfilment. And now?

She would cancel. When he called to confirm she would find some excuse, she had no idea what, or maybe she should be honest and tell him right out it was not a good idea.

Tomorrow she would go shopping in S. She would go back to T & M (& Son), the brand new department store into which she had earlier that day all too briefly ventured, only this time she would visit with intent. She would buy a dress, or maybe even two. She had not bought a dress, nor had one made for her, for years, other than the wedding outfits of course. And she would have her hair done. She would seek advice, she had become rather stuck in the mud so far as fashion was concerned, so far as everything was concerned. But then she had had little reason to be otherwise.

There was a plan.

6

'You called, Mrs Faraday?'

'I did, yes, Lily. I'm sorry to interrupt whatever it is you were doing. I need your advice.'

It was the following day and Claudia was in her bedroom, staring at herself in the full-length mirror.

'Advice, madam?' Lily pulled a face.

'This old thing. This thing I wear almost every day. Now be honest. What do you really think of it?'

It's true, and Lily had long since forgotten to remark upon it, even to herself, but of all the multitude of dresses that filled Mrs Faraday's wardrobe there were probably only four that she ever actually wore. One was the brown 'thing' she was wearing now, another was dark blue, one grey and the last one a faded patterned emerald green.

'It suits you, madam,' she said, a touch uncertainly.

'No, be honest. I'm sorry to put this upon you Lily, but I've become horribly aware that I only ever wear a fraction of the dresses that are hanging in my wardrobe, for reasons that I can't quite explain.' She thought for a moment. 'That of course I *can* explain: it's because I feel comfortable in them.'

'Of course.'

'I barely give a thought to what I put on in the morning nowadays, you know that. You used to make suggestions, in the early days, but even you have given up now. Isn't

36

that true?' Claudia was addressing Lily's reflection in the mirror.

'Well, I always did wonder why you never wore the emerald green, madam, now you come to mention it.'

'I've become stuck, Lily. Not only do I only wear four of the twenty or more dresses I own, but not one of them is less than fifteen years old.'

'They were made to last, madam.'

'I'm going to throw them all out.'

'Oh, my!' Lily's hand fled to her mouth.

'You can have them if you wish, I really don't care. What are you doing this afternoon?'

'I was . . .'

'Whatever it is it can wait. I want you to come shopping with me. For clothes. I want you to advise me. And honestly. I am aware that hemlines have risen quite sharply.'

Lily, involuntarily, bent down to touch her stockinged leg.

'They no longer droop somewhere vaguely about the ankle, except upon women of a certain age of course.' She glanced at Lily out of the corner of her eye. 'Long and floaty is out and the short, the coutured line is in, is it not?'

'Yes, you could say.'

'Even for someone of my age. Then we will go shopping, in T & Ms. Whatever they have to offer may not be the latest thing but they will certainly be an improvement. You have been far too polite to point out to me how dreadfully old-fashioned and middle-aged I have become.'

'Oh but . . .'

'But what? You were going to say I *am* middle-aged. Of course I am, but that's no reason to look it. Do you understand me?'

'Yes madam,' said Lily, and she gave a little curtsey, for

no reason at all.

~

For Claudia it was not so much a change of wardrobe as an overhaul of her entire being.

Abandoning the corset was like saying goodbye to an old friend, without whom she felt, literally, unsupported and rather disloyal. It was not so much the assurance of the departmental manager – who, on being told there was a Lady of Stature visiting her premises had been swiftly summoned to give Claudia her undivided attention and encourage her to part with as much money as possible – as the look on the face of her personal maid, whose smile grew bigger as the afternoon went on, that reassured her she was doing the right thing.

The new look rather suited Claudia's almost boyish figure. She could be properly proud and grateful for her modest bosom and her slim hips, both of which were set off to great advantage. But the biggest shock was in the hemline which, for the first time in history, now stopped at the knee; and this was where Claudia, whose legs were long and straight (her childhood nickname had been, for a while, 'Colt', which somehow morphed into 'Clot'), truly excelled.

And so as the watery sun began its daily descent the two women finally set off home, accompanied by half a dozen boxes piled high beside them in the back seat of the taxi.

~

The following morning however Claudia was greeted by a look of dismay.

'What is it, Lily?'

'I was just wondering what happened to yesterday's purchases, madam?'

'What do you mean? Are you worried because I promised you my old dresses?'

'Not at all, madam. I just thought, well, you know . . . '

'I'm keeping them for best.'

Gracious, what was she trying to say? That she'd spent a small fortune on a new wardrobe and then decided to keep it all for 'best'? What was 'best', anyway?

'I was thinking – forgive me for saying this madam, but I thought those dresses took years off you. They looked marvellous. And so I was looking forward to seeing you wearing them.'

Claudia took a deep breath. 'I tell you what Lily, you are absolutely right. Go upstairs right away and remove all my old dresses. I never want to see them again. No, wait, leave me the emerald green, and of course this one. The rest are yours.'

'Truly?'

'Truly. And thank you, Lily. I rather think that without you I'd have simply fallen back on old habits.'

'I rather think you might have, madam, if you don't mind me saying.' With which Lily gave her a grin that was just the right side of cheeky, and almost skipped from the room.

~

Ladies' maids talk to other ladies' maids, of course they do, and if you were looking for gossip it's here that you would find it. If a man wanted to know what his wife was secretly up to while he was away, or at work, he might do well to ask his wife's friend's maid. His wife's maid would be too loyal, and if she weren't then she would not remain her maid for long.

Up until this point when it came to Lily's turn for gossip she'd had to take a disappointing back seat. There had been the weddings, of course, and the (brief) visit of Mr Faraday, who had rolled up, checked out his future sons-in-law, muttered about the fuss, attended Harriet's wedding – which happened to come first – and gone again. Since then there had been nothing to report, not even the hint of something that Lily could embroider in the way that her friends embroidered their own tales; gossip being, naturally, a competitive sport.

This time, things were different. First of all was the surprising visit of the young man, who claimed to be a friend of Mr Faraday's but who Mrs Faraday appeared never to have met. Who managed to fix it so he missed the last train home and was forced to stay overnight. Then there had been Mrs Faraday's spontaneous visit to S, on her own, from which she had returned flushed and oddly exhausted. Following hot on its heels came another expedition to S, this time with Lily herself in tow, in order to replenish – or replace – her entire wardrobe.

Interspersed among all this had been a flurry of telephone calls, some of them quite late at night – and no, Lily was not disposed to eavesdrop, it was more than her life or her job were worth – and the next thing was her mistress announcing that she was planning a trip to London to stay with her daughter Jessica in Primrose Hill, and that it was quite unnecessary for Lily to accompany her. All of which suggested that Mrs Faraday Had Met Someone. Whether or not that Someone was the young man who stayed the night she had no idea, though since he was young enough to be her mistress' son it would make the whole business that much more scandalous.

All of which meant that as far as gossip went, Lily was in what might be called, for the time being at least, pole position.

7

Claudia did not really need an excuse to visit her eldest daughter. Jessica was a hospitable soul and always fun to be with. She was born laughing, Claudia was fond of saying, and had laughed and joked her way through every waking moment since. And now she was married to her mirror image, a merry fellow called Jonathan, or Jonno, who was something in export and import, Claudia wasn't quite sure, with ambitions to be a politician; a notion which Jessica claimed to be ridiculous since he was completely unable to take anything seriously.

The two of them would tell jokes in company that they, and no one else, found screamingly funny. But because laughter is infectious, and Jess and Jonno's doubly so, in no time at all and for no reason whatsoever, their friends would be as speechless with merriment as they were.

Their house was, predictably, shambolic. So Claudia's bed had first to be divested of the clothes that her daughter had piled upon it in preparation for, one of these days, donating to charity; Jessica being adept at postponing mundane tasks. Her mother's new look was not lost on her and at the first opportunity Jessica sat her down and interrogated her.

'So tell, Mother, what's going on?'

'In what sense?'

'All this.' Jessica gestured at her. 'New clothes, new

hair. Who is he?'

'I've no idea what you're talking about.' Claudia sat upright in her chair and wondered at herself. Sometimes her daughters made her feel positively immature.

'Oh please, Mama!' Jess giggled. 'You look ridiculously young. Somebody must have got at you and that somebody should have been me. I've been meaning to call you up and arrange a shopping expedition, and now you've beaten me to it. You look totally marvellous darling, I am so proud of you! Do I know him?'

It was preposterous, the daughter interrogating the mother in such a way.

'I just thought it was time I stepped into the twentieth century,' Claudia remarked primly, as if that was pretty much that. Not for Jessica, however.

'There must be more to it,' she declared. 'As it happens, Jonno and I are having a bit of a thing on Friday so you must stay on and invite him. What do you think?'

'What, dear, is a "thing"?'

'Oh you know, one of our get-togethers. We can't call it a *soirée* because that's so bogus and pompous, and it's not quite a party, or a dinner, so it's a thing. You know, friends round and sort of.'

"Friends round and sort of." And she'd had such an expensive education.

'They'd love you, the new you. Lots of fun and shenanigans.'

'We'll see.'

She didn't waste her breath reminding her daughter she was still married to her father. Clearly in Jessica's world a woman on her own was entitled to have as much fun as she could get, and why not? It gave Claudia permission, if she needed it, to do pretty much what she wanted. And come to think of it, that was exactly what Claudia did need: permission to be a part of the world again.

If only her daughter knew . . . She thought of the young man and that extraordinary night, and what Jessica would have made of it. To their daughters mothers are not sexual beings and do not lead sexual lives, perish the thought, and the idea that their own procreation was a result of a sexual act was something they conveniently ignored. Nevertheless if there was anyone Claudia might have confided in it would be Jessica, who never made judgements, or if she did, they were determinedly positive. Jessica was unable to bear a grudge or to think badly of anyone for long, if at all. Where this positivity came from was a mystery. Certainly it was not from Claudia herself, and not obviously from Gerald.

She wondered, as she continued to sit there while her daughter rushed off to do whatever she was rushing off to do: did today's new wives know any more about sex than their mothers when they were that age? If they did, it did not come from those mothers who, in Claudia's case at least, had never had that conversation about the facts of life with her three daughters that Claudia's mother had also managed not to have with hers. Innocence continued to wander unmolested down the corridors of ignorance. As a child Claudia was told babies were delivered by storks, and only to married couples. It was a wonder the world was able to function at all.

She felt guilty, of course. But there had never been a time, a proper opportunity; it was not something one discussed. And now that both the time and the opportunity were here, if she could ever get Jessica to stay still for more than five minutes at a time, it did not seem appropriate. Or rather, four months into her marriage was rather late in the day. And besides, if Claudia were honest with herself, were the subject of sex to be broached in the first place, which was highly unlikely, it would be the mother rather than the daughter who would want to be on the receiving end of any advice dispensed.

On the other hand, did Jessica know that it was possible for a woman to acquire sexual pleasure without *incursion*. And that there was a way in which a woman could reciprocate? To give pleasure to a man without the necessity of . . .

'What are you thinking about, Mother? You look quite flushed.'

Jessica, back from whatever she was doing, was looking at her with amusement.

Now. The opportunity was here, now.

'I was thinking about sex, darling. How little I know. Let me tell you about something that happened to me a couple of weeks ago. A young man came to visit – he'd worked with your father in Africa. He dropped by completely out of the blue and was forced to stay the night as he missed his last train home. Somehow the conversation switched to the subject of sex and the history of what he termed self-pleasuring. Then later on he introduced me to the clitoris for the first time in my life.'

What she actually said was, 'I was thinking I ought not to sit here daydreaming but start getting ready for my dinner engagement.'

'Do tell. Who is he?'

'His name is Douglas McAvoy.'

'Dougie? The one who . . . '

'The one who what?'

'You know – ended up not my father. Oh my goodness! Mama!' Jessica's eyes shone like a ten year old's.

'I don't know why you're so excited, Jessica. I am a married woman, remember.'

'I'm excited because *you* are, Mother. And don't try to tell me otherwise. Besides,' she bent down to peck her mother's cheek, 'you deserve a bit of harmless fun.'

And as Claudia rose to leave the room her daughter had the temerity to tap her playfully on the behind.

Harmless fun. Well, yes. Though why one's daughter should be encouraging one to spend an evening with an old lover was a bit of a surprise, and perhaps another sign of the free-thinking of the modern world. Yet sitting in her bedroom and looking out across the road at the trees and the slopes of Primrose Hill, Claudia found herself wishing she had never agreed to this ridiculous meeting. What was the point? Dougie belonged in the past, to another life completely, one she'd almost forgotten. Or had she?

In many women's lives, men's too perhaps, there is the one who got away, the one they end up not marrying, for whatever reason. And when life becomes difficult and one begins to grow regretful, that is when the mind turns to this person and wonders: *what if*?

What if she had married Dougie? She came close, very close. It was really just a matter of timing, but then what is life after all but a matter of timing? One meets a man at a particular time in one's life, maybe the wrong time, when one is too young, too green, not ready. Then when instinct, or perhaps social expectation, tells one the time is right, one has reached *un certain âge*, well then, let's see who is around.

Gerald it was, who was around. Gruff, plain-speaking Gerald, a clever chap with a good brain and a passion for archaeology. A man's man, more comfortable in the company of men than women. Who, unlike Dougie, barely looked at other women, let alone flirted with them.

Who barely looked at me, if the truth be known, thought Claudia. And if the truth be confronted face to face it was partly this that had attracted her to him. She had never been short of male admirers, the sort who followed her around like puppy dogs, eager to please, ready to pour compliments. Gerald was never eager, never obsequious, rather the opposite. If anything he was distant, aloof even, as if his mind were on higher things. He rarely paid her compliments and it was chance rather than anything else that threw them together. The less he flirted with her the more she wanted him. Yet it was those same qualities that first attracted her to him that now so distressed her.

Maybe it wasn't timing after all.

The young visitor had, without meaning to, brought Claudia some harsh truths: her husband did not think about her, was not interested in her or what went on in her life. She had known this all along, of course she had, but to have it pointed out to her so brazenly was rather humiliating. Yes, Gerald had been a good father and a perfectly decent husband in most respects, when he was around. He treated her well, he never strayed. Yet now she felt so distant from him it was as if they barely knew one another. Perhaps if she had taken a closer interest in his work, but he did not make it easy. He never invited her on any of his expeditions, not since the girls were born at least, never really talked to her about what he did. She knew virtually nothing about his work and he knew almost nothing about her daily life. It was a peculiar situation all round.

But then, if she really thought about it, there was another reason why she didn't marry Dougie, but she'd tucked that one so far back in the recesses of her mind she couldn't now bring herself to think about it.

Oh, but gracious me, look at the time. He'd be here in half an hour and she hadn't decided what to wear. Would it be her old favourite, the emerald green, or one of the new outfits she'd brought with her? The demure yet dashing pale blue two-piece with the velvet collar, or the deep red silk with the asymmetrical hemline? One did not want to look as if one was trying too hard, and yet . . . it had been such a long time and he would be shocked to see her so aged. Then again what did it matter? It was only Dougie.

She decided to wear the blue.

8

He was on the doorstep at six o'clock on the dot – Dougie had never had any truck with the notion of being 'fashionably late'. At the risk of appearing rude, Claudia did not invite him in. She did not want to sit and look on while he chatted aimlessly with Jessica, whom he had only known briefly when she was very small, having to endure her daughter's raised eyebrows and knowing looks, all of it done with great good humour, as always, but nonetheless.

It was still light on this lovely September evening and so Dougie suggested a walk in the park. It was not until they had climbed the hill and sat down on a bench to rest that she was able to look at him properly.

It is a well known and annoying fact that some men age better than most women, and so it was with Dougie. He had grown older, of course, better than Gerald, as it happened, but then he had always (unlike Gerald) taken care of his appearance. One could almost have described him as vain, but then Claudia was not averse to a little vanity if it kept a man in shape – a waistcoat straining over a protruding belly was not appealing. His eyes still sparkled, and his step was still springy and his walk brisk. She had to ask him to slow down at one point.

Having reached their park bench they turned to look at one another; and Claudia, to her embarrassment, or

48

perhaps because of it, found herself bursting into laughter.

'Am I that amusing?' he said.

'Oh dear Dougie, no, please forgive me. I've no idea where that came from. It is good to see you again, I wasn't sure it would be.'

'Whyever not?'

He had the most wonderfully warm and amused smile, more of a twinkle than a smile, as if he was enjoying his own private joke. Claudia had found it rather beguiling. In the old days they would tease one another about it.

'So tell us then,' she would say.

'Tell what?'

'What it is that's so funny.'

'Nothing. Life is not in the least funny, I can't help my face, I was born this way.' That sort of thing.

'You look marvellous,' he said in the here and now.

'I'm sure I don't. Not after all this time. You on the other hand, haven't really aged at all.' They were not yet at the stage of truth-telling.

'So. Where to begin.'

'Well, you know all about me,' Claudia said. 'And I know nothing whatsoever about you. Where have you been for the past twenty years? You seemed to just drop out of our lives, I even . . . ' She stopped.

'You even . . . ?'

'I even thought you might be dead. Killed in the war.'

'No. Fought in it, yes, got killed in it, no. As you can see.'

'Nobody seemed to know where you were.'

'Did you ask anyone?'

'I don't suppose I did. But your name never cropped up in conversation, as one might have expected it to.'

'"There's only one thing worse than being talked about, and that's not being talked about".' He looked serious for a moment, and then laughed. 'I've been abroad mostly.

India, Ceylon, Hong Kong and Indonesia, briefly. Australia for a while. Touched down in Kenya at one point.'

'Doing what?'

'Foreign Office stuff, you know.'

'And now? What brings you back to London?'

He was quiet for a while. He was looking away from her so she was able to study him at close quarters, and she thought, how much more interesting he looks now, how the lines and creases had given his face a definition it never had when he was a smooth-skinned youth. It was most unfair.

'My wife died,' he said eventually. 'Quite out of the blue actually. And I didn't feel like being away from home any more, on my own. So I more or less upped sticks and left, gave in my notice – retired, you could say – and here I am.' He looked into the distance towards Regent's Park and closed his eyes. 'I missed the smell and the poison of London air. Couldn't live without it.'

'I'm sorry to hear about your wife,' said Claudia. 'Did you have children?'

'Yes, one, a boy. Killed in the war. When he was sixteen.'

'Oh my goodness, I am so, so sorry.' It was her turn now to look up and away, as a mark of respect.

'These things happen. One is not alone in that sense.'

'I never had a boy,' she said. 'I so wished it, Gerald wished it in particular, but to have seen him disappear off to that dreadful war. . .'

'Thank heaven for small mercies. And now . . . ' He swivelled in his seat, turned toward her and rested an arm on the back of the bench behind her. 'You are looking splendid by the way, did I tell you that?'

'You did.' She giggled, again with a kind of childish awkwardness. It had been a long time since she'd received a compliment and now there had been two within ten minutes. 'You said you know what I've been up to.'

'I know what's been going on in your life – marriage, daughters fleeing the nest, husband out in the wilds picking over old stones. But you – I know nothing about you.'

'There isn't anything to tell.'

'Still at Hallywell.'

'Of course. I don't suppose we'd ever leave it unless we had to.'

'Doing what, precisely?'

'I told you, nothing very much.' He waited. 'Don't forget there were three weddings last year.' Why should she have to make excuses? 'I've hardly had time to draw breath since. I'm enjoying the peace and quiet, if you must know.'

Dougie gazed at her thoughtfully.

After a moment they got up and wandered down the pathway in the direction of Regent's Park, he proclaiming his delight at the greenness of the trees, at the balminess of his surroundings after the crude, blinding brilliance of everything he'd been used to.

'How I've missed the friendly fogginess of London,' he said, more than once.

He took her to a small restaurant somewhere off Oxford Street. They ate jugged hare and drank claret (he rather more than she), and at one point, in a lull in the conversation and as a way of filling a silence she said, 'I am sorry about your wife. You must miss her very much. What was her name?'

'Iris,' he said. And then, 'No, I don't really miss her. I can't say I miss her at all.'

'Oh!' said Claudia, and frowned.

'She was a good sort,' he went on. 'Put up with a lot. That's why . . . ' he stopped.

'Yes?' she said gently.

'There's altogether too much to say.' He took a rather long swig of wine and then changed the subject.

So they talked of inconsequential things, of the three daughters and their respective husbands, and their prospects. Of life in England after the war, such a long war it seemed, never-ending. Of losses and regrets and how the world looked so much brighter now, and the future too. She asked him what his plans were and he said he was going to become a writer.

'Truly?'

'Don't look so surprised.'

'But you mean, to make money?'

'Why not?'

Well. He always had been a dreamer. Now she came to think of it he'd always had ambitions to be a writer, but then didn't everyone at some point in their lives?

It was as they were about to embark upon coffee and *crème de menthe* – it was years since she'd tasted *crème de menthe* and she'd forgotten how delicious it was – that he said, 'Are you and Gerald happy?'

She was expecting this. 'Of course.'

'Astonishing.'

'I beg your pardon?'

'As I see it, if you loved him you would want to be with him, and you're not. So must be pining for him. On the other hand, if you are getting on with your life without him then you can't be missing him that much, which means either way you don't really love him. As I see it.'

'That is an outrageous thing to say!'

'Why? It seems to me perfectly logical. I would never have left you for such long periods. I would never have left you for a day.'

'Well then.' She couldn't think of anything else to say.

'I never understood why you married Gerald, never

understood what you saw in him, still can't. He hasn't got a gracious bone in his body. Never appreciated you. Took you utterly for granted.'

'That may be your view.'

'So?'

'I married him because he . . . ' she hesitated. She was about to say 'because he asked me', but the truth was, she couldn't actually ever remember him asking her. In fact she wasn't sure it wasn't someone else entirely who popped the question on his behalf, as in, 'Well you two, when are you getting hitched, then?' At which they had laughed, but then some kind of momentum took over.

'How about you? Was your marriage happy?'

It was her turn to divert the focus of conversation, but his response, which came immediately, was quite unexpected.

'She didn't like sex.' He stopped there, finished off his *crème de menthe*, signalled for the waiter and ordered two more. And it was not until the waiter had arrived, placed the fresh drinks upon the table and swooped up the empties and gone, that he continued.

'In fact, I think she despised it. She found it repellent. She found me repellent.'

Claudia was not at all sure she wanted to hear anything more on this particular topic, but there was no stopping Dougie now.

'She liked the bit before, and the bit after. But not the bit itself, if you follow me.' He chuckled and sipped his drink. 'She liked to cuddle up, she said she liked the warmth, the hugs, so I said she should buy herself a teddy bear. But the moment the hugs became . . . ' He tailed off, laughed lightly again and gazed into the middle distance.

He could be talking about me, thought Claudia, with a sense of shock. She too liked to cuddle up in bed with Gerald, she loved to feel his arms around her until . . .

'She'd lie there like a block of wood – not complaining, not doing anything, just lying there, waiting for it all to be over. So,' he turned to look Claudia in the eye, 'I felt I had to leave her alone, and seek my – satisfaction – elsewhere.'

'As in . . .'

'Yes. And there was never a shortage of willing participants, if you get my drift.'

She assumed he was talking about prostitutes and she thought, good gracious, how are the mighty fallen.

'Of course she found out, Iris. But she never said anything. She was a stoical old thing.'

But did you know about that secret spot? Claudia wondered to herself. Or did you, like Gerald, assume that sex was really only about the fulfilment of male need?

'But I didn't like myself. I didn't like myself at all. I hated myself, to tell you the truth.'

You pompous, egocentric goose, her thoughts went on. Was that all your life was about, liking yourself?

'I don't suppose Iris liked herself much either,' she said out loud.

He laughed at this.

'No, you're probably right.' He drained his glass, and then, 'Well my goodness, we made sharp work of that, didn't we?'

'That' being the second *crème de menthe*, which Claudia had not yet touched.

'Do you think I am a terrible person?'

'I don't know, Dougie, I don't really think it's any of my business.' She took a sip, to be polite, but she felt she'd had enough.

'But it is, you see. If you had only married me instead of that, that . . .'

'Be very careful what you say, Dougie. He is still my husband.'

'I know that, only too well. But I still don't understand

why you married him instead of me.'

'By the sound of it it's just as well.'

'No, you completely misunderstand me. I would never have been unfaithful to you. Never.'

'You don't know that. I might have been like Iris.'

'Might you?' He gazed at her in surprise. 'I don't think so.'

'Well, you'll never know, will you? Shall we get the bill?'

That was quite enough of that kind of talk.

He'd always been a womaniser, had Dougie. Terrifically charming, as womanisers are, and maybe a wonderful lover, though from his own description it's possible he was as self-seeking as the rest of them. Whose fault was it if a woman didn't enjoy the sexual act? They knew nothing. All over the world anxious young newly-weds went to their marriage beds white-faced with terror. Claudia's own sister was so frightened at the prospect of what lay ahead she was sick right through her wedding day (she did not tell Claudia this for many years).

Dougie stopped the cab at the end of the street.

'I want to ask you something,' he said. They were standing a few doors away from Jessica's house. 'I don't want you to give me an answer now, I want you to think about it.'

Now what?

'I want,' he said, 'to spend one night with you. Just one night. That's all.'

'What . . . '

'Don't speak.' He placed a finger lightly on her lips. 'Don't say anything. Think about it. I've been thinking about it for months. Years. One night. That's all I ask.'

She nodded. He walked her to the door.

'Goodnight.' He kissed her lightly on the cheek and walked off down the street without a backward glance.

9

If life is a random thing, as it undoubtedly is, is there any point in trying to plan it, let alone control what happens in it?

She could quite easily have married Dougie. He did ask her, after all.

It was at her family home near W, a modest place, not on the scale of Hallywell. There was a house party and the men had all gone shooting; a sport Dougie, having discovered he was a terrible shot, claimed to find barbaric, which was not very manly of him, although Claudia secretly rather admired him for thinking it.

He was not a particularly manly man, in the nicest sense. There had always been something rather feminine about Dougie, a sensibility and a sensitivity that was rare among the men of his set. He preferred the company of women to men, he'd always made that perfectly clear. He found their conversation more interesting, more emotionally profound, and interpret that as one might it made him a lady's man. Or so Claudia considered him.

The other women of the house were scattered about in the drawing room on that day, and outside on the lawn, and so Claudia found herself alone with Dougie in the library, which was more of a study really. They'd been sitting together on the window seat, not speaking, and without looking at her he'd casually taken her hand and held it in his, loosely. She did not try to pull away.

She did not pull away when he turned and leant towards her, cupped her chin in his other hand and started to kiss her on the mouth, nor did she resist when he gently lifted her to her feet and put his arms around her; in fact she went so far as to wrap her own arms around him in return, and so they stayed for a while, locked in close embrace.

But then she felt his hands move to her lower back, and beyond, as a certain part of him pressed against her, and she felt his breath start to quicken, and then he whispered into her left ear, 'Marry me.'

If it had been ten seconds earlier, if he'd asked her while they were simply embracing, while she could feel the warmth and the closeness of his body against hers and she was able to drift off on some magic carpet to a land of fairytale sweetness, before he . . . Before he began to force himself on her.

And so she said, 'No, I can't.'

'Why not?'

She did try to pull away from him then, but he held her firm.

'Please Dougie, let me go.'

'Tell me why not.'

'Because I'm engaged to Gerald.'

At which it was he who pulled back and gazed at her in stark astonishment.

'Since when?'

It was a lie, but a necessary one. 'Not in the technical sense maybe, but morally.'

'Morally engaged to Gerald? What in heaven's name does that mean?'

It meant that she and Gerald, while not officially, or even unofficially, betrothed, were considered by their friends to be a couple and had been so for some time, or that is how Claudia believed her friends saw it.

'That's nonsense and you know it.'

'Not at all,' she said.

He had continued to gaze at her for some time and she held his gaze for as long as she could bear and then, to her shame, she looked down and away from him, and it felt like – it was – a kind of admission.

But he never brought the subject up again. And lo and behold, two weeks later, the engagement was announced between Gerald Faraday and Claudia Sheringham, and Dougie joined in the celebrations and toasted the happy couple with what Claudia viewed as unmistakable irony.

~

She decided to stay on for a few days for Jessica's Friday 'thing', for what was to stop her? She was enjoying London, unexpectedly finding it less intimidating than her initial foray into S. So the following day she travelled by underground to South Kensington and spent an hour at the Victoria & Albert Museum gazing at the naked statues, and wondering how it could be that what the Ancient Greeks and Romans – and, according to the young man, the ancient Indians – considered beautiful was regarded in the twentieth century as indecent. After her initial self-consciousness (she felt like a voyeur and had to force herself to stay put) she came away believing there was nothing wrong with the naked body other than what was considered so by the beholder. That as the beholder, whatever embarrassment or inhibition she felt was entirely her own doing, the product of her upbringing and her own failure to challenge what she had been led to think of as acceptable.

TheIt meant that she and Gerald, while not officially, or even unofficially, betrothed, were considered by their friends to be a couple and had been so for some time, or that is how Claudia believed her friends saw it.

again the calm serenity of the inanimate statues contrasted so sharply with the frantic, hot-breathed, animalistic exertions of a man in the process of sexual congress that it was difficult to equate the two. It was the frantic bit that Claudia had difficulty with. When she thought back to the young man and how she had allowed him to . . . there had been no frantic behaviour, no loss of control or heavy breathing – not on his part at least. It had all been perfectly calm and, confess it with guilt as she might, enjoyable.

These were Claudia's thoughts as she stepped through the doors of the museum into the racket and bustle of the Cromwell Road. She found London, which she had not visited for some time, vibrant, crazy and dangerous all at once. In South Kensington she witnessed for herself examples of the latest craze that people called Bohemianism: women in flowered skirts, with shawls and patterned headscarves, men in what looked like pyjama trousers, with brightly-coloured waistcoats and non-matching jackets. And hats, on both sexes, that appeared to be made out of scraps, feathers, bits of bird and animals and goodness knows what else. This was the *milieu*, if that was the correct word, in which Claudia's middle daughter Harriet lived.

Harriet. She had married a poet called Leonard. ('A poet?' barked Gerald. 'What does that mean? Does he have private means?') Prue conjectured the only reason Harriet married him was because he shared a first name with Virginia Woolf's husband. Harriet and Leonard lived in a 'garret', as they called it, in Parson's Green, what Prue termed the 'poor man's Chelsea'; prices of property in what was regarded as the heart of Bohemia having been forced to ridiculous heights by the 'would-bes', thus rendering it out of bounds for the Real Things, who were by definition poor.

'You must look her up, Mama,' said Jessica. 'She'd be so offended if she knew you'd come to London and not seen her.'

'I'm not sure I have time, darling.' It was a feeble excuse, and they both knew it was not true. 'Perhaps you could invite her to your Friday "thing"?'

'Heavens no, she wouldn't be seen dead at one of our dos!'

Coming from Jessica that was a serious charge, and so Claudia resolved to put that particular adventure off for the time being, until she felt stronger.

That evening Jess, Jonno and Claudia went to the theatre, to see a revue featuring a young man with the unlikely name of Coward. Whatever was happening on stage was rather overshadowed by what was happening in the audience. Every time somebody said or did something comical Jonno laughed loudly, slapped his knee and called out 'Rollicking, rollicking!' When people in front of them turned round to see what was going on he mimed a frantic apology, flushed slightly, and then did it all over again.

'He can't help himself,' Jess whispered to her mother. She might have been talking about a child who'd been caught with his fingers in the biscuit tin. But she didn't tell him off – no, far from it, she was laughing along with him. Not only that, but at the funniest moments, at which Jonathan came close to falling off his seat, the two young things grabbed each other's hands and rocked backwards and forwards in utter helplessness; so that those around them, Claudia included, soon found themselves joining in and laughing more at their antics than at the antics happening on stage. At one point the star of the show, who had a particularly clipped, almost cutting way of speaking, broke off from what he was doing, stepped down to the footlights, peered into the audience and said, 'So glad you are having such a riotous evening, whoever you are. Next time we must swap places.' A comment that made Jonathan howl even louder than ever.

Watching her daughter and her daughter's nearly brand new husband, Claudia marvelled at what a fine match they were. She could see the attraction. He was one of the best-natured men in the world and he was married to one of the most generous-spirited women. He might not have been the brightest, nor the deepest thinker, and in truth a little of his rumbustiousness would have gone a long a way in Claudia's book. But as Gerald had said to her, gruffly but correctly, when at one time she had expressed her slight reservations about her future son-in-law: 'He is not marrying you, my dear.'

10

Soon it was Friday, very soon. Dougie had not telephoned and Claudia did not know whether to be relieved or disappointed.

His proposition had appalled her, then terrified her, as he had known it would. But as time went on curiosity took the place of blind terror and the more she thought about the prospect of a night with Dougie the more intrigued she became. It was her one chance of finding out not just how good a lover he was (though Claudia had never understood what it meant to be 'a good lover', in the abstract), but what it felt like to spend the night with a man who was not Gerald. At the same time would 'one night' mean just that? One never knew with Dougie. One night would inevitably lead to a request for another one night, and so on, and he was – or had been – so very much in love with her, so everyone kept telling her.

In love with her. What a sweet thought.

~

'Just a few people,' Jessica had promised. Now that it was upon her Claudia rather wished she hadn't agreed to stay on for her daughter's 'thing', but since she had, and since she had brought her scarlet silk number with her, she thought she might as well push the boat out.

She did feel good, even splendid, as she studied herself in the mirror. The deep red showed off her creamy skin wonderfully and gave her a sort of sheen that was really rather delightful. The scooped neck, back and front, sat just this side of respectability, or so she hoped. The bodice hugged her body closely down to the dropped waistline and the skirt, cut on the bias, knee-length and with the asymmetrical hemline, flattered her hips and, when she moved, swung in a manner that was almost coquettish. (Might someone ask her to dance? Would there be dancing? She did hope so.) Lastly came the stockings, silk of course, applied delicately and even sensuously by gently rolling them from the tip of the foot up the calf to the thigh, smoothing as she went. Inexplicably as she performed this task she thought of Dougie, and even more inexplicably she imagined him doing it for her. On her feet, simple court shoes with heels just high enough to set off her legs to their best advantage. The whole, though she said it herself, *à point.*

As for her hair, which she had had trimmed and styled, when it came to replicating the hairdresser's art she fell short, so it was Jessica who came to the rescue. Jessica, whose carefree beauty and casual manner belied an innate sense of natural style and alertness to fashion. With a few brushes and a couple of clever twists she managed to achieve what had eluded Claudia: her hair draped loosely to frame her face, folded in a coil at the back of her neck and deftly pinned; the end result a perfect mixture of sophistication and softness which, miraculously, took the eye away from what Claudia considered her least favourable attribute: her neck.

'And I think a touch of colour,' said Jessica, reaching for the rouge.

'Cosmetics? I don't think so darling.'

'I do think so, darling. Trust me.'

A dab on the cheeks, artfully applied to appear almost invisible, and another on the lips, which Claudia pursed, doubtfully.

'I suppose I'll get used to it,' she said.

'If I may be allowed to say so, Mama,' said Jessica, leaning over her mother's shoulder and addressing her in the mirror, 'you look sensational.'

It was a sentiment she expressed, in different ways, over and over throughout the evening. As in, 'This is my Mama, doesn't she look wonderful?' Or 'Guess who this beautiful woman is!' Comments to which Claudia did not in the least object.

They sat her on the sofa like royalty and told her to stay put while guests paid court to her. Which guests did, as instructed, sometimes awkwardly, often looking over their shoulder while they bashed away at the small talk, not wanting to miss anything more amusing going on the far side of the room. The front door seemed constantly open, with new people constantly arriving – 'Who are you? Oh, you've come with Rupert, welcome, welcome, any friend of Rupert's is welcome!' – until the room was so full you could not see across it. So these were the Bright Young Things Claudia had heard so much about, so beautiful, so glittery, so carefree. Young enough to have little memory of the war and hedonistic enough not to care, and who could blame them? These days who was to know what might happen next? There could be another conflagration just around the corner, so what was wrong with living in the here and now? She could learn a thing or two from these lovely young things.

'Mother-in-law!' It was Jonathan's idea of a joke, he never called her that normally. 'You may remember Stephen. Stephen, you may remember my Mother-in-law.'

'I do indeed, and please remind me of Mother-in-law's name?'

'Claudia,' she said, trying her best to smile.

He did look familiar, in a way, though she couldn't

immediately place him. He looked, come to think of it, rather like an older version of her son-in-law. Which of course is exactly what he was.

'I'm Jonno's father, we met at the wedding, oddly enough.'

He had the same ruddy cheeks, the same hearty laugh – he was Jonathan's prototype. Stouter, and greyer, yes, she remembered Jessica referring to him as the 'merry widower', which immediately made her wonder whether he was the reason Jessica had insisted on her staying on in the first place.

To her chagrin Stephen stayed by her side all evening. He was being solicitous, she realised that, but she'd have preferred to have been allowed to be a free spirit for a change.

'You're what, a stone widow?' he said, and guffawed. 'Is that what they call you? Husband away digging up old fossils? Or should that be a fossil widow?' He laughed even louder at this. 'Though that sounds impolite, I apologise. What do you think of the party?'

He was shouting to be heard above the hubbub and she didn't really want to shout back, so she smiled, and nodded what she hoped looked like her approval.

'I'd ask you to dance but I dance like a rhinoceros, so Jonno tells me!' he yelled.

The dancing had begun by then. There was a gramophone playing somewhere, jazz, the latest thing from America. It was vibrant and rhythmic, foot-tappingly so, and by now Claudia was ready to kick up her heels and join the throng, so she excused herself from the merry widower, gesturing she needed to 'powder her nose', and made a swift exit.

She felt tired suddenly. If she'd invited Dougie at least there'd be someone to talk to. She spent as long as she thought she could get away with before she began to make her way back to the party, but then she paused in the doorway. She saw Stephen across the room looking around for her so she ducked quickly out of sight. A tall young man standing nearby said, 'Avoiding someone?'

She laughed, and he laughed back.

'I spend my whole life doing that,' he said.

'Do you? Why? Do you owe people money or something?'

'You've guessed. There's a card game going on next door and I'm trying not to join in.'

'Why?'

'Because I don't trust myself.'

'So that's why you're standing not quite inside the room and not quite outside it. You're hedging your bets, is that the right expression?'

'You play!' he exclaimed, with delight.

She shook her head. 'My husband does. Or did.'

'Oh, is he dead?'

'No.' She couldn't help but laugh.

'He gave up, sensible fellow. I've been told I have an addictive personality, whatever that is.'

'Do you lose a lot of money?'

'No. That's the problem. Losing isn't the problem, winning is. Even I wouldn't play if I lost all the time.'

He spoke with a slight twang, an accent she couldn't quite place. And he wore a lounge suit with an open collar and no tie, which in present company said something about him but she wasn't sure what.

'How do you know Jess and Jonno?' He shouted down at her. He was very tall.

'I'm Jessica's mother.'

'Of course you are!' He snapped his fingers, took a step back and stared at her. 'Of course, the spitting image, mother and daughter, how could I miss it? Beauty spawns beauty!'

'Oh, please.' She blushed.

'You don't believe me. Well I tell you what, Jess's mother, let's dance!' He pronounced 'dance' in the American way, yet she didn't think he was American.

Claudia hadn't danced since she was Jessica's age, but in the unconventional yet strangely reassuring hands of her young partner she whirled and swirled with no other thought in her head except to show off her dress to its best advantage. She could see people staring at them, some in amazement, some in delight (Jessica in particular), and she felt suddenly invincible.

'You know the Black Bottom?' He yelled at her through the music.

'I beg your pardon?'

'Watch this!'

So she did, along with the rest of the room, as her tall partner demonstrated the latest dance craze from America, which involved hopping, sliding, swooping and a certain wiggling of the bottom that Claudia, and the rest of the room, found hilarious.

'Go it, Archie!' yelled someone.

'Get it up, you black-bottomed Aussie!' cried another.

Soon the whole place was clapping and stamping along with the music and Claudia thought she'd never had so much fun in her life. Display over, the young man grabbed hold of her once again and whisked her around the room in what she assumed was an Antipodean version of the foxtrot.

'You're Australian!' she said.

'Yeah, but don't hold it against me. You dance like an Astaire, did you know that?'

'Like a who?'

'Fred and Adele, haven't you heard of them? The latest dance sensation. *'Lady, be Good!'*'

'Oh, well, I'm deeply flattered!' she shouted back.

'You're not so bad yourself!' She was slightly breathless, or perhaps very breathless, now she came to think of it.

'Thanks, I'll take that as the compliment of the night. More?'

She shook her head. 'Thanks. I enjoyed that, very much.' She gently disentangled herself from his grip and turned towards the door.

'You're leaving?' He looked quite dismayed.

She wasn't quite sure where she was going but she did know she'd had enough excitement for the time being, and she didn't really want the merry widower latching onto her again as she was sure he would do. (She had seen him watching her dancing, mouth agape.)

'If you leave I'll be tempted back to the card table. Do you want that on your conscience?'

She placed a hand on his arm and looked closely into his eyes. 'Self-control, Archie,' she said, seriously. 'You can do it, if you want to.'

He put his hand on hers and squeezed it warmly. 'I've enjoyed talking to you, Jess's mother.'

'Claudia,' she said. 'Me too, Archie the Australian.'

Then quite spontaneously she leant towards him and kissed him on the cheek. Before she turned to go she caught sight of the merry widower gazing at them in horror, or maybe it was just surprise.

She climbed the stairs to her bedroom wearily. It was approaching midnight but the party was still on the wax. There appeared to be more people arriving than leaving, and heavens above if she'd been at home she'd have been in her bed two hours ago. Her bed. What a lovely thought.

She opened the door of her room and without turning on the light flung herself onto a canopy of fur and camelhair, and she realised, gracious me, they've been using my room as a cloakroom.

She lay there among the furs and thought, so soft, how

nice, I might go to sleep right here, on the top of them, or even in them. So she wriggled and burrowed until she was immersed, like a bird in a nest, in her bed of fur. It felt naughty, but very nice.

Then out of the corner of her eye she noticed a small, glowing red light in the corner of the room. The glow grew brighter, than dimmer, then wavered, and she saw it was a cigarette.

'Who's there?' she said as she snapped on the bedside light.

There was a woman sitting on a chair, her chair, in the corner, one leg crossed over the other, the cigarette in its holder dangling from her fingers. She had short bobbed hair and she was wearing a man's suit, which looked rather odd but also, Claudia was *au fait* enough with fashion to recognise, quite *à la mode*.

'Don't mind me,' said the stranger. She had a black line painted around her eyes. It gave her a haunted look.

'Oh,' was all Claudia could come up with.

'Is this your room?' The woman leant over and tapped the end of her cigarette into the wastepaper basket.

'It is actually.'

'Would you rather I vacated it?' She was making no move to go. She was looking at Claudia through her black-rimmed, laconic eyes.

'I suppose there's little point really.' Claudia lay back into the furs. 'It's not as if I can go to bed until everyone has gone, whenever that happens to be.'

'Don't count on getting much sleep tonight.' The woman took a drag on her cigarette. She was watching Claudia in a rather disconcerting way.

'That was such fun,' said Claudia.

'You're ducking out early though.'

'It's past my bedtime as a matter of fact.' Claudia wriggled back among the furs. 'I danced with an

Australian.'

'Bully for you,' said the woman. 'That'll be Archie Wentworth.'

'Archie, yes, he's quite a character.'

'So he likes to think. Says he's descended from convicts. His great-grandfather was transported to Australia for highway robbery.'

'Really?' Claudia lifted herself up onto her elbows. 'How thrilling.'

The woman shrugged. 'That's what he claims. And he's probably illegitimate. But then illegitimacy runs in the family apparently, so he's only keeping up the tradition.' She took a long puff on her cigarette.

'I'm surprised my daughter would know someone like that.'

'Archie doesn't need to be invited anywhere, he just turns up.'

Claudia sat up fully and took a proper look at the stranger. 'What are you doing here, come to that?'

'Waiting for someone.'

'Anyone in particular?'

'Someone who is not a lawyer, or company director or something in the City. Or heterosexual.'

Claudia's eyes widened. Was this her first encounter with what was known as a lesbian? That would account for the get-up, she supposed. Woman dressed as a man, it was obvious really.

The woman shifted slightly in her seat. She removed her spent cigarette from its holder, squeezed the butt between forefinger and thumb and placed it in her pocket.

'Is that what you usually do with your cigarette ends?'

'I couldn't see an ashtray, I assume you're not a smoker. I do have some manners.' She smiled, for the first time. It was an odd smile, it didn't really suit her.

'I thought there were some extremely dashing young

men down there,' said Claudia. 'Or . . . ' Now how could she put this? 'Or . . . '

'Or what?'

'Women too. Lovely, some of them. Having such a good time.'

The stranger shrugged again. 'Not my type.'

'Perhaps you came to the wrong party.'

'I think that every time. One lives in hope.' She sighed. 'You on your own here?'

'Yes. I'm Jessica's mother.'

'I know that. No husband?'

'He's away. He's . . . '

'No need to tell me.' The woman raised a hand. 'Not my business, what a woman does. We're all free spirits.'

'Why do you come to a party like this if you don't like the people?' Claudia felt vaguely defensive on her daughter's behalf.

'I was being provocative, darling.' She looked directly at Claudia and said, 'You ever had an affair with a woman?'

'Certainly not! What do you take me for?'

'I don't "take you" for anything. Just wondered. Woman on her own. Opportunity. No offence.'

'None taken. Nor did I mean to offend you. I mean, if that's what . . . that's what . . . ' Claudia fell back into her fur pillow. She felt so tired. She really did not want this conversation.

'You'll never know unless you try.'

You'll never know unless you try. Claudia thought of Dougie.

At that point there came a faint roar from downstairs.

'That'll be him,' said the woman, sliding to her feet. She stopped in the doorway. 'Want to meet him?'

'Who?'

'You'll see.'

What the hell, there was little point trying to get any sleep yet. 'All right,' she said, and she rose from the bed, patted her hair, and followed the young woman out of the door.

A crowd was surrounding the newcomer and it wasn't until her companion called out – 'Noël!' – that the crowd parted and there stood a dapper young man, tall, slim, rather good-looking, and faintly familiar.

'Nicholas!' the young man called back, raising a hand in greeting. Nicholas. She'd even adopted a male name, thought Claudia, momentarily stupefied. But as she watched the two of them greeting one another – a hug, a slap on the back, several slaps on the back, a slightly giveaway 'Nicky, dear boy' – it wasn't until then it finally occurred to her that her female companion was a male.

My word, she thought, the world has moved on.

'Noël, meet my new chum Claudia, Jess's mother.'

'Delighted,' said the newcomer.

'Good God!' boomed a voice from across the room. 'It's the man himself! How did he get in here?'

It was Jonno, pushing his way through the people. 'Noël Coward himself, well I'll be damned, how did you get here?'

'Taxi,' said Noël. 'How about you?'

Jonno roared with laughter. 'I was watching you only the other night. Rollicking!'

'Ah, so it was you.'

Of course, he was the man in the revue, the man who had addressed Jonathan directly from the stage. Noël Coward. Claudia had heard of him but only in the vaguest terms.

She looked around for her Australian friend. She wondered if he knew about Noël Coward, since he knew about the Astaires, but he no longer seemed to be there. So she turned to watch the exchange between Coward and her son-in-law.

'I always did want to go on the stage!' Jonno roared.

'I'm sure you'd knock 'em dead,' replied his companion, with a smile. 'If you like, I'll write a part for you.'

'You write plays too, do you? Well I must say. Would you put me into one of them?'

'Possibly.'

'I tell you what, my wife would make a wonderful actress. Very beautiful, as you can see.' He had his arm around his beautiful wife.

'So she is. Perhaps I would. Or perhaps I would write a play about her mother.'

Claudia started. He was looking right at her.

'I beg your pardon?' she said.

'Claudia, come and talk to Noël,' said Nicholas.

She couldn't think what on earth she'd have to say to someone like Noël Coward. She was still smarting with embarrassment at having mistaken his friend for a woman. She felt suddenly and totally out of place, like a small child who wants to go home.

11

After all that she was one of the last to go to bed. The clock had struck three a while ago and by the time she finally reached her bedroom the coats had gone.

She had found her second wind, thanks to the company. Noël Coward was only a vaguely familiar name to someone who did not frequent the West End. But there was an assurance about him, a confidence in the company of older people which most other young people didn't have. In fact it could be quite a giveaway when a Bright Young Thing, so apparently at ease with the world in general, became suddenly awkward and tongue-tied in the company of someone from an older generation; as if their *savoir faire* depended on an understanding among their peers that, 'Really darlings, this is all a game, and you know as well as I do not to take anything I say seriously.'

The conversation was nonetheless strange.

'Do you have a son, Mrs Faraday?' he asked her. They were seated together on the sofa upon which Claudia had spent a large part of the evening, partly with her son-in-law's father who, she was relieved to see, had gone. Opposite them sat Nicholas, Nicky, watching closely.

'Claudia, please. No, I don't,' she replied.

'A shame,' said he.

'But I do have three daughters. Will they do?'

'Perhaps.' He thought for a bit. 'I have never understood,' he went on after a while, 'why a woman should want to be younger than she is.'

'What do you mean?' demanded Claudia, momentarily offended.

'Gracious,' he said. 'You don't think I'm referring to *you*, dear Claudia.' He reached over and patted her hand almost paternally. 'I'm thinking of women of *un certain âge* who persist in falling in love. You would think a person would be glad to put all that terrible business behind her and get on with her life without all the mess. Wouldn't you?'

There was a pause. Both men were looking at Claudia.

'What mess?' she asked, eventually.

'Falling in love is a messy business, falling out of love even messier. Somewhere in between the sex and the mess and the games, life slips by without one noticing it. Real life, that is.'

'You don't consider falling in love real life?'

'No, I don't. Not in the way people go at it these days.' He smoked his cigarette through a holder, just like his friend. In fact their mannerisms were remarkably similar. 'Nowadays it's more to do with one-upmanship, skirmishes and scraps, fought to the death on battlefields.' He drew on his cigarette. 'Why would a person not want to put all that behind her?'

'I'm not sure,' Claudia began, tentatively, 'that falling in love is confined only to the young.'

'Ah!' Noël turned to face her directly. 'Now, there you have it. Tell me more.'

'I haven't anything to tell you!' She had regretted them the minute the words left her mouth, but it was late, and she'd had a certain amount to drink, and the company was making her feel reckless. 'Not really.'

She didn't want to meet his eye. She didn't want to

finish what she'd so thoughtlessly started, especially not in front of the man/woman called Nicky. As if he was reading her thoughts Noël, without taking his eyes away from her, said, 'Nicky, dear boy, do us a favour and get lost for a while, would you?'

For a long moment Nicky did not react. Then with studied deliberation he pulled himself to an upright position and sauntered slowly off.

'Tricky boy,' Noël murmured. He gestured for Claudia to go on.

'Why are you interested in what older women think?'

'I'm a playwright, Mrs Faraday. How can I expect to put myself into the shoes of a woman of a mature age, of any age come to that, without asking impertinent questions?'

'You're writing about an older woman who falls in love?'

'I'm *thinking* about writing about an older woman who *thinks* she's fallen in love. With a much younger man.'

'Because it makes her feel young again?'

'Pre-cisely.' He pronounced the word with great delicacy. 'One would think you'd been looking over my shoulder. Does that sound too absurd for words?'

'I'm not sure I'm the one to answer that. There may be other reasons.'

'Such as?'

'Because it's fun.'

'Ah!'

'Or because it just happens. As these things do, when you least expect them. Or want them.'

'Aha!' He waited, expecting her to go on. 'So some things never change, is what you are saying?'

'I think when one gets to a certain age and realises that the best of one's life is behind one, that is a sobering thought.'

He nodded. And waited.

'But then one starts to think maybe not. One still has a fair amount of time left in this world and one is not yet . . . incapable. And there are still – experiences – one would like to have, er, experienced.'

She felt ridiculously incoherent.

'There is a tension between what society expects of a person and what a person may expect, or desire even, for herself,' he said.

'Beautifully put.' She smiled.

'And in your case, dear lady, I have no doubt you have the courage to defy society's expectations.' He looked at her so warmly she wanted to put her arms around him and hug him.

'I do hope so,' she said.

It was at that point that Jonno approached, with a reluctant Jessica, who appeared to be pulling on his arm, to request yet again that the 'great maestro' (as he insisted on calling Coward) write his wife a part in his next play. So it was with the greatest of tact, and a maturity that belied his years – he was probably younger than most of the others in the room – that the Great Maestro explained gently that acting was, in fact, a profession generally undertaken by professionals. And while he had no doubt the beautiful Jessica, Mrs Faraday's daughter, would make a sublime actress it would not be easy to persuade a theatre management to take on someone with so little experience, especially in the West End. Even if she was, as he had no doubt, a superb Juliet in her school play. All of which was regrettable, but if Jessica did decide she wanted to 'take to the boards' he would be only too happy to introduce her to some Useful People.

Then, almost as an afterthought, he added, 'Since you have been the most generous hosts I feel bound to warn you that as professions go, you might find it easier and more lucrative to pursue a career in the coalmines.' Even Jonno got the message then.

The GM had a way of saying things that may not have been what a person wanted to hear but which made them feel the better for having heard them. Even Nicky seemed to have forgiven him, and between them, Nicky and Jonno, they managed to persuade the GM to perform one of the songs from his current revue for them *a capella*, since, regretfully, Jonno and Jessica did not possess a piano. Which he did, with great charm, directing it first to Claudia and then to Jessica and finally back to Claudia again. So Claudia ended the evening feeling quite the belle of the ball.

Before he left Noël Coward sought her out, and taking her hand he kissed it and said, 'Serendipity is a wonderful thing.'

'Do you think so?' murmured Claudia. Then, 'I look forward to seeing your play. What will it be called?'

He thought for a moment. '*The Whirlpool*.'

'Whirlpool?'

'It's the whirlpool of conflicting emotions and clashing motives that sweeps a person up and swallows him, like, like . . . ' he stopped and smoothed a hand over his hair. 'Not very inspiring, is it?'

'Like a vortex?'

'Vortex!' He snapped his fingers. 'That's it! *The Vortex*. That's much better. Thank you, dearest Claudia, thank you.' With which he kissed her hand again, and with a little bow he was gone, the faithful Nicky by his side.

~

The inevitable party post mortem took place the following morning over breakfast, which was attended by the younger members of the family in pyjamas and dressing gowns.

'I swear I only knew a fraction of the guests!' said

Jessica with a merry laugh.

The presence of the Great Maestro was the biggest mystery, but it was concluded eventually that he was there because of the man called Nicky, who himself had been invited by Jessica's friend Megan, who mistakenly thought he was sweet on her. Later on in the evening, in tears, Megan had confided to Jessica that Nicky was little more than a 'party junky', unable to resist an invitation, and that he not only had no designs on her he had spent most of the evening elsewhere.

'In my bedroom actually,' said Claudia.

When eyebrows were raised she went on to describe the scene that took place between the two of them, including the fact that she had thought that 'he' was a 'she' and moreover was a . . . (she could not quite bring herself to say the word lesbian, not in company, but it was understood), and who may or may not have had designs on *her*, who was old enough to be her – or indeed his – mother. At which point both Jessica and Jonathan roared with laughter, and then Jessica said, 'Poor dear Megan, she never could tell, could she?'

'Tell what?' queried her husband.

'The difference.'

'Difference?'

'Jonno you can be unbelievably obtuse. The difference between . . . ' she glanced at her mother.

'Don't mind me, darling.'

'He leans the other way. Bats for the other side. Actually I think he's been known to bat for both sides, but unfortunately not for Megan's.'

It was agreed that the presence in their house of Noël Coward was quite a boon, and would be a talking point for some time to come. And that he had definitely taken to Claudia, as had the strange Australian, whose name was –

'Archie Wentworth,' said Claudia. There then followed an

almost forensic discussion as to *his* provenance, which was never properly concluded.

'He wore a lounge suit,' said Jonno, with a puzzled frown. 'And no tie.'

'So?'

'Doesn't he know the *form*?'

'I've married a terrific snob, Mother, what should I do with him?'

Jessica laughed and tucked an affectionate, dressing-gowned arm into her husband's.

It was unanimously adjudged that one way or another, both guests, and by association Nicky as well, had added much to the gaiety of the proceedings and that the whole evening had been a wild success, even if it did break up at the rather late hour of 3 am.

'And if I may say so, Mother-in-law,' said Jonno, as he slurped his coffee (and he talks about 'form', thought Claudia), 'you were terrific. My father thought you were the bees' knees.'

'I am so pleased,' said Claudia.

12

It was almost a relief to get back to the dull tranquillity of her home.

It was as if she'd received a resounding push-start. Jessica had, in her happily forthright way, congratulated her mother on her 'pheromones', which word Claudia had to look up in order to establish it meant the sexual signals emitted by animals in order to attract the opposite sex.

She was shocked to think she might be emitting anything in particular, let alone something sexual. Yet how else to account for the sudden appearance in her life of so many admirers, whether male playwrights of unconventional sexuality or old lovers? Whatever it was, she was both secretly pleased and slightly unnerved. It was true that her encounter with Gabriel Carter had awoken something in her, something that had lain dormant for so long she could hardly remember whether she had ever been properly aware of it in the first place.

When Claudia was young, the more beautiful she felt, the more attention she attracted; or maybe it was the other way around. Something not dissimilar was happening to her right now. Prudence used to say the more sexually active a woman was the more desirable she appeared to the opposite sex. And while that was the sort of nonsense Prue was prone to spout, she understood now, did Claudia, there might be something in it.

If Jessica truly knew what had triggered her mother's pheromones as she called them, she would have been deeply shocked. Flirtation was one thing, so long as it was nothing more than 'harmless fun'. Whatever was happening to Claudia now as a result of her extraordinary encounter was, with the exception of the said encounter, still largely harmless fun in her view, and moreover made her feel a hundred times more alive. What could possibly be wrong with that? Having been asleep for so long, figuratively speaking, she had a lot of waking up to do.

~

She arrived home to several telephone messages and a letter.

'Mrs de Vere telephoned, madam, and a gentleman named,' Lily peered at the piece of paper she'd scribbled on, 'Perceveral Lightfoot.'

'Who?'

'That's what it sounded like. I did ask him to spell it out for me.'

Claudia assumed this must be somebody's joke, even Dougie's – who else could it possibly be?

'I told them all you were in London, madam, but I didn't want to give them your number. I hope I did right.'

'Thank you Lily, you did. And how were things while I've been away?'

'Fine, thank you madam. I enjoyed my days off.' Lily's eyes were shining more brightly than usual. Then she did an uncharacteristically coquettish little twirl and Claudia realised suddenly: 'You've had your hair done!'

'Yes, madam. Do you like it? It was you who gave me the idea.'

'It's very pretty indeed. How did I manage to do that?'

'It was you who started it really, when you had yours done, do you remember? And I thought, We women, it's time we took a good look at ourselves and made sure we're not getting stuck in a rut!'

She paused, and flushed. She was not used to being quite so outspoken with her mistress, but Claudia was highly amused. 'You've done very well, Lily. Perhaps too well. I'm afraid one of these days I might lose you.'

'Beg pardon, madam?'

'Never mind. I'll just get myself organised and then I'll be down for tea shortly, all right?'

'Indeed, madam.'

The letter was from Dougie. There was no indication he had also called pretending to be a Perceveral Lightfoot, rather the opposite.

My dear Claudia, he wrote.

You know what a thrill it was for me to see you the other day. You probably won't believe me when I tell you how glorious you were looking, so young, so full of life, it quite took me back.

You may have been wondering why you didn't hear from me again after my foolish proposition. Maybe you were glad, maybe you never want to see or hear from me again, I wouldn't blame you in the slightest. I was as taken aback by my own words as you were, as a matter of fact. Whatever courage, or stupidity, prompted me to say those things at the time left me seconds later, which is why I am writing to apologise. Were I a proper man I would have said all this to your face, but since it is so much easier to express oneself in written words rather than the spoken variety, that is what I am doing now.

I am asking if you will forgive me, or better still, pretend I never said anything in the first place, and that we might continue our friendship as if nothing had happened. I am staying with my sister in Highgate for the time being, and if you were to find yourself in London again in the foreseeable future it would of course be delightful to see you.

*Meanwhile I wish you all the merries and jollies and
so forth,*

Your devoted friend, Dougie.

Claudia thought for a moment and then, digging out a
pad of notepaper from her desk she tore off a sheet and
wrote,

Dear Dougie,

*Don't be such a fool. You are totally forgiven, if you think
you need to be. Why don't you come down and see me one
day soon?*

Love Claudia.

PS: Do you know a Perceveral Lightfoot?

And before she had time to rethink she'd folded the
sheet, packed it into the envelope, stuck it down and was
calling for Lily to collect it and put it into the post right
away, that instant.

'Is that before you have your tea, madam, or can it wait
till after?'

'Before. Right now.'

She was furious. Infuriated. A man of his age should
not be playing those sorts of games. With the pique still
rampant, she called up her friend Mrs de Vere.

'Prue, it's Claudia.'

'Darling! You're back from wherever you've been.'

'I was going to say the same to you.'

'You sound flustered, is there anything the matter?'

Claudia took a breath. 'Can't really explain on the
telephone, Prue. What about you, how are you?'

'Bursting. So much to tell you!'

'Well why don't you come down and stay for a bit and
we can let off steam together.'

'Let off steam? All right, if that's what you feel you
want to do. But gracious, I've only just landed back on
home turf. Would next week do?'

'Certainly. Just let me know which day. I'll be here.'

'Say Thursday?'

'Wonderful. Till then.'

'Till then.'

Claudia then turned her attention to Perceveral Lightfoot.

'Did he say why he was calling?' she asked Lily, who was still slightly out of breath from running to catch the post.

'No, madam.'

'Or any kind of message? A number even?'

'No, madam.'

'What did he sound like?'

'Sound like?'

'Young, old, foreign?'

'He sounded – well, he sounded older, I'd say, a bit like Mr Faraday, in a way.'

'But not Mr Faraday.'

'Oh certainly not, madam, he'd have said so. I just mean he sounded, you know, about the same age, and he spoke well, if you see what I mean.'

'Did he say he'd call back?'

'Not as I remember, madam.' Lily looked concerned. Her mistress was definitely not herself. 'Would you like your tea now, madam?'

'I think I'd better, yes, thank you Lily. I'm sorry.'

'What for?'

'I'm not quite myself, as you can see.'

'I never noticed, madam.'

It was not until the tea arrived, with the accompanying plate of *petits fours*, and she had sat down and closed her eyes and allowed Lily to pour it and place the cup and saucer into her hand, and she had had her first sip and felt the soothing liquid sliding down her throat, that Claudia finally began to relax.

~

Claudia and Prudence went back several years, BM (Before Marriage). Their friendship thrived on mutual admiration: Claudia had the looks and Prudence the personality. 'My dear, with my face and my figure I've got to have something to offer people!' Prue was fond of saying. She was small, and slightly dumpy, her face was round and perpetually shiny (despite attempts with powder puffs), and her hair a mass of hard-to-control curls, or frizz, as she described it. She spent her adolescence 'living down my name, darling' and got married quite late, in her mid thirties, to a man called Wilfred, who was something in the Foreign Office. He managed to quieten her down for the relatively short time they were married, until he died in mysterious circumstances in the war. Since when Prudence had reverted to her previous, imprudent self.

Like many friends, each envied the other. Prudence would have given anything – *anything* – to have had half the elegance and beauty (and the height) of her friend, while Claudia quietly marvelled at her friend's wit and extrovert personality, beside which she felt positively dull. Both in their different ways attracted people, different sorts of people with different motives, perhaps. 'At least you know people like you for who you are,' Claudia once told her friend, in response to which Prue, for once, had nothing to say.

Prudence thought her friend slightly straightlaced and (secretly) a little vain. Claudia marvelled at her friend's adventures while (secretly) only half believing them. Adventures had never been regular features of Claudia's life and she felt she lacked the knack of attracting them, whereas Prudence claimed they positively sought her out. Delving deeper, Prudence considered Claudia's beauty had arrested the development of other, less visible parts of her, such as her brain; while Claudia thought Prudence's recounting of her so-called adventures was nothing more than a way of drawing attention to herself. In Prudence's eyes Claudia used her absentee husband as an excuse for her lack of adventurousness, while Claudia thought her best friend ought, really, to mind her own business.

None of which less than complimentary thoughts got in the way of what was an enduring, profound and loving friendship.

~

The few days that followed Claudia's visit to London she spent quietly in the house, and wandering in the garden. It was still warm enough this late September to spend time outdoors without a coat, and she took to sitting on the ground beneath the ancient oak tree, her back leaning against the great trunk, feeling – or trying to feel – its pulse. If one closed one's eyes one could imagine anything, and it was on just such an occasion, as the sun was in position to shine directly, and softly, onto her upturned face, that she made her first acquaintance with Perceveral Lightfoot.

He was tall, taller than Dougie (and Gerald), lean, and cut a dash that reminded her of Douglas Fairbanks. He was strangely quiet in company, he preferred listening to talking, which was unusual in a man. This endowed him with a deep aura of mystery because he so rarely talked about himself, and when he did he managed to do so without revealing very much. No one seemed to know where he was from or what he did, or how he came to be among them in the first place. Someone said once he'd been a pirate, but Claudia assumed they were joking. To say he set his sights on Claudia from the word go is an assumption in a sense, because there was no telling what went on in his secretive mind. Yet Claudia was always acutely aware, whenever they were in company, of his eyes upon her.

There was one occasion in late summer, when the house was full of rather over-excited young people, that somebody decided, after dinner, that it would be fun to take a boat out and row to the 'haunted' island in the middle of the lake. There were only two boats however, so when Claudia declared that fourteen people, many of whom had had decidedly too much to drink, in two far-too-small boats, at night, without any light at all, was frankly idiotic and she would sit this one out, thanks very much, somebody – Prudence, probably – yelled out, 'Where's your sense of adventure, Claudie?'

So it was that she found herself, as she thought, standing alone by the lake watching her lunatic friends laughing and shrieking as they scrambled on board two violently rocking boats, that she heard a voice in her ear saying: 'They'll be in the water before you can say hello.'

It was Perceveral (he had not yet suggested anyone call him Percy).

'You're absolutely right,' she said, and then turning to him, she asked, 'Why didn't you go with them?'

He looked at her long and hard before replying, 'I didn't want to leave you here in the dark on your own.'

So they sat down on the grass, right there beside the lake, together watching the still-rocking boats with their near-hysterical occupants lurching away from them into the darkness. Then it went quiet, and still they sat there.

Then without saying a word Perceveral Lightfoot got to his feet and began to take his clothes off. Claudia averted her eyes until she heard the splash! as he entered the water. She watched him diving beneath the surface and then reappearing, shaking his head and laughing, and the spray from his hair, which was plentiful, splashed her and made her laugh, and stand up, and want to join him.

'Is it cold?' she called.

'Not a bit!' he said, and down he went again.

She hesitated. Then because his exuberance was so infectious, and because it was a beautiful evening, but mostly because no one was insisting or urging her to, in an instant she threw away twenty-something years of caution and stripped off all her clothes and stood there on the bank of the lake in the moonlight, stark naked. Her body looked luminous in the light of the moon, and as he re-emerged he looked up at her in open delight and called out, 'You are beautiful!'

With a little shriek she jumped into the water right by him. She'd never swum naked before and the sense of the water next to her skin – why, it was like taking a bath, only more, much more. There was water surrounding her and holding her and caressing her, and so she swam for a bit, and ducked and dived, and then she lay flat on her back and floated and allowed her head to relax and her eyes to gaze up at the watching moon for what seemed like an age. She felt so utterly free. She was aware of a movement beneath her and she knew as she lay there, open to the skies, to the world and to everything, that he was swimming under and around her and looking closely at every part of her, and it was unutterably thrilling.

They began to swim around one another, like a couple of fish, silver in the moonlight, chasing one another and diving and laughing like children; though not really like children, not at all. Claudia had never properly looked at a naked man's body before and she had always thought, assumed maybe, that it was somehow ludicrous. But this body was not ludicrous at all, this body was exactly like the sculptures she'd seen at the British Museum: white, solid, muscular, rounded, no sharp edges and no spare flesh on it at all. She found it quite extraordinarily beautiful and she wanted to stay there for ever, gazing at it.

Two bodies, barely an inch apart, almost but not quite

touching, treading water together, and so they stayed for several minutes until, with another of his quicksilver movements, Perceveral swung away from her, swam to the bank and pulled himself up out of the water. Then he lay down flat on his back on the grass and spread his arms and legs wide, like a starfish.

Eventually she scrambled out of the lake and onto the grass beside him, where she stood for a moment looking down on him.

'You are beautiful too,' she said.

He sat up and smiled at her. Then there came yells and laughter from the middle of the lake. 'Do you think they found the ghost?' he said.

'Maybe,' she laughed. 'They sound as if they're having a good time, anyway.'

'Not as good a time as we've had.'

He was still looking into the distance. So she reached for her clothes and began to dress, which with her wet body was not an easy task, but was eventually and quite uncomfortably achieved, and he did the same; so that by the time the two boats reappeared, still rocking dangerously and yet still miraculously intact, they were both fully clothed.

'Ahoy there, landlubbers!' came a male voice.

'How was it?' Claudia called out.

'Bit of a damp squib to tell the truth,' said the same voice. 'We couldn't see a darn thing.'

'And nobody fell overboard!' said another.

'It was really spooky out there,' she heard Prue's voice in the dark, 'and we could see moving shadows and all sorts. Another adventure missed, Claudie!'

To which remark Claudia said nothing, but smiled, as did her companion.

Prudence climbed out of her boat as one of the young men held it fast for her. She looked first at Claudia and then at Perceveral, then she frowned and said, 'You're wet.'

'I am. We are.'

'How come?'

'We went swimming.'

'What, fully clothed?' Prue's eyes were like saucers.

Claudia shot a quick glance at her companion. 'No.'

'Oh.' Then Prudence's face creased and she began to laugh. 'You!' She poked her friend sharply in the ribs. 'You dark horse!' She continued to look from one to another of them, hoping for an explanation, and when none was forthcoming she laughed some more, then turned and walked back towards the house.

By now the sun that had been warming Claudia's face had moved on so she was mostly in the shade. As she opened her eyes so the visions disappeared – the lake, the moonlight and the two naked bodies. She sighed, and pressed her back against the trunk of the tree, and for the first time she thought she felt the heart of the great oak, distinctly throbbing and pulsating right through her.

13

The phone rang early the following morning and to Claudia's astonishment it was her middle daughter on the line.

'You're up early, darling,' she said.

'Late, actually,' said Harriet. 'We're off to bed in a minute.' She yawned loudly, to emphasise her point. Of course. Harriet and Leonard led upside-down hours.

'I hear you went to stay with Jess and Jonno.'

'I did, yes.'

'How was it?'

This was not a straightforward question. Harriet and Jessica failed to see eye to eye, not to put too fine a point on it. It was not quite a feud, nor a falling-out, merely a case of two young women whose priorities and motivations were diametrically different. And whereas in Harriet's case she considered the lifestyle and profligacy of 'the two Js' beyond the pale, on Jessica's part there was not so much overt animosity as a sense of puzzlement as to why anyone, let alone a sister with whom she had shared an identical upbringing, with identical parents, should wilfully want to live a life so devoid of fun and creature comforts. To which Harriet's response would have been, 'There is more than one definition for "fun", you know, Jessica.'

They had never, to Claudia's knowledge, had such a

conversation but that is how she imagined they might have argued their respective cases.

Claudia was both mildly distressed that her two elder daughters did not get along, and mildly bemused, along with Jessica and for similar reasons, by the fact that both girls sprang from the same womb, and only two years apart. She knew she had never been the influence on her daughters that her own mother had been on her, deliberately so perhaps because her own mother had always dictated exactly how Claudia should dress, behave, speak and live her life, right up until the end (she died when Claudia was in her early twenties, before she married Gerald); which deprived Claudia of any sense of self-determination. Whether deliberately or not therefore she had allowed her daughters, within reason, to go their own sweet ways and make their own decisions, however wayward. She might not always have agreed or approved of these decisions but one thing she could say to herself, with pride and a bit of wistfulness, was that they were their own people, in a way she had never been allowed to be; thus all three had over the years developed a strong sense of independence which, as any mother knows, is a mixed blessing.

'It was fun,' was how Claudia responded to her daughter's question, realising as she did so she had used a contentious word.

'Huh,' came the reply. Then, 'So they're doing all right, are they? Jess and Jonno?'

That was another thing: deep down, or so Claudia thought, they did care very much about one another and were genuinely interested in what the other got up. So it was she, Claudia, and to some extent the youngest sister, Flora, who acted as conduits between the two. In fact, as was borne out by the next question, it was not Claudia that Harriet was calling up about, it was Jessica.

'What's their house like?'

'Beautiful. But a bit shambolic.'

'Huh.'

'It's a three-storey terraced house, in a lovely quiet street right across the road from Primrose Hill. You can see the park from the window, there's so much greenery.'

'I don't like greenery.'

Harriet did talk nonsense sometimes.

'Have you never been invited there? You and Leonard?'

'Oh yes, but what's the point? We don't get on with their friends and they think we're freaks,' said her middle daughter, not without a good deal of pride. 'So,' she went on, 'babies?'

'Darling, they've only been married four months.'

'So? I thought they wanted dozens. They'll have to get a move on if they want to churn out that many while Jess can still do it.'

'Gracious, she's only twenty-six darling.'

'Exactly.'

'Well then.' There was a pause. Was there something else?

'How are the two of you, anyway?' Claudia asked.

'Muddling along.'

Was it money? Was that the reason for the call?

'Do you . . . ' How should she put this? 'Is everything all right there, darling?'

'Of course, why do you ask?'

'No reason, I'm just being your mother. You're all right for money, are you?'

'Oh for goodness' sake, Mother!'

She had married a poet, after all.

'Perhaps you'd like to come down here one of these days,' said Claudia. 'It's been a while.' Since their wedding actually, which must be what, five or six months now.

'Maybe. Or . . . '

'Or?'

'I don't suppose you'd want to come here. Not when you've just been, to London that is. But you know, you'd be very welcome.'

Now this was a surprise.

'Darling I'd love to, but you don't have enough room.'

'There's a perfectly good sofa, if you don't mind roughing it.'

Hmm. Their way of life – up at noon, to bed at 6am – their parties, their friends, how on earth would they fit her into all of that? She was adaptable, up to a point only.

Claudia had only once seen the 'garret', as they insisted on calling it, in which Harriet and Leonard chose to live, and that was soon after they had moved in. She had tried to describe it later to Gerald who, having in the latter days of the couple's courtship interrogated Leonard in some detail as to his income, his capital, his background and his prospects, had eventually if reluctantly been persuaded he was not a complete dud and might just make a suitable spouse for his daughter. His response to Claudia had been predictable. 'One room, you say? And no proper kitchen! What, you mean they sleep in the same room that they *dine* in? What about hygiene? They what? One electric ring that they keep *on the floor*? What is this? This is slum dwelling! It's *fashionable*, did you say? You mean people *choose* to live like this?' But after this initial outburst he had never mentioned the subject again, either because he could not bring himself to think of it or, more likely, because he had not given it or them another thought.

And all this, Claudia thought later, though she did not voice it, from a man who spent a good deal of his life living in a tent.

But then, returning to the original question, there was no easy way that Claudia could refuse the invitation to stay with one daughter when she had so willingly stayed with another, which was why she ended up saying, 'I'd love to darling, one day quite soon.'

'Good,' said Harriet, and rang off.

Claudia pondered on the conversation for some time. There was definitely something Harriet was not telling her. The child who had never wanted anybody's opinion or advice on anything was now turning to her mother for just that. Which was alarming in one sense and reassuring in another, bearing in mind Claudia's above-mentioned relationship with her.

Of course it could have been something quite different which Claudia was too stupid to pick up on. Something to do with Jessica, or babies, although Harriet had sworn she never intended to have anything to do with the things – Christ no, there were enough people in the world already and anyway she would make a terrible mother, no maternal instinct and besides, she hated the brats, couldn't bear them near her, it was almost an aversion and yes, before you asked, Leonard agreed with her one hundred per cent.

Leaving aside any suggestion of the lady protesting too much methinks, Claudia did her best to explain, to all her girls, the joy they had brought her over the years, and continued to bring her, not to mention the comfort they might provide in her old age. Reassured that at least one of her girls would be delivering grandchildren, Claudia did not press the point. But then there was another possibility: that Harriet was pregnant and didn't know what to do.

In the end there was only one conclusion: that one of these days Claudia would have to grit her teeth and make the pilgrimage to Parson's Green.

14

Prudence had no children (Claudia never did quite find out why), but like many non-mothers she was not short on opinions as to how they should be brought up.

Her own upbringing had been, as she said, conducted remotely, by a mother who seemed barely to have realised she had brought forth two children into the world – one boy, one girl, in that order. She had consequently left their care and nurture completely up to their nanny and, when the time came, a series of maids and private tutors. Prudence prided herself as a result on her total lack of proper education or self-discipline which, she claimed, was the secret of the success she considered her life to be.

Following her own example children, in Prudence's view, should be left to their own devices to 'discover' themselves, and above all should not be expected to become carbon copies of their own parents, as so many mothers and fathers seemed to want them to be. By these criteria Claudia was a 'moderately successful' mother in Prudence's eyes ('eight out of ten, darling'), because while she had not imposed too many of her own views on her daughters she had laid down certain rules which ultimately kowtowed to society's mores, and thereby restricted her children's natural growth. So for instance in a social situation, *should* one's offspring decide, quite spontaneously, to take off all their clothes and jump into their host's lake 'starkers', as Prudence claimed to have once done (and Claudia in her fantasy had also done), by forbidding them to do so one was placing the opinion of others above the natural, and totally harmless, instincts of one's offspring.

Which view, as Claudia might have said, was all very well in theory but not necessarily so easy to abide by in practice. Besides which, by imposing her own view in this instance it could be argued that Prudence was doing the very thing she was accusing other over-authoritarian parents of doing. Which really negated the whole argument, which is what made the argument so much fun in the first place.

~

Mid-morning on the Thursday Prudence rolled up in her red MG sports car, chosen for its colour rather than its roadworthiness, mechanical condition, value for money, or any other quality by which motor cars are generally judged.

She was a good enough driver but liked to make out she was slightly crazier than she was (a tendency that could be applied to other aspects of her life), especially when she had a passenger, by driving chaotically and sometimes downright dangerously in built-up areas. Which naturally led to her husband having to remind her, time and again, with increasing weariness, 'The pavement is for the people, roads are for cars, dear.'

'Phew, darling, phew!' she exclaimed, immediately upon arrival at Claudia's front door. 'Rosie's making very odd noises, a bit like my old auntie Frank after too much Christmas pudding. But here I am!' (Rosie was the car.)

'Here you are indeed!' The two friends hugged and Claudia ushered Prudence into her drawing room, sat her down, asked her what she felt like eating or drinking, and how she was, all in a state of merry excitement. Because despite their differences the two women were always delighted to see one another and to know they were still enjoying good health.

'Nothing, thank you, not yet, and I'm extremely well,' said Prudence, answering the questions in sequence. 'Oh gracious, I am very pleased to be here. As for you . . . ' She took a long hard look at her friend and said, 'Well, what have *you* been up to?'

Claudia smiled. 'I just thought it was time for a change.'

'Yes, indeed. So. Well. We do have things to catch up on.'

And Prudence being Prudence she launched into her recent adventures without any sign of prompting from Claudia, in such detail that by the time Lily arrived to tell them lunch was ready she had reached the end of Day Two of her guided tour around the artistic spots of northern Italy. She had introduced Claudia to Pierre, the young man conducting the tour, Giovanni Martini (not his real name, needless to say), the lothario who was the first of many to proposition her, Martini's wife Spinoza (not her real name), who did all she could to make Prudence's life a misery, and sundry other bit-part players not important enough to introduce fully, at this stage anyway, or to have been assigned nicknames.

Claudia listened with patience and amusement, and a degree of scepticism.

'Did you actually get to see any *art*?' she asked.

Prudence seemed surprised by the question.

'Of course! That was what we were there for. Of course we saw some art, Claudie, what are you suggesting?'

Prudence's defensive, even slightly offended reaction was an indication of her suspicion that her friend did not believe her stories, or worse, did not listen to them. Or perhaps, and most likely, that she, Claudia, suspected the purpose of the tour was simply an excuse for Prue to meet and make mischief with as many different men as possible, which was, of course, largely true.

So it came to lunchtime, and the conversation digressed while Lily was in the room because maids have ears, and much as Prudence herself thrived on gossip about others she couldn't *bear* the thought that Downstairs might be passing on snippets of her own private goings-on.

The moment lunch was over however and they had retired to the drawing room, the saga continued. Claudia learned that Martini was a hearty drinker and an even heartier lover, and here, to Prudence's surprise, she interjected with, 'What do you mean exactly?'

'What? Mean exactly what?'

'When you say he was a hearty lover. What exactly do you mean by that?'

Prudence paused for a moment before replying, 'He put his heart and soul into it, that's what I mean.'

'In what sense?'

'What do you mean, in what sense?'

'Describe it to me. Tell me how it all came about.'

'Well, he . . . ' Prue was momentarily thrown completely off balance, and Claudia wondered, not without a slight feeling of malice, whether it was because the love-making never actually happened or whether she considered Claudia was overstepping the mark, even for a best friend.

'You want to hear *details*?'

'I do.'

'Well then. It was like this.'

It was Day Two, they were in . . . she couldn't precisely remember the name of the town because they were all, actually, rather alike, though it was where there were all those friezes by that fellow Belloni, or Bellini, or whatever his name was. They'd had a very long day and come seven o'clock Martini's wife Spinoza said she was tired and wanted a lie-down before dinner; so that left them, Prudence and Martini, on their own, in the bar of the hotel, downing martinis (hence the nickname) and chatting away like old friends, until quite suddenly he leant towards her and whispered in her ear, 'Why don't we carry on in your room?' Which is to say carry on drinking.

Prudence was neither surprised nor offended at the proposition, so taking the bottle with them they proceeded up the stairs, which creaked, and along the passageway to her room, which was at the end of it and fortunately far away from where Martini's wife was supposedly sleeping.

Once inside her bedroom Martini went straight to the window to draw the blinds and then without so much as a 'by your leave' he took his clothes off and went to lie, naked, on top of her bed, beckoning to her to do the same – 'with a certain impatience,' said Prudence, as if time were limited, which it was, so there was no point in her playing hard to get.

'So,' she concluded, almost abruptly in the circumstances, 'I took my clothes off and joined him on the bed and he had me.'

There was a pause.

'Just like that.'

'Yes. I mean we both knew what we were doing, there was no point in playing around.'

'And by "had you" do you mean he . . . '

'Had me, darling, yes. I can spell it for you if you like.'

'And did you like it?'

'And did you like it?'

Prudence shrugged. 'It was all right. A bit uncomfortable to begin with, you know, and he was quite big, and I didn't have any . . . '

'So, how long did it go on for?'

'Crikey Claudia, I wasn't timing him.'

'But – roughly?'

'Twenty minutes. Fifteen maybe. Dinner was around eight and this would have been – well, there wasn't a lot of time, put it that way.'

'So there was no lead-up to the . . . to the . . . '

'To the . . . ? Say the word, darling.'

'There was no lead-up.'

'Foreplay, do you mean? No, none at all.'

'Isn't that – less than satisfactory?'

'Darling, it was a mindless fuck, between two people who barely knew one another but fancied each other like crazy and didn't want to hang around. If you want to hear what *real* love-making was like you'll have to wait till Siena. And Pierre. On Day Nine, if I remember rightly.'

Claudia nodded.

'Anyway, you've never wanted to know so much before, what's going on?'

It was a good question. Try as she might, Claudia could not help but feel faintly sickened. It was the animalistic aspect of it all, the utter lack of *finesse*. She could not rid herself of the vision of two sweaty bodies copulating – such an unseemly word – on Prudence's bed. 'A mindless f---' indeed. If that was all it was, what was the purpose behind it? Where was the tenderness, the grace? Did she really want to sit and listen to Prudence's boastful, adolescent meanderings? It was like slipping back thirty years to their youth, when the main topic of discussion was their latest 'crush', and exactly what went on between them (very little), and what might go on between them if they played their cards right. And here I am, in my fifties, my friend as well, and we're going right back to our beginnings, as if all those intervening years had taught us nothing. It was quite dispiriting.

As for broaching the topic of her own sexual encounters, or fantasies, well, goodness, whyever would one want to do such a thing? Even with one's closest friend. She shivered.

'What's up Claudie? You look as if someone just walked over your grave.'

'It's nothing,' said Claudia.

'I am your oldest friend, remember. If you're shocked, or appalled, you only have to say so.'

She was both shocked *and* appalled, and dismayed. Dismayed at herself, at her continuing aversion to something that was supposed to be the most natural thing in the world, that was taking place somewhere or other every second of every day. She was dismayed that she had reached the age of fifty-two and understood nothing, that the visit of the young man, which she thought had woken her up, had done no such thing.

'You're off with the fairies, darling.'

'Yes, sorry. I feel like some air, what do you think?'

'Splendid idea.' Prudence got to her feet and straightened her skirt. 'What about a little excursion in Rosie?'

'Yes, why not?'

At last, safe territory. A little run through the country lanes with her oldest and, despite everything, her dearest friend. What could be more innocent, and enjoyable?

15

They headed towards the village of D for tea, the little car, driven far too fast, bumping and farting – Prudence's words – its way through the country lanes and occasionally slicing off corners and frightening the sheep. Claudia's heart was in her mouth for the most part but she would die rather than admit as much, and besides the countryside, which she rarely got to see, was looking so utterly glorious. She had no idea there were so many colours in the world, and all of them red. It was overcast and there was mist swirling through the trees, looking like smoke from little bonfires.

'I must say I miss the countryside,' shouted Prudence over the noise of the engine. 'Wouldn't want to live here though. Lovely to visit. Makes you feel at one with nature, all these animals and so on.'

The cows stared at them over the fences and Claudia wondered what might be going on in their minds as they stood there, chewing and impassively observing the little red monster bucking and barking its way round the corners, sometimes rather closer to them than was intended. It takes a lot to shock a cow, she thought, marvelling.

If one closed one's eyes and didn't worry too much about the danger and the fact that the roads were largely empty of other little red monsters, or monsters of any colour, one could find it quite exhilarating. Deep down Claudia simply hoped and prayed her friend did know what she was doing and would not needlessly throw them into harm's way. But she did not reckon, and neither did Prudence, on the tractor emerging from the field around the blind corner in front of them, which caused Prudence to swear, brake and swerve into the ditch, in that order, all in the flick of an eye.

There was a long moment during which Rosie, whose nose was firmly embedded in a ditch, gave a series of apologetic little coughs, and then died. Then there was a silence.

'Well, bugger,' said Prudence. 'Are you all right, darling?'

It was a difficult one to answer. One was alive, with no sign of broken bones, or even of whiplash. But at the same time not only had one's system gone into shock but one's faculties were so overloaded that to render an immediate and proper answer was out of the question. Which is why Claudia said nothing, causing Prudence to turn to her and say, 'Claudie! Speak to me!'

'I'm all right,' she said eventually, which was true in a physical sense yet could not come near to revealing her true feelings about her friend's stupid STUPID recklessness and her puerile insistence on SHOWING OFF, even to her, her oldest and dearest friend, who neither needed nor wanted to be impressed and wasn't anyway.

She was aware there was a third party involved and that that third party was even now standing by Prudence's window and shouting something which, fortunately, the window being closed, and miraculously not smashed, she could not make out. The expression on his face said quite enough however.

'Here goes, darling,' said Prudence, struggling to open

her door. 'Pray for me, won't you.' The door opened without too much resistance yet only offered up a small gap, it being jammed up against the side of the ditch, into which Prudence fought to squeeze herself, but squeeze herself she did. So Claudia watched the confrontation from the safety of the passenger seat, from where once again she could see but not hear what was transpiring. The farmer, whose already ruddy face had turned a kind of vehement purple, was shouting right into Prudence's face and, give the girl her due, she was neither flinching nor retreating. She was simply standing there and letting him have his say, or his shout, without moving an inch or making any attempt to speak. 'You make your bed, you have to lie in it,' Prudence was wont to say, and here she was, proving her own point in no uncertain terms.

Eventually he paused for breath, and Claudia saw Prudence begin to speak, and be interrupted, and stop speaking again. This went on for some time. Her friend did not try to curb the interruptions or break the farmer's flow. As time went on the interruptions became fewer and the vehement purple faded to its original ruddiness, and then the farmer took a step back from Prudence and shuffled from one foot to another and made what looked like a placatory gesture. She saw Prudence say something, at which he smiled and shrugged and turned to his tractor, from where he produced a rope which he proceeded to attach to Rosie's rear bumper, at which point Prudence tapped on Claudia's window and beckoned her to vacate the car so the farmer could pull Rosie from the ditch. This was no easier a task for Claudia than it had been for Prudence, for the same reason, although there being less of her she was able in a short space of time to wriggle through the gap in the door and go to stand by her friend on the roadside. Together they watched as the farmer manoeuvred his tractor (which was undamaged), with estimable deftness, bearing in mind its size and the width of the road, so that it was facing in the right direction. He was now able to attach the other end of the rope to his vehicle and thereby, with remarkable ease, gently release Rosie from the ditch; at which point all three protagonists gave a small cheer.

He then offered to tow the two of them with Rosie to the nearest town that contained a motor repair shop, but Prudence reassured him that this would not be necessary. It was not, she whispered out of the side of her mouth to Claudia, actually the first time she had been in such a situation and she was pretty sure Rosie was still roadworthy. So they climbed inside her again and Prue tried the engine a few times, and after another slightly irritated bout of coughing Rosie sprang to life as if nothing had happened; although, as the farmer was quick to point out, the front wing on the driver's side was not what it was and she should have that seen to right away, and who knows, it may have caused damage to the engine.

By now it was far too late for the teashop in D so Prudence was persuaded to turn around and head home again. Rosie drove as sweetly as ever; in fact, as Prudence commented, she was farting rather less than usual, so maybe she ought to be driven into ditches more often. However the front did look a mess, even Prue could see that, in fact she seemed more distressed by that than by anything else that had happened to them that afternoon.

Thus it was that Prudence was forced to stay on for a few days while Rosie was taken in for inspection and repairs, something that actually darling was well overdue as that *noise* was becoming more than a joke after all this time.

~

That evening they drank too much and laughed too much and Claudia told Prue about Dougie.

'Dougie? My goodness.' Prue was temporarily stuck for words. 'Oh my darling, that is serious. He was so desperately in love with you – you did realise that didn't you, at the time?'

'I suppose so.'

'And yet you turned him down. And we were all amazed, even Gerald.'

'Gerald?'

'Of course, didn't you know? That's why he was so backward in coming forward. He didn't think for a moment you'd accept his proposal, which is why he never proposed in the first place. At least that's how we all saw it.'

'Are you trying to say he never intended to propose?'

'I can't speak for him, darling, not to that extent, but it was all so blindingly obvious to everyone with eyes to see that you and Dougie were a pair, and were bound to be a pair. It would have been a pretty foolish thing for anyone to have stepped between you. Until you turned him down of course.' Prue shrugged and took another swig of her Drambuie.

'But I felt . . . ' Claudia stopped.

'You felt what?'

'I felt I was obliged, because we'd been together all that time, Gerald and I, it was assumed . . .'

'Only by you darling, certainly not by Gerald.'

'So how come he came to propose at all? If he thought that Dougie and I . . .'

'He only proposed when you turned Dougie down, if you remember.'

'But everyone was saying – even though Gerald never actually proposed – everyone was saying "When are you two getting married?", which they never said to Dougie and me.'

'Who cares what other people were saying? Just

because Gerald was on the scene first. We imagined you chose Gerald over Dougie because you didn't think he cared that much about you – typical of you, I might say. Everyone else, God knows, darling, they were queuing up to propose and the longer they queued and the more eager they showed themselves to be the more you ran the other way. We used to call you Miss Ornery. I'm not sure where that word comes from but it was what you were.'

Claudia frowned. How could one have such a different memory of something so important, perhaps the most important thing that had ever happened to her?

'Why you turned Dougie down in the first place is your business,' Prudence went on. 'I can only say in my view it was a mistake, if you want my view, which you probably don't.'

How could Claudia possibly explain why she'd turned Dougie down, even to her closest friend? Did she even know herself?

'So as I see it darling that gives you *carte blanche*. If you want it, of course.'

'Why should that change anything?'

'Because – Gordon Bennett do I have to spell it out for you? Gerald never loved you as much as Dougie did. And he probably doesn't now, let's face it.'

'How can you say that?' Claudia exclaimed.

'And there's no need to be so melodramatic. It was your doing, your doing entirely, Miss Claudia Ornery. If there was a Mister Ornery you should have married him, you'd have been perfectly suited.'

'Gerald did love me,' said Claudia, a touch defiantly. 'He said as much and I believed him.'

'Possibly as much as Gerald could love anyone. How was the sex?'

There was a pause while Claudia, whose mind was never at its most alert when the line of conversation veered so violently, as it tended to do with Prudence, absorbed the question. She was tempted to say it was none of Prue's business but instead she said, 'It was all right.'

'In that case you definitely owe it to yourself, and to Dougie. He's a wonderful lover.'

There was another pause, another long moment of absorption. Then Claudia got to her feet and headed for the door.

'Don't walk out on me!' her friend cried. To no avail. Claudia was out of the room and up the stairs and a moment later Prudence heard the slam of her bedroom door. She sighed, poured herself another Drambuie, sat there for another ten minutes or so while she downed it, and then slowly made her way to her own bedroom.

16

Breakfast the following morning was conducted in silence.

Claudia was disinclined to talk not just because she felt betrayed, which she did, but because she knew she had no right to feel so. If her best friend had gone on to have an affair with a man whom she, Claudia, had turned down, what happened subsequently was really none of her business. Which total lack of justification only made things worse.

Prudence was rendered mute not only because she was waiting for an apology from Claudia for walking out on her the night before – and how typical of her to walk away from a confrontation – but because she was unprepared to provide Claudia with any kind of explanation or apology for something that had happened twenty-something years previously, and which had nothing to do with her in the first place.

It was the kind of impasse that can continue indefinitely between friends who have known one another for so long that politeness, which is what usually puts a stop to the awkwardness of a prolonged silence, was no longer a consideration. Thus does the most advanced species on the planet conduct the business of communication.

It was Prudence who finally broke it. As she buttered

her toast, with more vehemence than the poor item deserved, she said, 'I can't bear it when you go all silent on me.'

Claudia did not reply.

'If you want me to go I will go, and willingly. I can't abide this steely silence. Speak your mind, for God's sake.'

'When I'm good and ready,' said Claudia.

That was more than someone like Prudence could tolerate.

'I hate it when you go like this. You always did go like this. Sulk, sulk, sulk. It drives me demented.'

'Then go, if you want to.'

There followed another silence.

'And it's not as if it does you any good,' Prudence continued eventually. 'If you're expecting me to explain, or apologise, I'm not going to do it, you know. I don't feel I have anything to apologise for.'

'I never said I expected an apology or an explanation.'

'Then I won't give you either.' Prudence bit down on her toast viciously. 'This is delicious jam, by the way,' she spoke with her mouth full.

'I'm glad you like it.' Claudia got up to refill her coffee cup and when she returned to the table she said, 'You were going to tell me about your other adventure. With the tour guide.'

'Pierre.'

'Yes.'

There was a pause.

'Well?' said Claudia, with as much bad grace as she could muster.

'You don't want to hear.'

'Oh for God's sake! Now who's being coy?'

'Darling.' Prudence replaced her cup with care upon its saucer and leant over the table towards the person who until very recently had been her closest friend. 'You –

really – do – not – want – to – hear. I could tell that right from the word go. You did not want to hear about my little fling with Signor Martini either – you were totally disgusted. It's a problem you have. In fact I think it is *the* problem you have.'

'I don't know what you're talking about.' Claudia did not meet her eye.

'Sex, darling. Sex, in all its raw, animal reality. You do not want to know. You hate hearing about it, you hate thinking about it, above all you hate having to do it. Well, it's none of my business but I can only say you don't know what you've been missing. What you *are* missing. Most of us don't get the chance after a certain time in our lives. For some reason sex doesn't happen to anyone over thirty-five, as anyone under thirty-five will tell you.'

Prudence picked up her cup again and watched Claudia over the rim.

'I only told you about Martini in the first place because you asked, you may remember,' she went on, replacing the cup without drinking from it. 'It's what happens when you're on holiday. It's harmless.'

'Not to his wife.'

'He did not like his wife and she did not like him. That was obvious from the start.' She lifted her cup again. 'It wouldn't surprise me if our little fling didn't put some of the spark back into their relationship. It's what happens in this crazy world.'

There was another pause. Prudence drank her coffee.

'More toast?' Claudia offered.

'No, thank you,' said Prudence.

Prue's problem, thought Claudia in the silence that followed, is she thinks she has a monopoly on truth. And because she is the way she is and I am the way I am, I am the one on the receiving end of her 'truth' in a way that she never is on mine. Whoever thought she was my friend anyway? We could not be more different – we see things differently, we have different priorities, different ways of leading our lives. What earthly right does she have to tell me how I should conduct my life, even bring up my children? How dare she!

What does it take, thought Prudence, to get this woman to fight back? She exhausts me. Why is it I'm the one who ends up talking nonsense? What makes us think we're friends in the first place?

'Did you really have an affair with Dougie?' asked Claudia at last.

'I don't have affairs, darling, I have one-night-stands. Someone needed to comfort the poor man.'

Claudia turned to look out of the window.

'Whatever makes us happy,' she said, and that was the end of that conversation.

After breakfast she took Prudence to see her tree, the great she-oak. She would have liked to have told her about the tree's heart, which she herself had felt, physically, just the other day; and she might have wanted to tell her about Sellors, the gardener, who had made her aware of the heart in the first place. She might even have wanted to describe what went through her mind as she watched him talking about the tree, about its age and its fecundity and how he loved it – or her, as he insisted on calling it; but she could hardly tell Prudence that without also telling her what had happened to her beforehand that had awakened whatever it was inside her that made everything that happened since, including that conversation, so significant. So she said nothing.

Prudence was unimpressed. Yes, the tree was tall and old and maybe it had mothered, and fathered, other trees in the wood over the years, or even centuries. But when it came to it, romantic though the countryside was, and nature and so forth, so long as you didn't have to live too close to it, or certainly not all the time, she couldn't see what all the fuss was about or what, in the end, was the point of trees in the first place. She suspected there was more to the tree than Claudia was prepared to tell her but she was not inclined to probe. Indeed, she suspected there was a lot more going on in her life that Claudia wasn't telling her but if that was the way she wanted it, so be it.

~

The set that Claudia and Prudence had moved in during their youth, along with Gerald and Dougie and countless others, was a moveable mixture of young men and women mostly living in London or the Home Counties, who got together for dinners and parties and weekend gatherings in the house of whoever's parents were the most tolerant or, more to the point, absent. There was canasta and gin rummy for the women and shooting and, wherever facilities allowed, fishing for the men, and croquet and tennis for all, and each new member was for a brief time the centre of attention simply for being new. Thus it was with Dougie.

Claudia and Prudence, and Gerald, had been part of the set for some time before Dougie stormed onto the scene. And storm he did. From the start he joined in everything, shooting with the boys, playing cards with the girls and bragging that he'd beat the lot of them at all of it. When it became obvious his enthusiasm for these sports was not matched by any aptitude whatsoever, that he had never handled a gun before ('not even in anger'), and barely knew the difference between a diamond and a spade, he had the whole party in hysterics. He was a natural clown and an accomplished flirt and everyone loved him, even the men whose women he apparently attempted to seduce. His only problem was his inability to convince anyone that he had a serious side.

If you'd asked her exactly when she and Gerald

became what others referred to as a 'pair' Claudia would have been hard pressed to come up with a proper answer. They had simply been around for a long time and somehow found themselves in the same group, partnering one another in croquet and on occasion in mixed card games. When the attentions of the male members of the group – who on the whole were, as Prudence described them, a pretty vacuous lot darling, to be honest – became too trying for words, Claudia found herself taking refuge in Gerald's company. Gerald never flirted, or spouted poetry at her or tried to fiddle with her hair, a particularly irritating and presumptuous habit that some of the boys indulged in. Gerald was upright and solid, his conversation was down to earth and to the point. He was intelligent, passionate about archaeology and ancient history and hugely knowledgeable about virtually everything. Dougie made her laugh, but Gerald made her think. And Gerald was there first.

But everyone loved Dougie and Claudia was no exception. He was irresistible. But he had neither the gravity nor the staying power to make him husband material.

Who thought that? Who said it? Did anybody ever tell Claudia that? Did Prue?

Why did she turn Dougie down? Was it the timing of his proposal? Or was it something else?

Does it matter why one does things? One does things for a reason, or perhaps for no reason at all, and one lives with the consequences. Doesn't one?

17

Sometimes, thought Claudia, one's friends can make one feel quite wretched. Prudence had always hated Claudia's aversion to direct confrontation and Claudia's awareness of this only made her more inclined to run from it; and so it went on in a circular fashion, as these things tend to do with people who know one another through and through.

Rosie was returned a few days later looking spanking brand new, and Prue's spirits lifted as Claudia's dropped when she realised how much more her erstwhile best friend loved her motor car than she loved her erstwhile best friend. Well no matter, she thought, I have my tree. In the end we all need something that doesn't answer back; a comfort, a solid, unjudgemental object in which we can confide without fear of recrimination. Maybe I should get myself a dog.

'Oh by the way,' it had quite slipped her mind until the moment of Prue's departure, 'do you know somebody called Perceveral Lightfoot?'

They were standing together outside Claudia's front door. Prue was leaning up against her precious motor car which, Claudia observed with dismay, she was absently stroking.

'Perceveral Lightfoot?' exclaimed Prue. 'You don't mean *the* Perceveral Lightfoot? Good God, darling, who

117

could forget Perceveral Lightfoot? Why?'

'He rang, apparently, when I was in London. Didn't leave a message. I couldn't place him at all, still can't. Who is he? Where does he come from?'

'I've absolutely no idea, darling, I've never heard of him.'

Prue gave a merry chuckle, took hold of Claudia's cheek and gave it an annoying little squeeze. Then she climbed into her car, turned on the engine – which started right away, and very sweetly – gave Claudia a cheerful wave and drove away.

Claudia watched her go with a mixture of relief and wretchedness.

~

Now what?

The trouble with real life is it has no shape, no structure. It's not like a book or a play, set out in discernible scenes by an omnipotent author who invents characters, gives them problems, spends the necessary time solving them until *voilà*, everyone goes home happily, or unhappily as the case may be.

Real life doesn't necessarily have that forward momentum that the reader, or the audience, demands. Real people – unlike their fictional counterparts – do not necessarily go on 'a journey', as writers like to describe it, so that at the end of the story they end up in a different place from where they started out. Real life is not nicely organised into beginnings, middles and endings. In fact, thought Claudia, books and plays have a lot to answer for.

That is how she felt as she stepped from her bath that night. Ever since the young stranger had come to call she had turned this part of her daily routine, the evening bath, into a ritual. What had once been a series of routine procedures – running the bath, climbing into it, washing, climbing out, drying, powdering, slipping on her nightgown and going to bed – was transformed into a conscious, not say sensual, ceremony. She took her time. She allowed herself to indulge in the sheer pleasure of lying in water that was just the right temperature, to be mindful of its effect on her body and of her body on it. Every tiny act was part of a self-conscious performance, as if she were being secretly observed. It was this that gave the whole ritual such a feeling of erotic poignancy. She was an actor in a play, or even a film, a glamorous film star with a beautiful body, made more sensuous and more beautiful by the unseen eyes gazing at her.

But that was all over. Ever since Prudence's visit, for some reason, the wind had gone right out of her sails. Taking a bath became just that. It was as if the young man's visit had never happened. Or worse, that it had indeed happened but in allowing it to go to her head she'd behaved like someone half her age.

She received a brief letter from Prudence thanking her for her hospitality and making no reference at all to the rift between them. She had telephone conversations with all three daughters, and imparted to her youngest, Flora, some of her concerns about Harriet; about which Flora was gently reassuring.

She spent a whole day writing to Gerald, struggling to find something to say that he might find interesting. She told him about the young visitor – Gabriel, she remembered his name now – but she didn't tell him he stayed the night, and certainly not what took place between them. She told him about her visit to Jessica and Jonathan and the party and Noël Coward, but not about her dinner with Dougie. She wrote about Prue's visit and how her friend drove her motor car into a ditch, but she said nothing about the feud that had developed between them. She mentioned conversations with Harriet and Flora, but nothing of her worries about Harriet.

She told Lily that should Perceveral Lightfoot call when she was out, to please make a note of his telephone number so she could call him back. She did not hear from Dougie. She sat in the window seat of the morning room with a book on her lap, gazing out at the trees and observing the dropping of their golden leaves one by one; and the slow dying of the trees and the increasing darkness of the shortening days echoed her own feelings about herself.

I am in the autumn of my life, she thought, and I know nothing. There's nothing ahead but winter and darkness and it is far too late to start learning new things now.

Life is terribly easy when you are young. She could never remember a day when she was bored, or short of something to do. She was part of the world then, and not just the hedonistic world of weekend house parties. Noël Coward had expressed surprise that a woman of a certain age would not want to put the business of falling in love behind her, and of course he was right – those days were agony. But what else was a woman of a certain age supposed to do with herself?

And so the weeks passed, September into October, and no omnipotent author stepped in to liven up the shapeless plot that was Claudia's life. She was back to counting the creaks as she ascended the stairs on her way to her bedroom at the end of the day, at which point she was sufficiently shocked to take action.

She decided to throw a dinner party. In the old days when Gerald was around they had entertained several times a week, so much so that he begged her to ease up and give him a break. They were informal gatherings for the most part, often quite spontaneous, and there was never a shortage of invitees. Of course that was BC, and so many of their friends were single and nobody cared if the numbers did not match up. In more recent days, on the rare occasions when Gerald was home and Claudia felt that in the short time he was around they had to catch up with *everyone*, because anyone who was *not* invited would feel snubbed, the dinners became bigger and more formal, and numbers absolutely had to balance; for every single man there had to be a single woman, which sometimes caused considerable angst.

Somehow since Gerald was away the invitations had dried up, and she assumed, perhaps wrongly, that her friends found his company more congenial than hers, and that without him not only did she upset the balance of male to female, she was frankly not scintillating enough to earn her single place at their table.

Now, she struggled to think who to invite, who would be likely to accept an invitation from a single woman whose husband was absent. In the end she drew up a list of fourteen people and, in the expectation that at least a quarter of them would refuse, she sent off invitations to all of them to dine with her a fortnight hence.

She wanted very much to see Dougie again and, in her heart of hearts she would have to admit it was this as much as anything that was the prime motivation behind the dinner party in the first place. If he accepted, *if*, he would have to stay the night (unless he had a motor car, which she assumed he hadn't, and was prepared to drive himself back to London afterwards). *If* he accepted and stayed the night, she would also have to ask someone else who would also be staying the night, for reasons that needed no explanation. *If* he accepted she would not invite Prue, for obvious reasons. In any case she was disinclined to invite Prue in the first place.

In the event all fourteen invitees, including Dougie – *'Thought you'd quite forgotten all about me, and yes, I would be delighted to stay the night'* – accepted her invitation, and Claudia was thrown into a mild panic.

18

The remaining member of the household, Phyllis, who took on the dual roles of cook and housekeeper while it was only Claudia living in the house, was not in the least put out at the prospect of fourteen to dinner. On the contrary, her eyes positively lit up at the thought of having something to do at long last other than make sure her one and only charge was properly fed and watered. She would call in extra staff to help in the kitchen, and with serving. Lily too felt the buzz of excitement, and the thought of having something to gossip about, after such a long period of frankly not much happening.

It didn't take Claudia long to get into her stride. She discussed menus with Phyllis, and organised for Sellors to act as chauffeur for the guests who, like Dougie, would be travelling down by train. It felt just like the old days.

Of her fourteen guests, seven men and seven women, very few of them knew one another, and nobody, that she could recall, knew Dougie. That was as well as she did not want to risk any indiscretions from the likes of Prudence, whom she had not invited, to mar what was intended to be a jolly and relaxed evening. She would, she hoped, be able to enjoy the company of Dougie without any fear that he might overstep the mark. She would wear her crimson silk, for the second time, as the first had been such a wild success, and she would have her hair done especially. She would make a proper event of it.

Halfway through the morning of the day of the dinner the telephone rang and a male voice announced himself to be Perceveral Lightfoot.

'Perceveral!' she found herself saying, as someone who is delighted to hear from an old friend.

'How are you?' The voice was not immediately familiar.

'I'm very well, how are you?' Now this was embarrassing. Was she supposed to know who he was and would it be an enormous *faux pas* to ask to be reminded?

'I called up some time ago and spoke to your maid. She said you were in London but she wouldn't give me your number, and it's taken me this long to find the time to call you again, I hope you'll forgive me. It's been such a long time.'

'Yes,' she said, uncertainly.

'I come and go, you see. Life takes you over, don't you find? Too many things to do, people to see, never enough time.'

'I suppose so.'

'And I was going to be around your way and I know it's ridiculously short notice but I'll be staying with chums just outside S and I thought, This is such a coincidence, I have to see if Claudia is free, and maybe she could even join me for dinner tonight.'

There was a pause as Claudia tried to digest all this.

'It so happens I have people coming here to dinner this evening,' she said. An image of the naked body in the silver moonlight flashed through her mind. 'But you would be welcome to join us.'

Did she really say that?

'What, tonight? How tremendously kind. Are you sure I'm not putting you out?'

She chuckled to herself and thought, What larks.

'Not at all, it would be good to see you.'

'Well I must say, that's remarkably lucky timing on my part. If you could give me directions from S I will be there at whatever time you tell me.'

So she did, and all the while she was laughing inwardly and marvelling at her behaviour because it was not like her to invite what could turn out to be a total stranger to dinner – except for Gabriel Carter of course, and look what happened there – but a bit of living dangerously might not be a bad idea. And there would also be something perversely satisfying about misbalancing the numbers, especially since it meant there would be a spare man.

Over lunch she did a bit of mental detection. He did not know the way from S, which suggested he had not been to Hallywell before, or not for some time. This meant that either he pre-dated Gerald, or their acquaintance had taken place somewhere else. His voice sounded completely unfamiliar but he obviously knew who she was, so not for the first time she found herself placing the blame on her deteriorating memory. The moment she saw him, even if as he said a long time had passed, she would remember him, she just needed a context. It all added an element of excitement to the prospects of the evening, and she even privately thought that it would do no harm at all in Dougie's eyes if there were an extra, and single, man attending.

In the afternoon Sellors drove her into S to have her hair dressed, and on the way she told him about the oak, and the fact that she thought she could after all this time feel the great tree's pulse. He was so excited he nearly put the car in the ditch, much as Prudence had done, and for the rest of the journey, there and back, he was positively beaming.

~

Dougie was one of the first to arrive, in the company of Caroline and Witt Andersen (with an 'e'), who was Swedish, or maybe Norwegian. They had all of them travelled down by train and were all three staying the night. So Claudia was unable to speak to Dougie in private initially, though he was able to nuzzle her neck, by way of greeting, and whisper something she couldn't quite hear but which sounded like 'Good enough to eat.'

Hot on their heels was her old friend Hermione, along with Sandrina and Henry Shuttlewick, with whom Hermione had cadged a lift. It occurred to Claudia that they could also have given a lift to Dougie, since they had motored from London and were returning there later, but for reasons she was not prepared to admit to she simply did not think of it at the time. Others arrived in quick succession, including Tim and Lady Lavinia Smytheson – the 'Lady' was from a previous marriage. Lady Lavinia examined Claudia through her lorgnettes and said, rather obscurely, 'Where's the cat?'

Of all Claudia's friends Lady Lavinia was the most naturally eccentric. Not only was she late for everything, she invariably travelled everywhere with her two King Charles spaniels in tow. Now Claudia loved dogs as much as the next person, but had to make exceptions in this case as they were, without doubt, the most over-pampered, overfed and neurotic creatures she had ever come across. For Tim and Lavinia to turn up on time, without the dogs, was a double miracle, and in a quiet moment when his wife was not looking, Tim whispered, 'Told her we were expected an hour earlier than we were and that you had a very ferocious cat,' and gave her a big wink.

Finally came a ring at the door and there was the largest man Claudia had ever set eyes on. He was six foot five at least, and broad with it, and since she did not recognise him he had to be the one and only Perceveral

Lightfoot.

'Claudia, how delightful!' He gave her a hug that all but crushed the breath out of her.

Well, at least he knew who she was, but she was darned if she could say the same about him.

19

The evening got off to a nerve-racking start. Dougie, bless him, aided by her friend Robbie – the kindest man in the universe, as someone once described him – acted as joint hosts when the temporary staff became confused over the drinks, and Claudia had to disappear into the kitchen to prepare the Béarnaise sauce, which was one of her specialities. Lady Lavinia toured the room with her lorgnettes, which frightened the life out of the women but convulsed the men, and baffled everyone by continuously calling on Topsy and Tinkerbell before being reminded by her long-suffering husband that, 'They're not here dear, because of the cat, remember?' To which Lady Lavinia replied, not without an edge, 'I am not seein' a cat anywhere.' Her tendency to leave off the final 'g' of 'ing' words was something Claudia found both divine and ludicrously affected, as did her husband's way of pronouncing words such as 'problim'.

By the time it came to serve dinner however all awkwardnesses seemed to have been ironed out. At one point as Claudia surveyed the length of her table she felt suddenly and overwhelmingly happy. There were all her friends, all thirteen of them and Perceveral Lightfoot, everyone appearing so relaxed and so happy and absolutely nobody looking left out, not even her friend

Hermione who, mousy though she looked on the outside was bright as anything if anyone gave her a chance to show it, which they rarely did. And here she was being listened to with great concentration by Robbie, wonderful Robbie, the Nicest Man in the Universe. It doesn't take much to make a person shine, thought Claudia. Just a bit of attention, that's all it needs.

There was Lady Lavinia, up to her usual tricks, training her lorgnettes without inhibition on the admittedly rather astonishing décolletage of Sandrina Shuttlewick. Sandrina, such a strange name, thought Claudia, made up, obviously, as was the rest of her; she called it her stage name though nobody had ever actually seen her on stage anywhere. She was a good twenty years younger than the genial and terrifyingly aristocratic Henry Shuttlewick, who obviously adored her and laughed at all her jokes, which made him unique in that respect.

And there was dear Dougie, down the far end of the table, sending Caroline Andersen into paroxysms of laughter. Claudia felt rather envious. She had placed him deliberately as far away from herself as possible, and Perceveral Lightfoot as close as possible on her right hand side, partly in order to get to the bottom of the mystery of who he was and partly to make Dougie jealous, in which joint tasks she failed miserably.

But she felt marvellous. This is what I'm good at, she told herself. Throwing dinner parties, getting people together to talk and laugh and forget about their worries and anxieties in the outside world. In her early married years, and to a lesser extent when the girls were around, it was what she was known for. I may not change the world, thought Claudia, but I can do my bit to give people a good time, and there's absolutely nothing wrong with that.

Dinner itself was a triumph. It was not only Claudia who thrived on entertaining, and Phyllis excelled herself.

As the gentlemen came to join the ladies in the drawing room afterwards the booming voice of Perceveral Lightfoot rang out: 'Do you have a billiard table, Claudia?'

'No, I'm afraid I don't, I'm so sorry.'

'Not to worry,' he boomed back. 'It's a ladies' household this, I can see,' with which, to Claudia's dismay, he pulled up a chair and sat himself down right next to her. On seeing this, Dougie, who was about to seat himself on Claudia's other side, instead took to perching on the arm of her chair, as if to claim priority by proximity.

'Love a game of billiards,' continued Perceveral, swilling the brandy in his glass. 'You can tell a lot about a man from the way he handles a billiard cue.'

'How do you mean?' asked Dougie.

'It's a curious mixture of force and cunning. Do you play?' He looked briefly at Dougie and, without waiting for an answer, continued: 'Force, strength – wham! – into the hole. And delicacy and cunning. Yes. Great game. Calls on all one's resources.'

That seemed to be it for the moment.

Claudia felt a slight tickle on the back of her neck. She shivered, and then realised what it was.

'Yep, nothing like a good game of billiards. A man's game, you know. Rugby, now there's another man's game. Not like cricket.'

Dougie was very gently running a finger along the back of Claudia's neck. She smiled and closed her eyes.

'Cricket is for gentlemen, not for men, if you follow me.'

He didn't need anyone to follow him, evidently, nor to comment, as he continued on, unstoppable.

'It's a class thing, I suppose. Football, that's another matter altogether. Can't stand football, don't know why. Funny that.'

'What about hockey?' asked Dougie. His finger had travelled the length of Claudia's shoulder and was now on the point of venturing beneath the sleeve of her dress. She gave a tiny gasp of pleasure.

'Hockey?' Perceveral seemed to give this a good deal of thought. Then he said, 'I've been invited to the royal household, did you know?'

'Well, fancy that,' said Dougie.

He gave Claudia's shoulder a little pinch and she shrieked, briefly.

'My thoughts precisely,' Perceveral droned on. 'Can't imagine why. Next month, the third of next month. Not sure of the etiquette, dress code etcetera.'

'Don't they make it clear on the invitation?' Dougie enquired politely. His fingers had retraced their steps to the small of Claudia's back, where they paused for a moment, before gently beginning to investigate the line of her backbone. Then he bent down and kissed her, right in the middle of her back. She moaned quietly.

'I expect you're wondering why – why the invitation in the first place. Well join the club. I expect it had something to do with Digby, remember Digby, Claudia?'

'Digby?' Claudia opened her eyes reluctantly. 'Digby who would that be?'

'Dig behind the cabinet and who knows what you will find?' said a low voice somewhere in the region of her lower vertebrae.

It was at that point that the party began to break up. One by one the guests were beginning to leave, so Claudia was forced to break the spell under which she had been happily falling and get to her feet to see them off.

'Wonderful evening Claudia, thank you so much.'

'It was lovely to see you looking so well.'

'Must reciprocate. Will reciprocate.'

'Give our regards to the old man.'

'Thank you Claudia, I did enjoy it.' This from Hermione.

'Are you getting a lift back to town?' Claudia asked.

'Well actually Robbie has offered.'

'I'm so pleased.' Robbie, who never seemed to have a girlfriend in tow. It would be too marvellous for words if these two could get together, it would vindicate the entire enterprise, if it needed vindicating.

'Tell me dear, do you have a cat or don't you?'

Claudia smiled graciously at Lady Lavinia. 'I do, but he's terrified of people, so he hides whenever visitors come to the house.'

'So Topsy and Tinkerbell could have come after all, well never mind.' Lady Lavinia kissed her hostess on both cheeks and smiled. 'Lovely evenin', Claudia, all the same.'

Soon they were all gone, including the Andersens (with an 'e'), who had retired to bed upstairs, and there were just the two men and Claudia.

Claudia gave a very big and rather obvious yawn.

'Oh, I am most terribly sorry!' Her hand fluttered exaggeratedly to her mouth. 'I quite forgot myself. It's been a long day.'

'Yes,' said Perceveral. But he continued to sit there, thinking. Then all of a sudden he got to his feet and said to Dougie, 'Can I give you a lift somewhere?'

'Thank you, no,' said Dougie, with a polite little bow.

'He's staying the night,' said Claudia.

'Oh.' Perceveral looked from one to the other, then: 'How's Gerald?'

'He's very well, so far as I know.' Claudia smiled.

'Still in Egypt, is he?'

'Egypt?'

'Well, that was the last I heard. Anyway, very good to see you again Claudia, very good of you to invite me. We must do it again some time.'

'Of course,' she said, as she ushered him to the front door and wished him goodbye, along with the dream of the naked silverfish.

'Where did he come from?' asked Dougie as Claudia returned.

'I have absolutely no idea,' said Claudia.

'Truly?'

'Truly. I didn't quite get the chance to ask him on the telephone, and I didn't quite get the chance to ask him at dinner, and by that time anyway it seemed a bit late to be asking a guest who he was exactly. So . . . ' She shrugged. 'Who knows? And after all, really, who cares?'

They stood there together, in the drawing room. The flickering light of the fire played on Claudia's flushed face.

'I don't think I've ever seen you looking so beautiful.'

'Oh Dougie, you do know how to pay a compliment.'

'Don't I just.' He took a step closer to her.

'What was it you were saying to Caroline Andersen, she was in hysterics.'

'I really don't remember.' His face was inches from hers. 'Probably the one about the farmer and the Frenchwoman's nose, to shock her rather straightlaced husband.'

'I don't think he's quite as straightlaced as he appears.'

'I really, really want to kiss you,' said Dougie, and so he did. Gently. On the mouth.

Over his shoulder Claudia caught sight of a young man leaning up against the wall and stifling a yawn.

She pulled back just enough to say, 'The staff, poor them, it's time we let them go to bed.'

'Only if they will let us do the same.'

'Dougie, stop.' She turned away from him. 'Do go,' she said to the sleepy waiter. 'We're all done now, we're off to bed.'

She ignored the snigger from behind her.

'Thank you, madam.'

'Lily will turn off and lock up.'

As the young man left the room so Claudia felt a pair of arms encircling hers and warm breath on the back of her neck. She leant into Dougie and shivered as his mouth nibbled her ear. 'My darling, let me come to your bed,' he whispered.

She could have said yes. She was on the verge of saying yes. Her whole body was telling her yes, and yet . . .

'No,' she said.

<h1 style="text-align:center">20</h1>

Claudia lay in her bath for some time. She felt both wicked and melancholy. I am a tease, she thought, and if Dougie wants nothing more to do with me it's my fault entirely.

She felt beautiful, and sexy, and annoying. She decided to go to bed naked, despite the temperature, and she lay there thinking of Dougie not so many yards away, also lying in bed, maybe naked, maybe not, also most likely wide awake, and thinking of her.

She was expecting a knock on the door. That is why she went to bed naked. If a young stranger could appear in her bedroom without invitation then surely Dougie, if he really meant it, if he *really* meant it . . .

She stretched, and she felt the folds of the sheet draping her body and the weight of the blankets bearing down on her and filling the space between her legs. She shifted slightly and stretched her legs wider apart and lifted her pelvis against the weight, and it was strangely exquisite. All alone. Can I do it all alone? she wondered.

She drew her hands into the warmth of the bed and began to touch herself, dispassionately, like someone taking an inventory, like a doctor. Two breasts, rounded and even, two nipples, upright and hard. A ribcage, a dip into a diaphragm and across the smooth plain of her stomach. She thought of herself as a landscape, with mounds and curves and hidden bits. Towards the base of the plain, on either side, the ridges of her hips. She pressed down on her upper thighs and slowly slid her hands along their length to the two lookout points of her knees. If she bent her legs they were the highest point on her body landscape, and if you were to stand on them you could see the length of her spread out on either side. On the far side, beyond her reach and out of her sight, were the steep, smooth slopes of her shins, down which a tiny creature could slither, or ski, past the slender pass of her ankles to ground level via the bumpy plateaux of her feet.

When she was a child she used to lie in bed just like this, knees bent skywards, and imagine she was inside a tent. She would pull the sheets right over her head and picture herself somewhere strange and exotic, a body inside a cocoon, the larva of a butterfly, watching herself metamorphosing, changing shape, child into woman, young into old.

She would like to be painted nude, she decided. She imagined being able to lie in bed and look at herself on the wall, to be able to see and feel her own nakedness all at once. Such narcissism, and why not?

Her hands skimmed down her inner thighs. As landscapes go, thought Claudia, mine is a complex one, each slope different to the other, and at the bottom of this particular slope, something altogether unique. The delicately rounded plateau of her *mons veneris* – 'mound of Venus', such a coy description – and covered in a fuzz of hair, for what reason she was unsure. And why, come to think of it, is this the part of the woman's body one never sees? Because it is secret, or private, or because it is ugly? Because here, right here, is the most complex, mysterious element of a woman's entire anatomy. So what exactly do we have here?

At the summit of the mound is a bone, and below the

bone there is a cleft in the mound and it is in this cleft that the secret of life is to be found. Moving her hand to this cleft Claudia parted it with her fingers to investigate what lay within it, and it appeared to her in her fantasy metaphor as a valley, moist and soft and very tender to the touch. At the further end of the valley was a deep cave, which could be described as the cave of creation, or perhaps it would be better described as an entrance, or exit, leading to and from a tunnel: to be entered into by the creator and exited from some time later by the created. Which really meant that at the end of the tunnel lay a kind of laboratory, otherwise referred to as a womb, within which miracles were wrought; without, after the initial moment of admission, and emission, any active human participation. For a woman, if not for a man, this part of the valley, or cleft, was what might be described as 'the practical section'.

But it was in the other section, the upper part, where the mystery lay, for this part seemed to serve no obviously practical purpose at all. Yet if God made woman then every portion of His creation must have some reason for its existence.

In the upper part of the cleft, which Claudia was only now investigating, lies a soft – how would one describe it? – cushion-like object which, when ignored, sits shyly and self-effacingly all but camouflaged in its surroundings. Touch this cushion, which Claudia now did, for the second time in her fifty-two-year-old life, and something extraordinary begins to happen. The tiny thing wakes up, and swells, and shoots a sharp message to the rest of the body, the adequate description of which has confounded poets throughout the ages, and which cannot be knowingly replicated in any other part of the body or indeed, by anything else in the world. The more attention this tiny but crucial point of the anatomy receives, as

Claudia's was now doing at the delicate yet gradually quickening fingers of its owner, the more it swells and the more intense the charge becomes, galvanising the body and causing it to writhe, like an electrified doll, of its own volition and in the most unladylike manner, and for its owner to moan, then groan, as if in pain, and then, careless of its surroundings, to cry out loud, as the charge builds and builds until it erupts into an explosion of total exquisiteness.

Claudia had absolutely no idea what had happened to her, or how a simple exploration of her personal landscape had ended up causing her to lose all sight of it, and of everything else for that matter. As she lay there, exhausted and panting, a thought came into her head that was so shocking it was almost heretical.

Maybe after all we don't need a male to give us satisfaction. That is what the young man meant by 'Nature's miracle'.

For some while she lay there awake, her hand resting comfortably on her secret spot as if in gratitude, or protection, and as a reminder to herself of her own continuing virility, and of possible adventures to come. Yet not tonight, for there came no knock on the door.

21

On her way down to breakfast the following morning Claudia heard shouts of laughter coming from the dining room.

'More farmers and Frenchwomen's noses?' she enquired, as she entered.

Her three guests turned to look at her with varying degrees of incomprehension.

'Your friend Dougie has just been insulting my country,' said Witt Andersen, with the faintest hint of a Nordic smile.

'Oh, he would do that,' said Claudia. 'He's terribly rude, please don't mind him too much. Dougie, what have you been saying?'

'I've been paying compliments, as a matter of fact,' said Dougie. He was spooning sugar into his coffee. 'I said I thought all Scandinavians were gloomy types but I have been proved wrong by your dear guests. Which only goes to show the dangers of national stereotyping.'

'I don't know why you think all Scandinavians are gloomy,' said Caroline Andersen, as she spread marmalade on her toast and took a large bite out of it before continuing, with her mouth full, 'Not that I am actually Scandinavian myself.'

'It's all that darkness, and that Ibsen fellow,' said Dougie.

138

'He was Norwegian.'

'Well, what was the other one called, Strindberg, he was no better.'

'He was Swedish,' said Witt. 'All Scandinavians are the same to the rest of the world. In fact to an Englishman all foreigners are much of a muchness, they can't really tell the difference between them, wouldn't you agree, Claudia?'

'Erm . . . ' She was hesitating because she didn't know the Andersens that well, and Witt said everything with the same deadpan expression, and besides, it was rather early in the morning and she hadn't yet had her coffee.

'Not at all,' said Dougie, saving the day. 'I can tell a Chinaman from an Indian any day of the week. I can even tell a Queenslander from a Texan, in a darkened room, and I'll bet that's more than any Scandinavian can do.' He grinned, winked at Claudia and said, 'Good morning Claudia, did you sleep well?'

'Yes, thank you Dougie. How about you?' This was addressed to all three of her guests, two of whom nodded and murmured, 'Very well, thank you.'

'I thought I heard you cry out at one point.' He was stirring his coffee and not looking at her. 'Did you have a nightmare?'

'Not that I recall. Or maybe I did. I'm so sorry, I hope I didn't wake you.' She turned away from him to hide the flush.

'I had the most extraordinary dream, as it happens,' said Dougie.

'A pleasant one, I hope,' said Witt.

There was a pause.

'Well?' said Claudia, rather against her better judgement. 'Do tell.' She took a seat next to Caroline across the table from the men.

'Oh, do you really want to know?' Dougie looked

around at the assembled company.

'I love dreams,' said Caroline, clapping her hands together like a child.

'It's not particularly interesting but anyway,' Dougie drank his coffee and cleared his throat. 'There was this Frenchwoman and this farmer, and one day they . . . '

'Dougie, that's enough,' said Claudia.

'What?' Dougie looked at her in pained innocence. 'How do you know I didn't dream about a Frenchwoman and a farmer?'

'Because . . . Well, go on, what did you really dream about?'

'There was this Frenchwoman, and she was holidaying in' – he looked at the Andersens – 'Sweden?'

'Denmark,' said they, in concert.

'Not that it makes the slightest difference,' said Witt.

'Denmark it is. They do have farmers in Denmark, I imagine. So this Frenchwoman, her name was Coco, after Coco Chanel, you know? She was on holiday and she was invited to a party in Copenhagen, and at the party was this young man who turned out to be a farmer. They were chatting, after a fashion, since she spoke very little Danish and he virtually no French, and in the course of it they stepped out onto the balcony so they could be alone, *toute seule*, you could say. It was clear that they were becoming highly attracted to one another and so he began to proposition her, which caused her some anxiety. So when he suggested they go somewhere quiet, to continue their *tête à tête* away from the prying eyes of others, she said, in French and quite distinctly, "no", or rather, "*non*"'.

Dougie paused to take another sip of his coffee, and over the rim of his cup he saw Claudia watching him closely.

'How did she know,' Caroline ventured, after a moment, 'what he was asking her, if she spoke no

Danish?'

'He was making it perfectly obvious, from his gestures, and so on, and his manner,' said Dougie, 'which are universal, more or less.'

Caroline frowned and nodded slowly.

'So the farmer went off, leaving the Frenchwoman on the balcony,' Dougie continued. 'She hung on for a while, chatting to this person and that, and then she decided it was time to go, so she collected her coat and said her goodbyes and so forth and off she went. To her surprise, the farmer was waiting for her just inside the front door, and he said to her, or she thought he did' – he glanced quickly at Caroline – '"All right then, are we all set?" And she replied, "No – *non* – I told you, *non*. Don't you understand me?"

'"Well,' said the farmer. "I understand the word *non*, or *no*, or even . . ."' he looked to the Danish couple for guidance.

'*Nej*,' said Witt.

'"*Nej*". It's a straightforward word, not hard to interpret – this is me talking, not the farmer by the way – and yet . . . and yet . . .' He leant forwards conspiratorially and two of his listeners did likewise.

'You might think, how can one simple and straightforward word have more than one meaning? What is difficult about understanding the word *non*, or *no*, or even *nej*?' He leant back again and so did the Andersens, and Claudia thought the whole thing looked like a scene from a bad play.

'So?' said Caroline, after a pause. 'Is that it?'

'Not quite. To the Danes, you see, *no*, or *non*, or *nej*, when spoken by a foreigner, a woman, means the opposite.'

Witt laughed out loud at this.

'Is that not so, Witt?'

'Carry on,' said Witt.

'It is a little known fact,' said Dougie. 'You see, a woman on her own at a party, in Denmark, is on her own for one reason only.'

'So she can pick up a farmer,' offered Caroline.

'Getting warm. Which only goes to show . . .'

'Dougie that was hardly a dream. Where were you in all this?' Claudia asked.

'I'm coming to that. You see, strange though it may sound, the farmer was me.'

'Ah,' Claudia laughed. 'And the Frenchwoman?'

'The Frenchwoman,' Dougie looked closely at Claudia and she scowled a warning back. 'The Frenchwoman was a Frenchwoman. Or perhaps an Englishwoman pretending to be a Frenchwoman.'

There was a silence.

'I'm not really sure I understand that dream,' said Caroline, eventually.

'The meaning of dreams is never clear-cut,' said Witt. 'They require some creative interpretation.'

There was another slight pause.

'Do you want me to explain it, or will you?' said Dougie, to nobody in particular though it was obvious he was addressing Claudia, who right at that moment got up from the table and walked away from it to emphasise her total lack of interest in this line of conversation.

'Looks as if it's up to me then.'

Dougie rested his elbows on the table and thought for a moment.

'One likes to avoid national clichés, as I've explained. But at the same time a cliché is only a cliché because it contains a hint of truth, *n'est-ce pas?*'

No one seemed inclined to disagree.

'However,' he went on, 'when it comes to the sexes, that is when clichés often come into their own. For example . . . '

'Dougie, I really don't think our guests want to hear any more,' said Claudia, returning to the table with the coffee pot. 'More coffee, anyone?'

'Oh, I do!' said Caroline. 'Or I think I do. Want to hear more, I mean.' She looked at her husband for reassurance but he had resumed his customary inscrutability.

'I could give you an example,' Dougie continued, 'as in my dream, of occasions when a woman has said *no*, or *non* or even – though not from my direct experience, since I have never had the pleasure – *nej*, when it's perfectly obvious she means *yes*, or *oui*, or . . . ' he hesitated.

'*Ja*,' Witt supplied.

'Thank you. Now I acknowledge that for the most part *no* means exactly that, but there are times, enough times to be significant, when it clearly means *yes*. So the unsuspecting male has to be *very* careful to be able to distinguish between the two.'

'Dougie, you are the biggest male chauvinist on earth,' said Claudia. She tried to make it sound lighthearted, and failed.

'Why,' questioned Caroline, her brow wrinkled, 'would a woman say no if she means yes?'

'Again, I was coming to that,' said Dougie. 'This is the crux of the matter, this is where it takes care, and delicacy, and above all experience, to be able to tell the difference. I'll have a top-up Claudia, if that's all right.' He lifted his cup in the direction of the coffee pot, which Claudia was still holding.

'Help yourself,' she said, abruptly, slamming it down on the table in front of him and sitting. She was aware of the two pairs of Scandinavian eyes fixed on her in curiosity.

'Thank you.' And so he did, and once he was done he continued, 'There are a number of reasons why a woman says *no* when she means *yes*. Firstly, it's because she does not know her own mind, or because she has not yet made it up, which amounts to the same thing. Secondly, it is because she likes to play hard to get, which is a skill at which many women excel. Thirdly, and most likely, it's because she is torn between her instinct and her sense of propriety. In other words, between what she wants to do and what she knows she ought to do. What society expects of her, let's say.'

There was another long pause. Dougie drank his coffee and then he looked up at all three of them in turn, smiling pleasantly.

'*Compris*?' he said.

'Well, I think you are being rather tedious, and really quite rude,' said Claudia. Her hands were fluttering, she couldn't stop them. She looked at the Andersens. 'I hope you don't think all Englishmen are quite so boorish,' she said. 'Although if it comes to national stereotypes you'd have every reason to think so.'

Nobody was responding. This was turning out to be torture.

'Actually,' she babbled on. She was just filling the silence now. 'If there is an English stereotype it's a pompous man in a waistcoat and a moustache telling people what to do.' She laughed, a little hysterically. 'Speaking English, no matter where he is, and when people don't understand what he's saying, simply raising his voice and speaking v-e-r-y s-l-o-w-l-y, as if to a child. Isn't that right?'

Please, she thought, for God's sake someone help me.

'The English stereotype,' said Witt, 'is complex. What you say is true, maybe, but there is more. The stereotypical Englishman is polite yet secretive, and he belongs to a club the name and the nature of which he will never divulge, especially to a foreigner, in which there are rules and codes of behaviour that are so opaque, and multifarious, that even if a foreigner were to get hold of them he would be able to make neither head nor tail of them.'

There was another hiatus. Caroline was looking at Claudia.

'I think you overestimate the average Englishman,' Claudia responded. 'The average Englishman is a small boy who would prefer to be still wearing short trousers and sitting on nanny's lap eating ice cream.' She smiled sweetly at Dougie.

'You've lost me completely now,' said Caroline.

'Pay her no notice, Caroline,' said Dougie. 'She has no idea what she's talking about, do you Claudia?' He leant over the table towards her and gave her hand a squeeze and she flinched.

'I think maybe that's the end of this particular conversation,' said Claudia.

22

The Andersens left soon after breakfast to catch the train back to London, but Dougie did not go with them. He stood side by side with Claudia in the front doorway waving them off.

'Not so gloomy after all, I thought, didn't you?' she said.

'Maybe,' said Dougie. 'Though he'd have every reason to be, married to that flibbertigibbet.'

'Oh Dougie, that's not very kind!'

'I'm not a very kind person, Clot.'

Clot. It was years since anyone had called her that.

'Where did that come from?' she asked.

'Clot? I don't know, dear Clot, I suppose I dragged it up from the deepest recesses of my mysterious mind.'

They were the years of nicknames, when they were young. Clot was an anagram of Colt, which is how Dougie and others thought of Claudia all that time ago, all legs and skittishness. But what did she call him?

'What did we call you then?' she asked him. They were still standing together in the doorway. 'Let's go inside,' she said, and so they did, and she closed the door behind them.

'Loofa,' he said.

'Loofa, yes, that's right. Why did we call you that?'

'It was "fool" backwards. I've no idea where the "a"

146

came from.'

'Fool, yes, I remember now.'

There was a slight pause.

'You will stay to lunch Dougie, won't you?'

He thought for a while before replying and when he did, he was not looking at her.

'I don't think so, Clot. I should be on my way.'

'Oh.'

'I just have something to attend to upstairs, and then, if you'll excuse me . . .'

He backed away from her almost formally and she watched as he bounded up the stairs, taking them two at a time like someone half his age, and she partly wondered whether he was doing it for her benefit and whether he was even now standing on the top landing trying to catch his breath.

Dear Dougie, thought Claudia as she wandered into the empty drawing room. He could make some woman very happy, and she hoped one day he would.

She regretted that ridiculous conversation over the breakfast table and she didn't want him to leave before they had, in a sense, made things up. There was something deeply melancholic about Dougie, behind all the bluff; there was a solid door beyond which he would from time to time retreat and which nobody, not even Claudia, not least Claudia, could penetrate. Yet he knew her so well. That ridiculous conversation had in its oblique way hit the nail on the head and she knew it. He could see right through her, which was both alarming and thrilling.

The leaves were definitely turning now and the wind had got up, stripping the trees and creating a thick carpet on the lawn beyond the window of gold and orange and brown. A lot of work for Sellors, thought Claudia, and maybe she would offer to help him. It would give her something to do.

He was still so remarkably young, Dougie, spry even, much younger than Gerald, though there can only have been a couple of years between them. Of course he kept himself fit, she imagined, with his trim body and his quick mind. There was a lightness about him, the way he spoke, thought, told jokes, the manner in which he moved his hands, which was almost effeminate. Not that there was anything effeminate about Dougie, not at all.

She had been looking forward to spending some time alone with him, once everyone else had gone. They would go for walks together and maybe play the odd hand of gin rummy, which Dougie was always absolutely hopeless at. He claimed he did not have enough 'guile', which made the assembled company shriek with laughter, she remembered. All those years ago.

'Do you remember that, Dougie, how you claimed to be too guileless to play gin rummy?' She turned to ask him as he appeared in the drawing room doorway, clutching his overnight case in one hand and what looked like an envelope in the other. She felt she had to keep him talking so she could delay his departure, maybe get him to change his mind – what could he possibly have to rush back to London for?

'Did I?' he said.

'Yes, it was such a hoot. You of all people. Pretending to be absolutely hopeless at absolutely everything. It was one of the things we loved about you.'

'Well it was true. It still is.'

'What do you mean?'

He laughed. 'Nothing really. Look, I have to be on my way Claudia. Thank you so much, it was the most magnificent evening. And you looked, well, breathtaking.'

'Thank you, Dougie.' She felt the prick of tears in her eyes. 'I'm so glad you came.'

'I just need to give you this.'

He handed her the envelope and her heart felt suddenly like lead.

'What is it?'

'It's the usual, it's me finding it easier to write things down than to say them. Read it when I've gone.'

'No, I'm going to read it now.'

'Please, Clot.'

'No!' She was not going to let him get away with it this time. 'You will sit down and I will not let you go until I've read this letter and we've had it out.'

She took a seat on the sofa and waited, and after a moment, with a heavy sigh and a slightly overdone shake of the head he sat down on an armchair opposite her and stared at the floor.

'*Dear Clot,*' she read. She looked up at him but his eyes were still fixed floorwards.

'*I realise this is a cowardly thing to do but as you know only too well, when it comes to matters of the heart I find it easier to write down my thoughts than to try to express them to you face to face.*'

She chuckled, but he was still floor-gazing.

'*Last night was agony, there is no other word for it. I realised from the moment I saw you in that utterly gorgeous red number something I've probably been denying myself all my life, that I am hopelessly in love with you and that I've been so ever since I met you a million years ago and I suspect I always will be. Yes, so now you know.*

So like the court fool in Shakespeare I hide my broken heart behind jokes and barbs, but jokes and barbs are wearisome things after a while. Why you turned me down last night, after I felt so much warmth from you, I have no idea and I suspect you don't either. We complicate things, we humans, to an absurd degree sometimes, and I think perhaps I've had enough of the games after all these years and it's time for me to be on my way for good.'

Claudia lowered the letter for a moment to look at Dougie, but his face was now all but buried in his chest.

'Oh Dougie,' she breathed.

'You don't have to read any further,' said a muffled voice from beneath his scarf. 'Not now.'

Claudia resumed the letter.

'My darling girl, all I wanted to do is to take you to bed one time, to feel your skin against mine, to touch you, kiss you, enfold you, smell you, to snuggle, to caress, and finally to make gentle and sweet love to you in a way I suspect no one has ever done in your entire life. Well, let's put it another way, there is only one person who has had the good fortune to make love to you and that is your wretched husband, though why I should call him wretched I've no idea, but I rather imagine he does not appreciate his luck, nor do I imagine he satisfies you as I would like to satisfy you.'

Claudia found her voice beginning to break up. She cleared her throat.

'Please don't go on.' His voice was muffled not only by a scarf but by gritted teeth.

'But a man has to know when to go. I suspect I will dream of you, I will fantasise about you, I will think about you constantly but I will never see you again. I'm sorry to sound melodramatic, not to say like a character in a cheap novel, which is worse, but there is no other proper way of saying it.

Goodbye dearest Claudia and take care of yourself. I will hear news of you from time to time I've no doubt. Your old chum, Loofa.'

Claudia lowered the letter and let it lie in her lap for a long moment.

'May I go now?' said Dougie.

Then she tore the pages through once, twice, three times (with a struggle) before throwing them onto the fire.

She was both embarrassed and moved, and faintly angry. She had not meant to humiliate Dougie, as she realised she had done, unwittingly, without knowing the contents of the letter. But it was so typical of him that he was incapable of being serious in person – hence the veiled 'dream' he recounted at breakfast, the full meaning of which only she and he properly understood – and only able to express his real feelings in writing, if indeed they were his real feelings. A bit of her was flattered, of course, but his behaviour made any response very difficult. One thing was resoundingly clear however: if Dougie's feelings were genuine then she should tread very, very carefully.

'Please stay for lunch, Dougie,' she pleaded.

There was a short pause before he replied. 'If you insist,' he said.

So Claudia rang for Lily and told her Mr McAvoy would be staying for lunch, and maybe beyond that, to which Lily responded, with a smile, 'Very well, madam.'

23

'Tell me about Shakespeare's clowns,' asked Claudia over lunch.

Dougie began to sing,

'When that I was and a little tiny boy,
With a hey and a ho and a hey nonny no,
A foolish thing was but a toy,
And the rain it raineth every day.'

He carried on in prose. 'They were the wise fools,' he said, 'the ones the aristocracy hired to make them laugh and to tell them where they were going wrong, in jokes of course. Except for Trinculo, he was just a fool.' He took a bite of cold chicken, chewed and swallowed before continuing.

'It was an old tradition going way, way back to the ancient Chinese Empire. It was said the building of the Great Wall took one life for every metre of its length, and that's a lot of metres and lives, and once it was done the Emperor looked at it, stroked his chin and said, "H'mm, now I think of it, it could do with a lick of paint," which of course meant another several thousand lives. But his clown made such a joke of the whole idea that in the end he dropped it.'

There was another short pause as Dougie took a drink and worked his way through the next mouthful. Claudia, her chin on her hand, watched him across the table.

'It was the same Emperor,' he went on, 'who declared that the smallest coin to be minted should be a ten-yen piece, which was a day's pay for a peasant, only nobody dared to tell him as much. So his clown took him to the local bar and ordered ten drinks for him, and when the Emperor said he was thirsty but not *that* thirsty, his clown told him that since one drink cost one yen and there was no such thing as a one-yen piece he had to drink his way through his money's worth of ten yen. And that when, as was inevitable, his Great Emperor-ness decreed the smallest currency to be a one hundred yen piece, then he'd have to work his way through a hundred drinks, and so on. Fortunately the Emperor saw the funny side and relented.'

'Perhaps we could all do with our own personal clown,' said Claudia.

'I think so. I definitely think so,' said Dougie. 'You want to hear some more? You're going to be sorry you started me off on this. Tamberlaine the Great, he hired a jester because he made him laugh, so he was able to say things to the great man that no one else would dare. One day Tamberlaine was looking at himself in a shaving mirror and burst into tears because he thought he looked so ugly and old, so everyone around him started crying too, in sympathy, but his clown cried longest and loudest of all, and when Tamberlaine asked him why, he said, "You only see yourself when you look in the glass but I have to look at you all day".' Dougie chuckled, and dabbed at his mouth with his napkin. 'They built a shrine to the clown after he died; they thought he had some kind of mystical power.'

'And do you believe you have some mystical power?' asked Claudia.

'Indeed I do. I have the mystical power to mess up my life like no one else I know.'

Claudia frowned. 'I really hate it when you talk like that, Loofa.'

'Why, does it sound self pitying?'

'It sounds defeatist.'

'Clowns of course, Shakespeare's clowns anyway, with the exception of Trinculo, were very serious people. Serious and quite often rather depressed. It's a serious business making people laugh and their lives depended on it. Literally. Which is enough to make anyone depressed.'

'Are you depressed, Dougie?' she asked him.

'It's quite difficult to stay depressed for long, life is too absurd.'

He finished his food and placed his knife and fork together on his plate.

'I should take you to see some Shakespeare one of these days, he knew all about the absurdity of life.'

'I'd like that,' said Claudia.

She contemplated him across the dining table. The sadness was something new, she'd never noticed it in him when he was young. When they were young, they were frivolous, and carefree, without a thought for tomorrow, and that is how it was meant to be. She never thought about anything in much depth, and now she felt guilty, like a featherbrain, which is what she felt she was and had always been.

People seemed to come and go in one's life and one never became really attached to anyone because that was not the way things worked. Friends became friends by chance, because you happened to be in the same place at the same time, rather than because one shared a bond with them. Her erstwhile friendship with Prue proved that point. Some of the people she used to mix with, now she came to think of it, were probably quite unspeakable, but it didn't matter because they were all there together, sharing the same nonsense games and generally having fun.

'A penny for them,' said Dougie.

'I was just thinking, how little we really got to know one another, when we were young.'

'You believe so?'

In addition to which, on top of the gaiety and the hedonism, were the hormones – those wretched things that got in the way of one's judgement, that made one person seem far more exciting than the other and often for all the wrong reasons.

'I was just a featherbrain, I suppose,' she said.

'So were we all,' said Dougie.

But if that were the case, if she really were a featherbrain, how did she come to end up with Gerald?

'The only one with anything very much up there,' Dougie tapped his head, 'who ever managed to keep that on this,' he indicated his shoulders, 'was Gerald. So you see you weren't such a featherbrain after all.'

'Explain, please,' said Claudia.

'I just mean you made the right choice.'

He was looking at her mildly, blandly even, as liars and prevaricators invariably do. She rather wanted to kick him in the shins, so to avoid doing so she got up from the table, and as she rang for Lily she said, 'I think we should have a walk in the garden, before the sun gets too low, what do you say?'

'Excellent,' he said, springing to his feet.

'And Lily,' Claudia turned to her maid as she came into the room to clear the table, 'I believe Mr McAvoy will be staying for dinner. Is that not right, Dougie?'

Dougie shrugged. 'Anything you say.'

'And the night.'

Lily looked up and, despite herself, stared from one to the other rather baldly before saying, 'Very well madam. I hadn't stripped the bed anyway.'

'Then it seems as if you know more than I do,' said Claudia with a slight edge, which was rather lost on Lily.

Not all was lost on Lily, however. Since the dinner party, which like a swan had been all grace and perfection on the upper side but chaos and confusion underneath – what with all the new staff they'd hired for the occasion who didn't know a skillet from a frying pan and, understandably, had no idea where anything was kept, so that she and Phyllis between them had had to spend the best part of the morning hunting down kitchen implements and restoring them to their proper place – she had been storing everything in her head and imagining, as she went about her business, exactly how she would describe the scene to her friends and colleagues on their next gossip night. She would pick her words carefully because, after all, she was deeply fond of her mistress, who rarely said a harsh word to her and who, she sensed, was desperately lonely and had been at a loss ever since her daughters had fled the nest.

So she would recount with genuine pleasure the meeting between her mistress and Mr McAvoy, who was a bit of a 'card' (it was not a word she normally used but it fitted him to a T, she thought), and who told jokes with such a serious expression she was never sure if they were jokes or not, but she learned to laugh anyway.

Right now for instance, as Lily was clearing away the lunch things, she stopped to watch the two of them strolling across the lawn towards the wood, so easy together, laughing and chatting away like old friends. She thought how she would describe the spark in her mistress' eyes whenever she saw them together, how affectionate they were, how now and again her mistress would reach out and touch Mr McAvoy on the arm, fleetingly, not like husband and wife (she had never seen such intimacy between Mrs and Mr Faraday), more like, well, lovers. Or maybe old lovers. For that is what she presumed they were. Why just now, as she looked on, she saw them stop, just before the clump of trees, and Mr McAvoy place an arm around Mrs Faraday's shoulder and with his other hand, point towards the sky, and Mrs Faraday, shielding her eyes against the low sun, look in the direction he was pointing at and let out a burst of laughter and then turn towards him; and so, still with his arm around her shoulder, they continued to wander out of sight among the trees, where they were about to get up to who knows what.

24

Claudia took Dougie to introduce him to the great oak. She told him how Sellors the gardener thought it might be over four hundred years old and how it might have mothered and fathered most of the surrounding trees, but she didn't tell him about its beating heart. Dougie stood underneath the tree, looking up, and wondered out loud of all the stories the old oak might have to tell, all it had seen and witnessed over the centuries. Of Gerald, for instance, as a young lad – for he had been born and bred at Hallywell – sitting at its foot, with his collection of stones and bones and fossils, examining them closely and making tiny little notes in his spidery little handwriting in his tiny little notebook. 'I expect he was quite an earnest little boy,' said Dougie, to which Claudia did not respond.

They strolled on through the trees to the pond beyond, and Claudia began to tell Dougie about the house party and the imaginary lake of her fantasy, where . . . and there she stopped.

'Go on,' said Dougie.

Claudia pulled a face. 'I'm not really sure that I should.'

'Did it involve me?'

'No, I'm afraid it didn't.'

'Then perhaps I don't want to hear it.'

Claudia laughed, briefly. 'Actually I think you may have been there.'

'May have been. Pretty vague, my sweet.'

'Prue certainly was.'

'And Gerald?'

'I'm not sure. There were a whole heap of them – you – all piling onto boats and laughing and shrieking like crazy, and I was just there on the bank looking at them and thinking, Really, who *are* all these people?'

'Then I definitely wasn't there.'

'And as they were rowing away I realised there was someone else, standing right there beside me. And no, it wasn't you.'

She was gazing across the pond and there was a faraway look on her face.

'Then this – person – all of a sudden he took off all his clothes and dived into the water, and he was dipping and splashing and fooling around and it looked so gorgeous. So I joined him.'

'Naked?'

'Of course.'

'I don't believe you,' said Dougie.

'Then don't believe me. It was a fantasy, remember?'

'Ah, of course.'

There was a short pause.

'Then what?'

'Well, nothing really. We swam around together, in and out and under and over and around one another, like a couple of fish. He had the most perfect body I've ever seen. It was silver. In the moonlight.'

'Have you ever seen a naked man's body?'

She didn't answer this.

'Did you make love in the lake?' asked Dougie. 'In your fantasy?'

'As a matter of fact, no. But it was a very sensuous

experience. Afterwards he climbed out of the water and lay there, flat on his back on the grass.' She took a breath. 'He was beautiful, and I told him so.'

'Very romantic,' said Dougie. 'Who was he, anyone I know?'

Claudia was silent for a very long time and when Dougie turned to look at her, she was trying to suppress a laugh.

'Well?'

'It was such a lovely story and I didn't want to spoil it.'

'Who was he?'

'He was Perceveral Lightfoot.'

'Good God.' Dougie laughed shortly, and then he stopped and said, 'When exactly did you have this fantasy?'

'That would be telling.'

'So tell.'

'A couple of weeks ago, perhaps.'

Dougie thought for a moment.

'Do you often have fantasies?' He had his hands in his pockets and he was idly kicking the leaves beneath his feet.

'I'm not sure that's any of your business,' said Claudia, lightly.

'All right. But answer this one then. Did you have fantasies before, when you were young?'

'Of course! Didn't everyone?'

'What did you fantasise about?'

'Oh, the usual, you know, knights on white horses, who paid homage to me and pampered me and made gentle love to me and then – rode away.'

'Interesting. And now?'

Claudia shot him a sideways look, then she turned and wandered back in the direction of the wood and, after a moment, Dougie followed.

As they walked he told her the story of King Lear and his Fool, how the old man turned his back on the only one of his three daughters who really loved him, and how the only person who could tell him to his face what a fool he was was his Fool.

'So it was his Fool who told the old king he was a fool.'

'He helped him to discover his own foolishness,' said Dougie.

'And what happened in the end?'

'Sadness, and redemption, and self realisation.'

'And what about the Fool?'

'He sort of vanishes from the scene without explanation. A *deus ex machina* in reverse, you could say. Maybe Shakespeare just got bored with him.'

'He'd served his purpose so – pouf!' Claudia made a gesture of dismissal. 'If only that happened in real life.'

There was a moment before Dougie said, 'What do you mean by that, exactly?'

'That you could find someone who knew you better than you knew yourself and wasn't afraid to tell you where you were going wrong.'

'And if there were such a person would you listen to him? Or her?'

'Ho hum,' said Claudia. She thought fleetingly of Prue.

Lily, once again looking out of the downstairs window, saw two people walking thoughtfully and solemnly across the lawn towards the house. They were not speaking and there was a bit of a space separating them. Her first thought was they'd had a row, there was some kind of rift between them. But the more she looked, the more she realised they might just be two people who were so comfortable in one another's company they did not feel the need to talk.

The rest of that day confirmed Lily's latter impressions. Mrs Faraday and Mr McAvoy spent the evening together in what looked like warm and friendly companionship. After dinner her mistress took it upon herself to teach her friend gin rummy, which her friend made huge play of not understanding, and getting all the rules wrong and finding the betting too confusing for words. Her mistress pretended to be cross but she could see, could Lily, that she was putting it on and in the end, both of them ended up in fits of laughter.

Then it was the following morning and there was the all-important business of what, if anything, had happened overnight. The first clue came at breakfast-time. Mr McAvoy arrived first, and on his own, and seemed mildly surprised to find Mrs Faraday not there. 'But then she never was an early riser,' he said, almost to himself, but loud enough for Lily to hear and to process.

'Dear Lily,' he said. Then, 'You do love your mistress, don't you?'

This was an odd one, but Lily swallowed and nodded and said, 'Yes sir, of course.'

'We have things in common, you and I,' he said. Then he seated himself at the table and became lost in thought.

'Would you like a cooked breakfast this morning, sir?' Lily enquired.

'What sort of a life is it for a woman down here on her own, do you suppose?'

Lily was not sure if this was addressed to anyone in particular so she did not immediately respond.

'Mm?' He looked up at her. 'What does she do with herself all day? No, don't answer that, it sounds as if I'm prying.'

He went back to pondering the table and Lily hovered uncertainly. 'I think,' she ventured, after a moment, 'she misses the girls. I'm sure she does, as a matter of fact.'

'Of course. And her husband? No.' Again he made a dismissive gesture. 'I have no right to ask you these questions. Forgive me Lily, what were you saying?'

'I was asking if you'd care for a cooked breakfast, sir. And to answer your question, I think Mrs Faraday is rather used to Mr Faraday not being here, after all this time. In fact,' she went on in a bit of a rush, 'if you come to think of it he's not been here for longer than he has been, if you see what I mean.'

There was a pause, during which Lily blushed, and then Dougie looked up at her and smiled and said, 'Thank you Lily, just toast and coffee for me.'

This time he really was leaving, and as he was about to depart he pressed a ten shilling note into Lily's hand and said, 'Look after her for me, Lily. I know you do anyway. She is very precious.'

'Of course, Mr McAvoy,' she said.

She tried not to watch his leave-taking but she couldn't help noticing the look on her mistress's face, and how she continued to stand in the doorway for a long time after he'd gone, in the cold, before she shivered suddenly, turned and came back inside the house.

Later, when she went up to strip the bedclothes from Mr McAvoy's bed there was every sign that he had spent the night in them. Moreover when it came to making her mistress's bed she couldn't help but notice – because despite her youth she knew a thing or two, did Lily – that there was no indication that anything untoward or, in Lily's eyes, interestingly scandalous, had happened.

25

'*Allez, Maman, courage* – only one more flight!' said Harriet.

'That makes it . . . '

'Five. Top floor. It's a garret, remember. You can't starve on the second floor, or you can do, but it doesn't have the same ring.'

'Just give me a minute.' Claudia held onto the banisters as she tried to catch her breath. Her heart was hammering so hard she thought it would pop right out of its socket. It was a long way, for sure, and the stairs were steep and very uneven, but there was something else that was making her not want to arrive at her destination before she had to.

The decision to visit her middle daughter was made spontaneously and immediately after the dinner party and the brief yet strange spell with Dougie, partly as a distraction from events that Claudia felt were beginning to spin out of control, and partly out of concern. And partly because, let's face it, she really couldn't put it off any longer.

'What happens when . . . you . . . ' she panted.

'When we have visitors? They hurl stones at our windows, which usually miss so they have to shout, which is all right in the summer when the windows are open, and we throw the keys down to them. I didn't want to do that with you because I thought you might not catch them and they'd end up down some gutter somewhere.'

Harriet always did have an uncanny way of being able to finish her mother's sentences, whether because what Claudia had to say was so terribly predictable or whether their minds travelled along similar paths, who could tell.

'The last flight is the most rickety, so watch your step. Mama. There's absolutely no rush. Take your time.'

There was only so long one could stand there clutching one's chest. Best to get it over with. So, bracing herself, Claudia staggered up the remaining flight of stairs to her middle daughter's garret, as she was so proud to call it, on the top floor of the ramshackle Victorian terraced house in Parson's Green.

She'd been there once before, briefly, soon after Harriet and Leonard had moved in, and she had a memory of one quite sizeable but distinctly shabby room, with grubby walls, a threadbare carpet, a couple of broken-backed sofas and not much else. What greeted her now therefore was a rather marvellous surprise.

It was much larger than she remembered it, and so light and airy, with windows in every wall. The room itself took up the whole of the top floor, and it was partitioned off in higgledy-piggledy fashion by screens, painted – by Harriet herself, her mother assumed – in a mix of styles and colours, and some of them draped in brightly coloured silk.

There was silk everywhere – silk at the windows, silk on the chairs, silk on the screens, and in such colours! Crimsons and scarlets, pinks and violets and emerald greens. The floor was covered in deep, soft layers of Persian-style rugs laid randomly and at odd angles on top of one another.

Gerald would have taken one look, laughed out loud and declared that his daughter was living in a *souk*. But

Claudia thought the whole place was, in a crazy kind of a way, utterly charming.

'Oh my darling!' she exclaimed. She went to stand in the middle of the room and gazed around. 'It's delightful.'

'My humble domain,' said Harriet, with a coy little smile. 'I'm glad you like it, *Maman*.'

'Oh but I do, I do. It's so *imaginative*! Did you do this all yourself or did you get help?'

Harriet went to sit on one of the silk-clad chairs and tucked her feet up underneath her.

'What do you mean, help?' she said. 'Not professional help, if that's what you mean.'

'You did it all yourselves?'

'Mostly me, actually. In fact entirely me.'

'Well my clever little darling, who'd have thought it?'

'Just because it's a garret doesn't mean it has to be squalid.'

'I would hardly call this a garret,' said Claudia. 'Whatever the word means. And one does hear things, doesn't one, about the Bohemian set.'

'This is Bohemian,' said Harriet, with a hint of defensiveness. 'Perhaps you've just got an odd idea of what Bohemianism is.'

'Where did all this *silk* come from? It looks like a display room.'

'We have a friend in the wholesale business. He gives us the odd offcut. It's amazing what you can do with practically no money at all. Most of what you see is secondhand, acquired from here, there and everywhere and given a lick of paint. That's all.'

'But you have such an *eye*. Where's Leonard, by the way?'

'Some of it is copied, actually. From books. Those screens for instance, they're not Japanese at all, they're old theatrical props, we got them from a friend in the theatre props business, they're painted to look Japanese. And those rugs are *faux* Persian from a market in the King's Road. It's all *faux*. I've even got a *faux* fur rug on my bed. *Faux* is the thing, you see.'

'So you both live and work in here, do you?'

'Sort of. I've even got some *faux* crystal champagne glasses, perfect for drinking *faux* champagne out of!' Harriet laughed merrily. She had a tinkly laugh – not like Jessica's, which was hearty, or Flora's, which was soft, and sing-song – but there was a touch of the manic about it.

She was sitting now on her chair with her knees drawn up to her chin and her arms hugging her knees, a bit like a small child, and she was rocking backwards and forwards as she laughed, as she used to do when she was little and when there was something wrong.

'Is there anything wrong, darling?' asked Claudia.

'Why do you say that?' Harriet's voice was sounding quite shrill.

'Nothing really.' Claudia sat down on one of the plump sofas, the one swathed in cobalt blue, leant back into the aquamarine and orange cushions and gave a deep sigh. 'And it's every bit as comfortable as it looks.'

'I thought you'd never come,' said Harriet. She'd gone back to kneeling on her chair again.

'Oh darling, I am so sorry, I know it's taken me a while. I wanted you to settle in properly, you know.'

'You went to stay with J and J.'

'Yes, I did. But then I didn't . . . . To be honest I wasn't sure what to find here, you know. Bohemianism and so on.'

'You didn't realise I was living in a palace.'

'Why do you keep saying "I"? Where's Leonard?'

'Well, a sort of palace. It's just habit, that's all. I did most of the work, so I think of it as mine. Figure of speech really. Do you like this?'

Harriet stood up to show off her skirt. It was knee-length, and patchwork, a myriad of colours and fabrics and, frankly, rather Romany, thought Claudia.

'It's very unusual. Did you make it?'

'Yes, from offcuts. It's patchwork, so it doesn't cost anything to make. I'm selling them.'

'Are you really?'

'I get the pieces of fabric from friends in the business – sometimes they're just remnants from the ends of rolls, you know, but it doesn't matter – and I just make them up. I have a sewing machine, secondhand of course.'

'You clever girl. Where do you sell them?'

'To friends. And markets. And shops. All sorts. Every one is different, unique. People will pay quite a lot for something that's absolutely unique. Oh, whoops!'

'What?'

'"Absolutely unique." You're not allowed to say that. There's no such thing as "absolutely" unique. It's "unique" or nothing.'

'Is it? Who says?'

Harriet sat down again rather abruptly, then immediately stood back up again and said, 'Would you like something? A cup of tea?'

'Leonard says,' said Claudia. 'It's the sort of thing he would say, isn't it? He is a poet, after all. You never did tell me where he was, is he away?'

'As a matter of fact, yes. I have the most exotic Indian Darjeeling tea, a friend gave it to me, would you like to try it?'

'All right, thank you.'

Claudia stood up and followed her daughter to what she feared might be the single electric ring on the floor that constituted her kitchen. But no, once again she was pleasantly surprised. True, the kitchen was a part of the room but there was a proper gas cooker, and a sink, though no larder, all of it tucked away behind more screens in a corner of the room.

'You don't mind living among the cooking smells, then?' she asked her daughter as she padded after her.

'What cooking smells?' Harriet did her tinkly laugh again as she filled the kettle.

'You do cook, don't you?'

'Not if I can help it. People bring food with them and we share it.'

'That's a fine arrangement.'

'Everybody does it.'

Claudia watched in dismay as Harriet heaped several teaspoons of tea into a teapot and poured the water on top of them before it had even properly boiled, and without heating the teapot beforehand. Surely some time in the course of Harriet's youth her mother had taught her how to make tea properly, so this was yet another small act of defiance.

Harriet's look was not unlike that of some of the young things Claudia had encountered that day in South Kensington when she had visited the Victoria and Albert Museum. Her hair was cut short in a bob that swung when she moved her head, and she wore a fringe that came close to covering her eyes so that Claudia had to consciously stop herself from reaching towards her to tuck it out of the way. Her blouse was, in Claudia's eyes, rather at odds with her patchwork skirt in terms of style and colour, but no doubt in the world of Bohemia this was *à la mode*. Overall, Claudia was not sure whether her non-conformist daughter was not after all simply conforming to another style and culture altogether.

'So where is Leonard exactly?' she asked as they were sitting back down again and drinking tea that was so strong it made Claudia gasp.

'He's in Venice,' said Harriet. Then yet again she

sprang to her feet and said, 'Would you like a biscuit of some kind? I think I have some. I can't offer scones or cakes, or . . .'

'Harriet will you just sit down and talk to me?'

Harriet stared dolefully at her mother from beneath her fringe. She looks just like a dog we used to own, thought Claudia. He was on the manic side as well, and almost as restless.

'So Leonard is in Venice,' said Claudia, 'and why aren't you with him?'

There was a short pause before Harriet spoke. 'He didn't want me there.'

'Why not?'

'He's with his muse.'

'His what?'

'His muse. He can't work otherwise, he says.'

'Oh.'

Claudia drank her tea. You could get used to it, she supposed – the tea, not the fact that her daughter's husband appeared to be up to no good.

'That's upsetting,' said Claudia. 'Are you upset?'

'Really not. It was always understood it was an open marriage, we could do what we want, on our own if need be, we didn't have to be in each other's pockets all the time.'

'But you've only been married for . . .'

'Seven months,' said Harriet. 'And three weeks. Give or take.'

'Oh my darling.' Claudia laid a hand on her daughter's arm but Harriet did not react. 'These open marriages, so-called,' she went on. 'They never really work. Or rather they may work for the husband – it's the wife who's the one left behind while he goes off and does what he wants with whoever he wants. Is it anyone you know?'

'Who, his muse? No.'

'Well, I think you should pack up everything and come home, right away.'

'Mother, you absolutely do not understand!' Harriet's eyes, what her mother could see of them, were flashing. 'I knew you wouldn't understand, that's why I didn't want to tell you. It's absolutely all right! I tell you!'

'Well, I just don't believe it.' Claudia was bristling. 'The moment he gets back I'm going to give that husband of yours a piece of my mind. And his lady friend, whoever she happens to be.'

There was another pause. 'It's a he,' Harriet mumbled.

'I beg your pardon?'

'His muse, it's a he.' Harriet tossed her head, another habit she'd acquired, presumably so she could occasionally catch a glimpse of the outside world beyond her fringe.

'Oh, it's a man. Well.' Claudia took a deep breath. 'Well, that's all right then.'

'What do you mean?'

'If he's just a chum.'

'He isn't just a chum, Mama.'

There was only a limited number of times one could ask one's daughter what she meant, so Claudia thought for a long moment, as she tried to process the information she was receiving, before she said, 'I think you really need to spell things out for me, Harriet, I don't think I'm quite following.'

'It's not a problem, Mama,' said Harriet. 'It happens all the time. Men go with men. Women go with women even. Some people go with men *and* women.'

There was now another pause which went on for so long you could hear, distantly, it being five floors above street level, a motor car travelling the length of the street from one end to the other.

'In that case,' said Claudia eventually, 'why were you

so reluctant to tell me?'

Harriet gave a lengthy sigh. 'Because I knew you'd make a fuss. Which, let's face it, is exactly what you're doing.'

With which she got up from her chair, grabbed the teacups with one hand and the teapot with the other, and stormed off to the kitchen area, and the only thing that was missing was the bang of the kitchen door.

26

Claudia took herself off for a walk shortly afterwards, despite the fact that it was beginning to get dark on this December day. She wanted to put some space between herself and her daughter.

It was not that she was unfamiliar with homosexuality, of course, or even with bisexuality – though she found the latter harder to come to grips with than the former. It was not even that this particular poser was happening so close to home, though that too was a consideration; liberalism was all very well at a distance but when it was part of your own family, well.

No, what disturbed Claudia most of all was her daughter's reaction to her husband's behaviour. As a mother one naturally wants one's offspring to be happy and independent and generally managing to cope with the world, and Claudia had always felt that her daughters had achieved all of this, long before they were married. Of the three, Harriet, as the one in the middle, had always been the odd one out, the non-conformist, though Claudia wondered if this was not simply her reaction against her more conventional siblings.

What really concerned her was the feeling that, though she would protest otherwise, Harriet was not a natural Bohemian. She was not so radically liberal-minded that she really did not object to her husband, within a year of marriage, swanning off to foreign parts with a male lover. That whole business about open marriages, she wasn't fooling anyone. One could see it (if one could penetrate beyond the fringe) in her daughter's eyes, hear it in the tone of her voice. But knowing this, or sensing it, was one thing. Doing something about it another. What was a mother to do?

Claudia walked on, in no particular direction. She had a memory of Harriet and Leonard some time ago mentioning, almost apologetically, as if it might compromise their Bohemian sensibilities, that the flat they were about to move into was not far from the river, though you really wouldn't know it. That was another thing: the rejection of all things society deemed desirable, such as the proximity of a river to what was, in Claudia's eyes, an otherwise distinctly unprepossessing part of west London. It all seemed like a foolish game, a party act, this turning everything on its head.

The sudden appearance, around the corner, of a parade of shops reminded Claudia of another purpose behind her aimless wanderings. A girl who could not make a cup of tea was unlikely to have given much, if any, thought to dinner, and without consciously looking for it Claudia was not aware of the existence of any food in the corner of the room Harriet called her kitchen. Mind you in this respect it was a case of the blind leading the blind, and so Claudia found herself standing at the counter in the butcher's shop and pointing at what she thought were pork chops, and asking for two of them; following which, next door in the greengrocer's she picked up some cabbage, and a couple of pounds of potatoes, and some cooking apples for the sauce; all of which arduous and unfamiliar exercise did an excellent job of wiping from her mind, if only for the moment, all filial worries.

And so she returned to Harriet's garret in a marginally

better frame of mind. 'Embrace the difference,' she told herself, as she negotiated, steadily, the five flights of increasingly uneven stairs.

'What's that?' said Harriet, peering into her mother's shopping bag.

'It's food, darling, we have to eat.'

'You needn't have bothered,' Harriet shrugged. 'Somebody's bound to turn up with something.'

Which is exactly what happened. Just as Claudia was getting used to spending a quiet evening in with her daughter – companionably chit-chatting about this and that, looking through Harriet's art books to see where she got her inspiration from, and her collection of patchworks; and, on being offered a skirt or even a bedspread if she wanted one, declining politely, with a gentle laugh, saying she didn't think they were *quite* her thing; to which Harriet responded by saying it was perfectly all right, she wouldn't dream of imposing anything on her mother that wasn't her thing (in which remark there was a good deal of meaning) – there came a loud knock on the door, and there stood a skinny girl in a long skirt, clutching a ceramic dish, and behind her several others, all of them holding bottles and pots and bags of who knows what.

They were the first of around a dozen visitors who piled in, one after another, laughing and generally making quite a lot of noise, briefly nodding at Claudia and then making themselves at home on cushions and chairs or on the bare rug. Pots and plates of food were spread over the floor and glasses were filled with something that was referred to as pink champagne but tasted more like cheap claret and lemonade (which is what it was, and surprisingly refreshing it was too). One young man wearing what looked like an Indian tunic produced an accordion and began playing, which led others to sing along, not always the same song and hardly ever together, adding their own percussion in the form of cutlery banged on plates, and hands and feet slapping the floor. When Claudia expressed concern for Harriet's neighbours, the majority of the assembled company raised their hands and said that as those very same neighbours they gave themselves permission to go on making as much noise as they liked.

Someone thrust a plate of 'ratatouille' into Claudia's hands. It looked like nothing on earth and tasted like vegetable stew with random spices, and Claudia thought longingly of her pork chops. She worked her way through it and then sat back and, unbothered and largely ignored, observed the goings-on.

As the evening progressed so the party gradually split into small groups. In one corner a handful of people, Harriet among them, immersed themselves in animated discussion. Others gathered around the accordion player, swaying to the music and occasionally breaking into song, and now and then getting to their feet and moving to the music, which ranged from gypsy rondos to what sounded like East European laments. A pair of young women took it in turns to comb one another's extraordinarily long hair. Others surrounded a device that Claudia believed to be a hookah, passing the pipe from one to another and inhaling some sweet-smelling substance that reminded her of the Middle East and, unexpectedly, of Gerald.

The two women, Claudia then saw, had turned from hair-combing to the altogether more intricate, and intimate, business of exploring each other's bodies. They began by unbuttoning one another's blouses and reaching inside to fondle their friend's bosoms. Then removing their upper clothing altogether they flicked their hair over their heads and took it in turns to drape their crowning glories across their friend's naked chests, and all of it in full view of the assembled company. But the assembled company, with one exception, took not the slightest notice.

Claudia was transfixed. She found herself transported back several decades to the dorm in her all-girls boarding school where, one evening after the Christmas ball a group of rather over-excited young things decided to divest themselves of their flannelette pyjama tops and explore one another's breasts. There was a bit of tentative prodding and stroking but it was really just a game, and it was accompanied by distinctly unsexual and marginally hysterical giggling. While she could not recall any feelings of sexual arousal at the time, the recollection of it now, as she watched the two women, gave Claudia a surprising thrill.

'Are you all right, *maman?*'

She felt a hand on her shoulder and jumped, like a guilty schoolgirl.

'Oh, hello darling. Yes, I'm fine, how are you?' She hadn't until that moment felt like a voyeur.

'What exactly are they doing?' she asked.

'That's Albert and Bertha.' Harriet slid onto the sofa next to her mother.

'*Albert?*'

'That's what they call themselves. It's a performance piece. It's about the sexual duality of the divided self.'

'I beg your pardon?'

'They're exploring the notion that human beings aren't simply made up of male and female but that we're all a mixture of both, and that same-sex, or homosexual attraction is integral to everyone to a greater or lesser degree.'

Claudia blinked. She thought to say something but decided otherwise.

'Sometimes they invite onlookers to participate,' said Harriet.

'Do they indeed?'

'That's why I thought I'd better come and rescue you.'

Well, what was a middle-aged mother of three supposed to make of that?

'And you, darling, what were you discussing over there? It looked awfully earnest.'

Harriet gave a deep sigh. 'Ireland.'

'Oh, that.'

'Can I get you anything, Mama?' asked Harriet.

'No darling, thank you. In fact,' Claudia stifled a yawn, 'I think if you don't mind I shall conk out on one of your sofas, behind one of your screens.'

'I'll get rid of everyone,' said Harriet, getting to her feet.

'Oh, not on my account, darling.'

But Harriet was already clapping her hands and announcing to the assembled company, 'Time to go, everyone, my Mama needs her beauty sleep.'

And so, eventually, they did.

27

There was not much beauty sleep to be had, not for Claudia, not that night. It was not the discomfort of the sofa that acted as her temporary bed (which was in truth not uncomfortable at all), nor the lingering aroma of cinnamon and Turkish tobacco, but rather the buzzing of her mind that kept sleep at bay.

The idea of women pleasuring one another was bizarre, and despite the protagonists' claims, apparently endorsed by her daughter, quite unnatural. Moreover as a public display it was of course beyond the pale, yet searching her soul Claudia found she was in fact neither disgusted nor appalled, nor, even, embarrassed; all of which said something about her that was mildly puzzling.

'We are all experiments.' It was Gerald who had said that, once, in a very different context.

The following morning she and Harriet took a bus to Knightsbridge, and from there they walked to Hyde Park. On the way Harriet regaled her mother with the origins of the Irish Free State, a topic which so engrossed her that she appeared to forget altogether her proclaimed antipathy to 'greenery', and Mother Nature in general.

Claudia did her best to keep up with her daughter's conversation but her mind kept straying. Part of her marvelled at Harriet's knowledge and concern for serious matters such as the plight of the Irish people and their struggle for independence against what she called the 'tyrannical' British government. At the same time she was distracted by little mannerisms Harriet had acquired, all to do with her fringe, such as her habit of sticking out her lower lip and puffing sharply upwards, which made the said encumbrance momentarily flutter up and away from her forehead; or the way in which in order to get a proper view of anything she had to tilt her head back and peer down at it, which lent her an air of disapproval. Then when least expected, into Claudia's mind popped the image of the two women and the things they had done with their truly astonishing hair, and equally suddenly and unexpectedly the image of Dougie, that day when she had read aloud his letter to her, what agony she must have put him through, how could she have done such a thing? All of which managed to take up the entire half-hour journey from Parson's Green to Knightsbridge.

For her part Harriet was completely aware that her mother was not listening to a word she said (which was nothing new), but a bit of her still wanted to prove to Claudia that she was who she was: a modern, free-thinking and independent young woman who cared about the world around her; who had rejected the societal constraints under which she had been brought up but was not yet ready to embrace nihilism; who considered Freud a prophet; who was not in the least perturbed at her husband's sexual proclivities and who, one day when she was ready, which was not yet, was perfectly prepared to herself experiment with homosexuality. While a large part of Harriet had rejected most of the world of her upbringing, another only marginally smaller part of her still sought approval from the mother who had imposed it on her.

The park, on this cloudless, crisp and sparkling December day, was simply beautiful, Claudia thought.

'How much further you can see when the trees are bare, don't you think, darling?' she remarked as they strolled round the Serpentine; at which Harriet merely shrugged, but then she nodded, in a kind of acquiescence. 'I suppose so,' she said.

There were few people around: the odd rower on the water, some children playing, a dog here and there – you would never think you were right in the heart of a busy city. They stopped for lunch at the Serpentine café, and once they had finished eating Claudia laid a hand on her daughter's and said, 'Now tell me darling, truly, without jumping down my throat. Are you really happy or are you just putting on a brave front?'

Harriet tried to pull her hand away but her mother held on fast.

'I'm fine,' she said, but without much conviction.

'Because you don't have to put up with this situation, you know that. You can give Leonard an ultimatum.'

'You don't . . . ' Harriet began, and then sighed, and looked up and away at something, or nothing.

'I don't understand,' said Claudia. 'You're right, so I really need you to explain it to me.'

Harriet brushed her fringe to the side of her face so her mother was able, fleetingly, to catch sight of her eyes, which looked to her to be insufferably sad.

'It's complicated,' she said eventually.

Claudia waited. She was still holding her daughter's hand, very tightly.

'When I told Leonard I wanted to marry him . . . ' Harriet began.

'*You* told Leonard you wanted to marry *him*?' exclaimed Claudia.

'Please, Mother, do – not – interrupt.'

'Sorry darling, I'll shut up.' Claudia pressed her lips together to prove her intention.

'Yes, I told him I wanted to marry him, and he said he couldn't marry any woman because no one would ever be open-minded enough to put up with . . . ' she paused.

'With his predilection.'

'If you want to put it that way. We discussed it, at length, as we discuss everything. He told me he couldn't live without . . . and that it was best to be completely honest about it, and I admired him for that.'

Claudia grunted, quietly.

'He said it all happened quite spontaneously. He was with . . . and they were reading poetry together – Anton's a poet too.'

'Anton? He sounds foreign.'

'Mother. '

'Sorry darling. Go on.'

'It was late at night and the poetry was very intense. I think it was probably Rimbaud. And they were sitting close together and the atmosphere was so electric and they were both feeling so emotional. And it just happened. They ripped off one another's clothes and made love, there and then.'

Claudia blinked, but said nothing.

'I was actually a bit disgusted when he first told me. But then he described it, and it was . . . '

'He described what they did together? To you?' Claudia eyes were wide and she gripped her daughter's hand even more tightly.

'Yes. He said it was quite different to making love to a woman. It was more – it was all muscular physicality, like men wrestling, which Leonard says anyway is a homo-erotic sport, like a lot of men's sport.'

'"Homo-erotic"?'

'Whereas with women it's all tenderness, and stroking, and mystery and discovery. Man on man on the other hand is another thing altogether. It's more equal. It's knowing. The excitement is in the knowing rather than the discovery, if that makes sense. I thought it was beautiful.'

She paused there.

'Go on,' said Claudia, gently. She was stroking her daughter's hand now.

'He said he would keep his two lives quite separate, that when he was with me he would be with me totally, and we would never meet, me and Anton. But that he couldn't give him up. And so I told him I could live with that.'

She had addressed all this to the tablecloth, and now she looked up for the first time and through her fringe at her mother, not without apprehension.

'My friends all think I'm remarkable,' she went on, 'to be so understanding, so self-sufficient. And the fact is, when we are together, Leonard and me, it is so . . . ' she struggled for the word, 'so intense, so passionate. I love him totally, *Maman.*'

'I understand, darling.'

'I'm not quite sure that you do. You see this business of one person "owning" another person, it doesn't really cut it with me. This monogamy – whose idea was it in the first place? Society's. Why should we not be free to live as we want to live, without hypocrisy? How many people have clandestine lovers? Isn't it morally better to be open about these things? Open and honest? It leaves me free to do what I want, too.'

'And what is that? What do you want?'

Harriet went back to studying the tablecloth.

'I don't really know,' she said. 'I just know I don't want to lose him.'

And then, from behind the curtain of her fringe, two great big tears rolled down Harriet's cheeks and plopped onto her empty plate.

'Oh my darling,' said Claudia. Now she took her

daughter's hand in both hers, and when she spoke her voice was trembling slightly. 'Just listen to me. How you live your life is entirely up to you, although I won't pretend to understand it. But just know that you must do what you think is right, not what Leonard thinks, or your friends, not what you think will impress your friends but what you really want. Otherwise you're just falling into the same old trap we all fall into, doing what is expected of us, rather than . . . And know, my dearest sweetheart, your old home is always there for you, as am I, if ever you need it.'

'Thanks, *Maman*,' said Harriet, and she squeezed her mother's hand.

Claudia's heart was partly broken, yet partly revived. The heart after all is a muscle, and like any other muscle if not used regularly is prone to atrophy. She was very deeply moved, more so than she had been for a long time, and while she grieved for her unhappy daughter she also rejoiced in the knowledge that she, and her heart, were still truly and completely alive. And moreover that her daughter, for good or ill, or more likely both, had discovered genuine love.

Travelling back on the bus they sat together holding hands and not talking at all. At around the halfway point, at Sloane Square, Harriet laid her head on her mother's shoulder and that's how they stayed for the remainder of the journey.

28

While she was in London there were people Claudia felt she really ought to get in touch with. There was Prue, to whom she hadn't spoken since that senseless quarrel, and of course Dougie. And then there was her old friend Hermione.

Hermione was ten years younger than Claudia and had never married. She had never even, so far as Claudia was aware, had a serious lover. She was, as unkind people were wont to describe her, mousy, not to say downright plain, and so quiet you didn't know she was there half the time. When people tried to recall who was present at such and such a social event they inevitably remembered all the guests except for . . . oh yes, there was one other, now who on earth could that have been? That, invariably, was Hermione.

Yet Claudia was extremely fond of her. She was shy, certainly, yet highly intelligent and extremely intuitive, and when in company with friends she trusted she could be remarkably witty, even acerbic. She said once to Claudia that without wanting to sound snobbish she was rather discerning about her friends. 'Shy people usually are,' she explained. 'If you're a talker you don't necessarily care who it is you're talking to, so long as there's a face there with ears on it. But if you're a listener, well, you want to make sure what you're listening to has some value.' And she had burst into gales of laughter. 'If you see what I mean,' she ended, apologetically.

So Claudia was truly flattered because she knew Hermione did not have a great deal of friends but that the friends she did have she cared about very much. In today's world, when so many people appeared to 'collect' other people in order to fill up some mystical address book, that was rare, and all the more special for it.

Moreover Claudia had an ulterior motive for her visit. She wanted to find out what happened after the dinner party, when Robbie (the Nicest – and the most serially Single – Man in the Universe) had driven Hermione home afterwards.

They had lunch at Hermione's maisonette the following day. She lived in Camden Town, which Claudia regarded as rather racy, and definitely not a part of London one would want to venture into at night. She had lived there for as long as Claudia could remember.

'How lovely to see you,' said Hermione, her face shining, as it did when she was genuinely pleased to see someone.

She was very small, and her hair, which had remained much the same indeterminate colour ever since Claudia had known her – which was a good twenty years – was tucked into an untidy bun. That was another thing about Hermione, she possessed not a grain of vanity. She wore skirts of uncertain length over heavy stockings and sensible shoes. Her blouses were buttoned to the neck and she had a penchant for cardigans which looked as if they might have been knitted by her mother, or even her grandmother. She wore neither jewelry nor cosmetics. She washed her face with soap and, when she could be bothered, softened it with cream which she made herself out of goodness knows what.

For Claudia's dinner party she had gone to town and

bought herself a dress, but it was the kind of dress one only found nowadays in sad shops down side streets in suburban towns, whose stock had and would continue to remain defiantly unchanged and untouched by the fashions of the day. Hermione prided herself in being 'understated', which itself was an understatement of massive proportions. But Claudia knew that beneath the blue-stocking exterior lay a witty, wise and utterly delightful person.

'How are you and what have you been up to?' she began.

'Huge amounts and nothing at all,' said Hermione. 'I work hard and then I come home and read about the Byzantine Empire, isn't that thrilling?'

'Is it?' asked Claudia.

'So that's me in a nutshell. Your turn.'

Hermione poured them both a glass of sherry and they sat talking, and talking. Claudia told her friend about her daughter Harriet – not everything, obviously, but enough to paint a broad picture of a girl who she thought was trapped in a way of life that she could not naturally embrace. Hermione listened and nodded throughout, and said, 'You can't blame the young for having the courage to experiment, otherwise how else would we ever evolve? And she was brought up in *such* a respectable household.' She went on to remark how lucky Harriet was to have such a loving and *understanding* mother, that not many mothers would even try to see eye to eye with her, let alone spend nights sleeping on a sofa next to the kitchen, *and* with the bathroom down a flight of stairs and shared with several other households.

All this made Claudia feel so much better about everything, and so the sherry bottle became gradually emptier.

But what of Robbie? No, she wasn't going to ask

straight out, so by way of encouragement she told Hermione something about Dougie. Hermione again nodded in her fashion and said, 'I could see there was something going on that night. I did wonder.' Then she paused, waiting for enlargement, and when none was forthcoming she added, 'Probably just as well.'

'Why do you say that?'

'Who knows what you'd be getting yourself into with Dougie. He takes life so seriously.'

'Dougie? But he's always joking and making fun of things!'

'Yes, I know. But underneath all that, you know . . . '

For a moment Claudia was tempted to tell her friend everything about the Dougie conundrum, even to seek her advice. She was after all the *soundest* person she knew, despite never having had – to Claudia's knowledge – a serious relationship in her life. But even while she was pondering such things her friend pre-empted her.

'I would be very careful with Dougie.' Hermione was looking gently at Claudia. 'I believe he could be too easily crushed, and I don't think . . . ' She stopped.

'You don't think what?'

'I don't think you should play with him. Not,' she added quickly, with a little flutter of her hands, 'that I'm imagining you would do such a thing. But he is quite vulnerable, don't you agree?'

For an extraordinary moment Claudia wondered if Hermione and Dougie hadn't – but no, that was impossible, yet how else would she know so much about him?

'Especially now, I think,' Hermione went on, 'with you on your own, and he also.' She shrugged. 'But I do think – and please forgive me for saying this as it's really none of my business – if you did want to embark on something with Dougie then you should consider your position with

Gerald very seriously.'

Never before had Hermione expressed her opinion quite so baldly. And the truth was, as ever, she was absolutely right.

Claudia was considering her response when there came the sound of the front door opening and then closing and footsteps tapping along the hallway past the sitting room and up the stairs. Claudia half rose from her chair.

'Who's there? Is it a burglar?'

'No, no,' said Hermione with a smile. 'It's a friend of mine.'

'Robbie?' She said it before she could stop herself.

Hermione laughed. 'Good gracious no. Anyway, you were telling me . . ?'

'Was I? But if it's a friend, why don't you invite him in? Am I not allowed to meet him?'

'All in good time,' said Hermione. 'We were talking about Dougie, and you were saying how he jokes all the time, which is often a mask for someone who is deeply serious.'

'You're probably right, as you always are.' But Claudia's concentration had gone now; she was preoccupied with the Person Upstairs.

'You're a dark horse,' she said to Hermione, and Hermione merely nodded and smiled.

They then had lunch, which was a bowl of clam chowder, homemade – Hermione was an astute housekeeper and a very good cook – and they chatted about other things. Claudia wanted Hermione to come and visit her and asked what her plans were for Christmas.

'We'll be spending it here, just quietly,' she said.

Claudia nodded. Getting information out of Hermione was like pushing a heavy boulder up a steep hill. '"We"', she said, 'being . . . ?'

'You'll find out soon enough.'

There was fruit and cheese to follow and some dessert wine, which was not something Claudia usually imbibed but it went surprisingly well with the Stilton.

'You should open a restaurant,' she said.

'As a matter of fact I have toyed with that idea,' said Hermione, 'only my cooking is so unfashionable, like the rest of me. Also once you're having to make money out of something it ceases to be a pleasure. I prefer to keep it as a hobby. Anyway I already have a perfectly satisfactory job.'

Claudia was not at all sure what it was that Hermione did. She had told her, on many occasions, so to ask her once again was out of the question, but as far as Claudia could remember it entailed regular hours and an office, and desks and typewriters and shipping, or export and import, or maybe both. The world of work and commerce was something Claudia had neither experienced nor ever properly understood.

After lunch they retired again to Hermione's little sitting room for coffee. And as Hermione was pouring the first cup, the door opened and a woman entered.

'Joyce!' said Hermione, getting to her feet with that shining smile on her face. She greeted the young woman with a hug. 'Meet my old and dear friend Claudia.'

'I'm delighted to meet you,' said Joyce. She had short, curly blonde hair and a very pretty smile and, as they stood there side by side, with their arms around one another's waists, Claudia noticed they were almost exactly the same height.

'Oh! said Claudia. 'Did you just come in, a while ago?'

'Yes. I didn't want to disturb you while you and Hermione were catching up on your news.'

Claudia looked from one to the other. Hermione could barely contain her giggles.

'Yes,' said Hermione eventually, through her laughter.

'Joyce lives here too.'

'Oh, you share it, I see.' Then Claudia said, to Hermione, 'you never told me you had a flatmate.'

'Joyce is not my flatmate,' said Hermione, still smiling. 'She's my lover.'

Once again Claudia felt the world lurch. She stared at both the women in turn, and at the look on her face so they burst into laughter together.

Twice in as many days she had come face-to-face with a situation that was so far from her regular frame of reference she was finding things very difficult to process. First Harriet, and now this.

'Well, my word, I would never have guessed.' It was the best she could come up with.

'Why should you?' said Hermione. She was holding her friend's – her lover's – hand.

'How long have you been together?'

The two women looked at one another.

'Six years, is it?'

'Seven.'

'Is it really?'

'Seven years in January.'

'Well there you are then.' Hermione turned to Claudia. 'Long enough to count as a marriage, don't you think?'

'I had no idea!'

'Are you shocked?' asked Hermione. And then, 'Of course you are. I'm sorry to spring it on you so suddenly but I didn't know how else to do it. Of course nobody knows, no one else, outside these doors.'

'Then I feel deeply touched,' said Claudia, though it wasn't the emotion uppermost in her mind at that point.

She sat back down again and they did likewise. They were looking at her and then looking at one another and bursting into little bouts of laughter and then looking back at her again, like schoolchildren who've been sent to the headmistress and are waiting to see what sort of punishment she's going to inflict on them.

Claudia smiled wanly back at them. She wanted to feel pleased, delighted even, she could see how happy Hermione was, how truly and completely happy, she was almost envious. But it was a step too far for her at that particular moment. It was cataclysmic, an overturning of the natural order. She felt quite faint.

She wanted to leave right there and then. To her shame she could think of nothing to say and she was horribly aware of her obvious dismay. But she stayed put, if only to show her solidarity, and besides, to do otherwise would look downright rude.

So the conversation continued for a while and the atmosphere became easier until Claudia had all but forgotten the two women facing her were not just friends but, yes, lovers. There, she'd said it, albeit to herself, though she couldn't bring herself to imagine what two women got up to together, in the bedroom, that is. She was embarrassing herself even thinking of it. But the more they chatted the more the embarrassment was replaced by a kind of *curiosity*. After all one would never have known, if one had met these women at a dinner party, or anywhere. They seemed so *normal*.

'You see?' said Hermione at the front door as Claudia was leaving, 'it wasn't so hard, was it? Were you fearfully embarrassed?'

Claudia looked at Hermione for some time, and closely. She exuded a kind of calm happiness that Claudia herself had never, or not for some time, herself experienced.

'I . . .' she stammered, then said honestly, 'Yes, I was, to begin with. But I'm truly glad for you Hermione, truly. I just need a little while to get used to it.'

'There's really nothing to get used to,' Hermione shrugged. 'Just think of us as a couple of good friends, and if you can accept us then please accept Joyce too, as a new friend. She's a lovely person and she does make me happy.'

'I can see that,' said Claudia.

She made Hermione promise to bring Joyce down to visit her in the country, very soon. Yet even before she'd reached the pavement she was wondering how she was going to explain to Lily that her two female visitors would be sharing a bedroom.

29

Hermione could show those so-called Bohemians a thing or two, thought Claudia as she entered the bowels of the Northern Line. She was just the sort of woman Bohemians would scoff at, with her regular nine to five job, the same one she'd held down for at least ten years, the same train into Town, the same one out of it, as regular as clockwork, as right as rain, mousy little Hermione. But who knows what goes on behind people's front doors?

When she arrived back in Parson's Green Claudia found Harriet hard at work at her sewing machine. 'I've suddenly got all these orders,' she said, without looking up. 'Goodness only knows why, from a new outlet in Kensington High Street, terribly posh. The word must have got around.'

'So you have no objection to doing business with the bourgeoisie?' Claudia remarked, mildly, peeling off her gloves.

'One has to eat,' said her daughter.

'Well darling, you know if you're ever short of money you only have to ask.' Claudia fell back onto one of the sofas and kicked off her shoes.

Aware that the treadle had suddenly stopped she looked up. Harriet was gazing fixedly into space and she said, with great deliberation, 'Don't you ever offer me money again, *Maman*.' With which she returned to her work with added ferociousness.

Claudia stared at her daughter for a blank moment. Then she turned to look out of the window. The sun was setting in between two buildings and as it did so it peered briefly yet sharply through the clouds, throwing a sudden golden light across the room. Claudia absently watched a speck of dust, caught in the beam, as it flitted aimlessly, up, down, around and in circles before disappearing into the shadows, and for a moment she felt a strong sense of identity with it.

'I think,' she said, 'I'll go home tomorrow.'

Harriet did not reply.

'Did you hear me, darling?' She turned to look at her daughter. Harriet pulled her work out from the machine and tore the cotton thread with her teeth, a habit Claudia had tried in vain to rid her of some time ago, telling her she risked damaging her teeth, to which Harriet had responded, 'It's only cotton, for goodness' sake.'

'You've had enough then,' said Harriet.

'Darling, of course not, I just feel it's time. Especially since you have all this work on your plate all of a sudden.'

'You stayed with J and J nearly a week.' She was fumbling with the garment she was making. She had not looked at her mother once since she'd walked in.

'Yes, but – goodness me, what is this? I had appointments.'

'And of course it was a lot more comfortable. It's all right, you don't have to explain.'

Claudia turned to look out of the window again. It was beginning to snow, lightly. She suddenly longed to be home, in her own place, and in her own bed, where nothing particular happened and there was no one to whom she had to be accountable.

Perhaps she'd been a bad mother. Having allowed the

girls to grow up in relative freedom, to be, within reason, themselves, just perhaps they had mistaken this freedom for indifference. It had been a bone of contention with Gerald, when he was at home, which in the old days he was more often than he was now.

'They make a lot of noise when they're together,' he'd remarked on one occasion. 'Why is that?'

To which Claudia had responded by shrugging and saying, 'They're young.' Which had earned her a long hard stare.

But she also remembered the time when her friend Laura had brought her daughter Charlotte to visit, and had spent the entire time talking for, about and over the top of the poor child, and in the third person, as if she wasn't there; as in: 'Charlotte is very shy and awkward with people, you know, so we're thinking of sending her away to Switzerland when she leaves school to acquire some sophistication.' After they had gone, her own girls had exploded into laughter and outrage, saying what an appalling woman she was and no wonder her poor daughter couldn't say boo to a goose, she wasn't allowed to get a word in edgeways. And it was Harriet who had said, 'Thank goodness you're not like that, Mama,' and given her mother an affectionate hug.

Anyway, thought Claudia, it's too late to go back on anything now.

She had been looking forward to confiding in Harriet about Hermione, how she'd only now discovered that one of her oldest friends had turned out to be – *like that* – and who would have guessed? She even thought, stupidly perhaps, it might have given her a little more credibility in the eyes of her Bohemian daughter, to think that her boring old stick of a mother had such an unconventional friend. But Harriet's head was once again bent over her machine and her foot was pumping up and down on the treadle as though her life depended on it, which in a sense of course, it did.

'Besides,' said Claudia, 'Christmas is approaching, there's a lot to do. Are you coming down?'

'What?' said Harriet, after a moment.

'I asked if you were going to be coming down for Christmas. It's not long now, you know.'

'I don't know,' Harriet replied. 'It depends on Leonard.'

It depends on Leonard.

'That's to say,' she looked up from her work for a moment, 'we haven't discussed it. He may want to spend it with his parents.' She smiled weakly, even apologetically, at her mother. 'Can I let you know in a day or so?'

'Of course darling. It would be wonderful to have you all down together.'

Harriet nodded, and continued with her work. But at least the frost had thawed just a bit.

~

Despite the thaw Claudia felt sad. As she sat in the café at Paddington station the following morning, waiting for her train, which was delayed on account of the snow – which was not heavy but which nonetheless seemed to disrupt the railway timetable every time it put in an appearance – she wondered whether, as a mother, she had after all made some wrong decisions about herself.

Gerald's absence had not been easy to come to terms with, and those absences had become longer as the years went by. Yet Claudia had tried so hard to keep her loneliness from her daughters – from everyone, in fact. It was important for her to present herself to the outside world as a self-sufficient, independent and contented woman. To some extent she believed the person people took you for was the person you might become, and that as a mother it would be quite wrong for her to show any kind of weakness to her daughters. After all, they also had to put up with an absentee father, it wasn't easy for them either.

But was this the best example to present to her children? By appearing to walk through life without a qualm, was she inadvertently making it harder for them to show their own vulnerability? If she never confided in them why should they confide in her? Stiff upper lip, stuff and nonsense. She laughed, briefly and rather surprisingly, out loud.

'You're spilling your coffee,' said a male voice.

Indeed she was. The cup was in her hand, and had been so for some time, but at an angle, and the coffee was dribbling steadily onto the table in front of her. She righted it, and dabbed rather uselessly at the puddle on the table with her napkin, so by the time she looked up to see who had alerted her to her misadventure, the man had seated himself at another table and was staring out of the window with, she couldn't help but notice, a similarly mournful expression.

He was younger than her, but not by much, dressed quite smartly, and handsome in a weary kind of a way. He wore a soft Trilby hat which, as she watched, he removed – revealing a partly balding head – and placed absently on the table, all the while looking out across the concourse. Claudia was suddenly reminded for no reason she could think of of Noël Coward, the famous actor/playwright she had met at Jess and Jonno's, and of the strange conversation they had had about an older woman falling in love with a younger man.

That got her thinking about the man in the café, who only now, as he took a sip of his drink, glanced around, nodding briefly at her, before turning again to look vacantly through the window. She wondered if he wasn't perhaps a victim of one of these hopelessly all-consuming love affairs which, by the way Mr Coward, no woman ever quite manages to put behind her because, like some awful disease, just when you think you are immune they sneak up on you and take hold of you like a vice.

She was almost tempted to go up to the stranger and try to get into conversation with him, to find out what it was that was making him so sad. Perhaps he had just said farewell to his lover, knowing they were never going to meet again, because . . . ? Because they were both married and they had had a brief encounter, quite by chance, maybe in this very café, and had unexpectedly fallen in love and begun an affair before realising that duty was more important than their individual happiness; so their love affair had to come to an end and they had to part, knowing they were never going to be properly happy again. It would make, thought Claudia, a marvellous play, with just the one set, the café, and these two people and perhaps the odd character in the background, like the woman behind the counter. If she ever met Mr Coward again she would tell it to him. She thought it might appeal to him, especially if the woman were older than the man.

Just then there was an announcement and the sad stranger got to his feet, placed his hat on his head and walked out. Perhaps he's catching the same train as me, thought Claudia, as she finished her coffee and collected her things together and, giving it just a minute so nobody would think she was actually *pursuing* the stranger, she walked out of the café and across the concourse to the departure board. There he was, gazing up at it. She glanced at him sideways and then up at the board to see her train was departing in twenty minutes, and by the time she looked back at him he had gone.

30

Once again there were messages awaiting her at home. Mrs de Vere had called, twice, and Mrs de Sanchez de . . . de . . . Lily could never quite get Flora's married name right, but anyway it was Miss Flora, who'd wanted to talk to her mother about Christmas arrangements.

It had snowed a fair amount, and it was still snowing, and unlike in London, where it so quickly turned to slush and mud, here in the country it was pristine, and so white in the wintry light it almost hurt Claudia's eyes to look at it. Like a child she had to don her warmest coat and boots right away, and walk across it, listening to it squeaking beneath her feet, and stopping every so often to look behind and see her footprints quickly vanishing which, when she really was a child, she thought was hysterically funny and proved she was invisible. She walked to the great oak, she felt almost duty bound now, it was like going to greet an old friend. The snow clung to the tree's branches and fell, in dollops, upon her as she stood beneath it, gazing upwards, until a particularly large clump fell right into her eyes, making her blink wildly and shake her head and laugh out loud.

She was glad to be home.

She was looking forward to Christmas. She hoped, she really hoped, everyone would be there, all the girls and their husbands, except for Gerald, of course. Once

Christmas was over she would invite Prue down for New Year, perhaps with Dougie; that way they could both act as a kind of foil for each other, or perhaps what she really meant was a protection. She had contacted neither of them while she was in London, partly out of cowardice and partly, in the case of Dougie, because of what Hermione had said about him. She had fully intended, or so she thought, to enjoy a brief fling with Dougie. After all, she'd thought, why not?

Why not. Well, what sort of a reason was that for an affair? Dougie was not a why not person, not now, not any more. If it were a case, as it had been once, of choosing between Dougie and Gerald then it deserved a rather more considered motivation than Why not.

Talking of which, she thought she would pay Gerald a visit to wherever it was he was working now. Egypt? Or perhaps Palestine. It might well not happen, but it was something to think about.

~

Flora arrived first, on her own, with her dog Sally, who was, she explained, 'a failed sheepdog'. Flora lived in Shropshire with her Spanish husband Carlos, where they ran a stud farm, he being the youngest in a long line of racehorse breeders from Toledo. Carlos was with his father, who was in the country looking at other stud farms, and would follow on in a few days, at around the same time that Claudia expected Jess and Jonno and, who knows, with a bit of luck, Harriet and Leonard.

Of all her daughters Flora, the youngest, was without doubt the most mature and level-headed. She and her husband lived what she described as a simple 'homespun' life in their timber cottage, set in the heart of rolling countryside half a mile from the nearest road across a dirt track. There she baked bread and made soup out of home-grown vegetables and herbs while her husband 'toiled in the fields', as she put it; though as these things go it was quite high-class 'toiling', in a business that commanded huge amounts of money. Flora painted an idyllic picture of a country life far from the madding, and maddening, crowds and anxieties of city life, where she spent whole hours just listening to birdsong and watching the wildlife frolicking outside her kitchen window.

'All that nature. Enough to make a person puke,' said Harriet once, sticking a finger down her throat to emphasise her point.

But Flora was no country bumpkin. She had golden hair and honey-coloured skin and her eyes were a deep, warm brown. Everything about her was wholesome. She exuded good health and good feeling and she wore soft, fluffy clothes in earthy colours that draped themselves over her body with no hard edges anywhere. She was as extremely natural as her elder sister was determinedly artificial. They are the light and the dark, thought Claudia, once again marvelling at how such disparate beings could have emerged from the same womb.

It was good to have the chance to spend time alone with Flora without the company of her slightly disconcerting husband. They went for long walks, around the garden – the snow had virtually gone by now, leaving just the faintest traces of white clinging to the edges of the grass – and through the wood, where Claudia stopped at the great oak, upon whose trunk Flora laid a gentle and almost proprietary hand in passing. Sally went with them, or rather ahead of them, collecting a stick on the way which she chewed and then casually dropped without a backward glance, in the assumption that one or other of them would pick it up and throw it, and she would run and grab it up and chew it some more; so in very little time it was so small that no one else but she could find it, which caused her to have to double back and pick it up and then drop it again, staring at the two women dolefully as if to say 'pay attention', before trotting off again.

As they circumnavigated the surrounding fields, avoiding any that contained sheep, which would, Flora promised, send Sally berserk (she being a failed sheepdog), they discussed the subtleties and fascinations of horse-breeding, of which Claudia knew nothing. She learned how you can tell a good deal about a horse from simply watching it walk, from the evenness of its step, the way the legs moved in their sockets, the position of the head. She listened to tales of skulduggery and forgery, of the false claims undertaken by some of the more unscrupulous operators, who thought nothing of painting a white stripe on a horse's nose, or spreading varnish on its coat, so that it matched the picture in the catalogue of a certain other famous thoroughbred which commanded a greater stud fee than their unprepossessing nag.

Carlos, Flora assured her mother, was as honest as the day is long. He was passionate about his work and knew more about horses than anyone in the business, being as he was the son of a noted stud farmer. Talking of whom, said Flora, turning upon her mother her large, doe-like eyes, she wondered if she'd mind if he, her father-in-law, might spend Christmas with them since he would otherwise be on his own, as his wife had to stay at home to look after her ailing mother.

'Of course,' said Claudia, with a slightly sinking feeling, as she had been looking forward to Christmas with just the close family, but how could she possibly say otherwise?

'Oh good,' said Flora. 'I hoped you'd say that. He's quite entertaining and terribly polite, almost formal, I'm sure he won't get in the way. And of course I'm not suggesting he should stay, obviously not, he can put up at the Feathers, it's no distance. Besides, he has a car, and a chauffeur.' At which she looked at her mother and raised her eyebrows slightly.

So that was that. No one ever could resist Flora.

Then Claudia told Flora about Harriet, and Leonard's trip to Venice with his male lover. Flora looked startled for a moment, and then she said, 'Well, it's what Hattie chose for herself, the non-conformist life. But it's a bit of a test for her, to say the least.' She laughed gently. 'And I wouldn't worry about her anxiety Mother, you always did tell me she was born with an anxious little frown on her furrowed little brow.'

'Yes, I believe I did,' Claudia recalled.

'Will they be here for Christmas?' Flora asked.

'I hope so.' Claudia pulled a face.

'Dear Mother, you are not to worry. We are all grown up people now, even Jess, after a fashion. We are all going to have a very jolly time.' So saying she tucked her mother's arm into hers and gave it a warm squeeze.

'Thank God for you, Flora,' said her mother.

~

In the event everyone arrived, and on the same day, Christmas Eve. First Jonno and Jessica, by car, followed a couple of hours later by Harriet and Leonard, by train. ('We did offer them a lift Mama, but they wouldn't have it,' said Jessica, with a shrug.) Leonard wore an orange corduroy suit – 'Rust, actually, *Maman*,' said Harriet – and a red cravat. He had hair down to his shoulders and a beard, and he seemed in a remarkably chipper mood.

'Mrs Faraday, season's greetings and the top of the afternoon to you,' he said, bowing flamboyantly and kissing her hand, which she found both silly and endearing. Harriet giggled and nudged him and Claudia half wondered if they hadn't been drinking on their way down.

Once they were all settled and unpacked and had

refreshed themselves with tea they set to decorating the Christmas tree, a family Christmas Eve tradition, only this time the menfolk were involved. While the girls hung baubles, tinsel and the little porcelain angels Claudia had inherited from her grandmother, the boys took it upon themselves to arrange the lights.

Leonard climbed the stepladder to fix the star on the top of the tree and as he did so he burst into song:

'Deck the halls with boughs of holly,

Fa-la-la-la-la, la-la-la-la.

Then Jonno joined in, with his booming bass, and the two of them sang along in a kind of harmony for a moment until Leonard, without warning, suddenly switched to:

'Ding dong merrily on high,

In heaven the bells are ringing,

Ding dong verily the sky

Is riven with angels singing.'

And so Jonno joined in again with the chorus:

'Glor-or-or-or-or-or-or-or-or-or-or-or . . .'

But as he drew breath to complete the Gloria, Leonard switched again:

'Gaudete, gaudete! Christus est natus,

Ex Maria virgine, gaudete!'

Which rather naturally silenced Jonno. 'I say old man,' he said, genially, 'we don't do Latin here as a general rule.'

'Tempus adest gratiae,

Hoc quod optabamus,

Carmina laetitiae,

I don't know what comes nextus!' belted Leonard, and then: 'Voilà!' he proclaimed. He signalled to Harriet, who flicked a switch and as if by magic the lights on the tree lit up and the surrounding company, with the exception of a discombobulated Jonno, burst into a round of applause.

Claudia, who was looking on, with Flora, glanced at her daughter and raised an eyebrow. It did not take a genius to see what was going on here.

Meanwhile Sally the failed sheepdog, whose barking had been hitherto ignored, became so over-excited she started spinning on the spot, after which she staggered into the corner and was quietly sick.

31

The Spanish contingent arrived just in time for dinner, dressed appropriately and clutching a case of champagne.

Claudia had always found Flora's husband Carlos on the intimidating side, with his polite-to-the-point-of-formal manners, his slicked-back hair and his perfectly manicured fingernails. Nor had she really taken to his father, who was also called Carlos and shared his son's immaculate appearance and professionally-acquired suaveness. Why anyone would want to name a child after themselves was bizarre, in her opinion, not to say confusing, and indicated a kind of arrogance, as if one's offspring were allowed to be no more than a minor replica of oneself. Then again perhaps that's the kind of thing you might do if you were a professional breeder, thought Claudia, as if by perpetuating the name you stood a better chance of perpetuating the purity of the bloodstock. It didn't help that Carlos Senior insisted on calling his son Carlitos, in public – an appellation that appalled and humiliated poor Carlos Junior so profoundly that he noticeably winced every time the name was mentioned. The family, led by Flora, tended to call him Carl.

Despite her misgivings Claudia, for form's sake, placed Carlos Senior next to her at the dinner table, which turned out to be less arduous than she expected. He was polite but not aggressively so, complimenting her on her table, her house – '*muy elegante*' – her appearance, and her three beautiful daughters. They talked about the weather, and English Christmas traditions, families in general – he had two sons, Carlitos and his younger brother Guillermo, who also worked in the family business back home in Toledo – his ailing mother-in-law and the dutiful wife who had stayed at home to look after her. And so the time passed quite painlessly. After a while Harriet, who was on his other side, began quizzing him about the political situation in Spain, which she considered to be profoundly dangerous, an opinion with which Carlos Senior appeared to concur, genuinely or perhaps diplomatically, and Claudia was able to turn her attention away from Carlos '*grande*' to poor Carlitos '*pequeño*', who hitherto had been sitting silently on her left.

The family was on best behaviour throughout the dinner, to Claudia's relief. Leonard had calmed down to the extent that he was almost mute, and she recalled Harriet explaining some time ago how her husband was prone to what she termed 'manic depression', which she professed was a form of mental ailment manifesting in extreme mood swings, but which Claudia thought was no more than a fancy expression for something rather more mundane, such as a way of seeking attention. While all around him had changed for dinner Leonard remained defiantly, if predictably, clad in his orange corduroy, and he stayed that way for the duration of his visit, from time to time changing his cravat and even, at less formal times such as breakfast for instance, dispensing with it altogether.

On Christmas Day the entire family minus Harriet and Leonard attended the morning service at St Mary's, their local parish church. On their return the female members of the family set to laying and decorating the dining table and, in the case of Flora and Claudia, helping out in the kitchen. Lunch consisted of goose, stuffed, with cranberry sauce and a cornucopia of vegetables, followed by Christmas pudding, soused and set alight in brandy, and all of it accompanied by copious quantities of champagne. Jonno and Jessica told jokes at which everyone – including Harriet and Leonard – laughed even though they didn't understand them. Leonard emerged from his shell to spout poetry, at some length and with much enthusiasm, and the two Carloses entertained with traditional Spanish carols. All in all it was a truly festive family affair.

There was only one tricky moment, when Claudia opened her Christmas parcel from Jessica and Jonno to reveal a gramophone, at which Harriet went suddenly and extremely quiet. 'Obviously I can't compete with *that*,' she muttered.

'But darling, it's *lovely*,' her mother murmured back, as she undid the wrapping on a beautifully hand-made sewing basket. 'It means so much that you made it yourself, thank you sweetheart.'

Later on, in the evening, the gramophone was put to use and the house rang to the sound of New York jazz. The drawing room carpet was rolled up and Jonno gave an uninhibited and slightly grotesque display of his version of the Charleston, and then Carlos Senior sprang lightly to his feet, offered his hand to Claudia and told her he was about to teach her how to tango and he would brook no refusal.

Claudia was an accomplished dancer but knew enough about the tango to realise she was about to make a complete fool of herself. In the circumstances however her partner, holding her loosely yet firmly, by applying just the right amount of subtle pressure on her back, led her with such skill there was no mistaking which way she was to go or what she was to do. It felt positively liberating, exhilarating even. For the first time she began to understand the definition of the dance as, in the words of the famous writer George Bernard Shaw, "The vertical expression of a horizontal desire".

She felt quite flushed. And then it was all over and he was smiling at her and bowing, but this time she didn't really mind, even when he took hold of her hand and held it for longer than necessary – even that felt totally in keeping with the whole festive experience.

The storm erupted, as it was eventually bound to do, over breakfast the following morning, before Claudia came down. It began, she learnt later from Flora, with a lighthearted remark from Jonno addressed to Leonard, to wit that he had 'come in fancy dress'; at which Leonard turned on his brother-in-law and asked him, rather aggressively, what he thought he meant. Jonno, disregarding the aggression, responded to the effect that there was a dress code in this house and that to ignore it indicated a childish lack of respect, to which Leonard said something about people dressed up as penguins and not knowing how preposterous they looked, which remark Jonno asked Leonard to repeat, which he did, louder and with added emphasis.

During this exchange Jessica had entered the room and, clocking the situation, commented mildly that perhaps Jonno had a point; at which Leonard rounded on her, which led Jonno, whose face, normally ruddy, was beginning to turn an indignant deep red, to intervene and perhaps unwisely to laugh and make out the whole thing was a joke. Then Leonard said, bluntly and with his face very close to his brother-in-law's, that Jonno's jokes were never funny and the only reason anyone laughed at them was out of a misguided sense of tight-arsed ('yes Mother, sorry, but that's the word he used') politeness.

The argument broke up the moment Claudia entered

the room. She had heard enough outside the door to get the gist of it, but one look from her to her two sons-in-law was enough to pitch them into a deathly and sulky silence. Jessica and Flora tried their best to break the ice by talking about the weather, but the atmosphere of resentment prevailed right up until Carlos Senior arrived on the doorstep.

'Did I interrupt something?' he asked.

'Just a silly spat,' said Claudia, with a weary sigh. 'Don't mind them.'

'Was Carlitos involved?' asked Carlos.

'No,' said Flora. 'He hasn't come down yet.'

'Thank God for that,' he replied.

'Have you had breakfast, Señor Sanchez?' asked Claudia.

'I have, thank you,' said Carlos, with a gracious nod.

There followed a long silence, broken only by the crunching of teeth upon toast and the gurgle of coffee poured from a jug. Carlos, still standing in the doorway, his hands behind his back, looked from one to another of the assembled company in puzzled query, but no one but Claudia was prepared to meet his eye.

She pulled a face at him, as if to say, 'Children, what can you do with them?' He smiled, then gestured with his head for her to follow him. Once outside the door he said, 'Should we make a rush for it?'

'I beg your pardon?'

'Out,' he said simply.

'Where?' asked Claudia.

Carlos shrugged. 'Anywhere! Away from *los chicos molestos.*'

And before she had time to think of an excuse Carlos Senior had taken hold of her arm and steered her through the door, barely giving her a moment to grab her coat and bag, and into the waiting car outside.

32

'**W**here to?' said Carlos, as they headed down the driveway away from the house.

'You're asking *me*?' said Claudia. 'It was your idea.'

'It is your country,' he said. He wrenched the car rather clumsily round the corner into the road. 'Show me something beautiful, please.'

He'd given the chauffeur some days off over the festive season, he explained, which presumably accounted for his rather erratic driving and his tendency to forget which side of the road they should be on. Fortunately there were very few cars about at that time, it being Boxing Day morning and snow threatening. The clouds were low, and heavy, as though struggling to contain the weight of an impending snowstorm. From time to time the sun pushed its way briefly through the gloom to throw a ribbon of light across the open fields, before it disappeared again.

Under Claudia's direction they drove to an escarpment overlooking Salisbury Plain, where they pulled off the road and stopped. She pointed out the white horse carved into the chalk hillside, just discernible in the lightly-falling snow, which was believed to date back to the time of King Alfred. Carlos was delighted, he said that Pegasus had flown into the hillside and imprinted himself there, and what a beautifully proportioned animal he was, if a little long in the leg. He would like to mount his back and fly across the world.

She told him they were looking over thousands of years of history, of prehistoric standing stones, such as Stonehenge (just out of sight), of Iron Age hill forts, burial grounds and Roman roads. If her husband were there he could tell Carlos everything he ever wanted to know about the place and its history, and it would take him all day, or perhaps even a week, if he let him.

As they sat there together on the escarpment in Carlos' hired car, so together they imagined scenes of Romans and Anglo Saxons, Druids and Iron Age farmers in their mud huts and Roman villas – a panoramic collage of history rolled into one composite whole. He said he thought the English countryside was astonishing, so neat and organised with its tiny fields and its tidy hedgerows, what meticulous people the ancients must have been. He marvelled at everything they saw and everything she said, and she even began to think some of it might be genuine.

At one point he got out of the car and beckoned for her to follow him, and she did, walking ahead of him, treading carefully through the snow. As they paused to take in the view the other side of the ridge she felt a soft thump upon her back and she turned, expecting to see a truanting urchin, but there was only Carlos, looking at her innocently, hands behind his back, so she picked up a handful of snow and chucked it right back at him, and there ensued the most exhilarating snowball fight.

Soon the clouds began to give way and release their burden of proper snow, so, pink-faced and laughing, they raced one another back to the car and drove off. As they descended into the valley once again he asked her where they were going, and when she replied that perhaps they ought to go home as the family might be worrying, he snorted and said, 'They're children, who cares what they are thinking? Let us give them time to sort themselves out and we'll go back when they've grown up a bit.' Which made Claudia laugh yet again, and when he suggested lunch at the Feathers she readily agreed.

At the lunch table she asked him why he had named his son Carlos, after himself.

'Excuse me?' He seemed not to understand the question.

'Don't you find it confusing?' she asked.

'It is a sign of his pedigree,' said Carlos. 'He is Carlos Sanchez de Valeira, successful stud farmer, son of Carlos Sanchez de Valeira, successful stud farmer, son of Carlos Sanchez de Valeira, not quite so successful stud farmer, son of José Sanchez de Valeira, builder.' He shrugged, as if the logic were obvious.

'That's very modest,' said Claudia.

'Like the horses, they take the name from the sire. And sometimes from the dam,' he added as an afterthought.

'What if Carlos had decided not to follow in his father's footsteps?'

'But he did.' It was a stupid question, obviously.

'I see,' said Claudia, though she wasn't sure she did. 'So does that mean if Carlos and Flora have a son he must be named Carlos too? And he must also follow in the family business?'

Carlos shrugged again in his Hispanic kind of a way, lopsidedly. '¿Quien sabe? Who knows? It is up to them.'

'Or to him perhaps.'

He shrugged again, in acquiescence this time. 'I think you are rather shocked,' he said. 'As if I were proposing a form of eugenics. Which of course I am, in a way. Horse breeding after all is all about eugenics; why waste time on the weaklings?'

Claudia began to fear for Flora. Does she know what she married into? she wondered.

'Now you are thinking of Flora,' he said,

disconcertingly reading her mind. 'Naturally. If I may say so, she is the perfect dam for Carlos.'

'I'm so pleased,' said Claudia, as archly as she could. 'And I hope for your sake they will produce many winners, who may or may not choose to continue the family business.'

'Ah, you misunderstand me!' He threw up his hands in mock frustration. 'I am talking about her beauty and her intelligence and her calm. All of this is perfect for Carlos, is it so wrong of me to say that?'

'Not at all, it's the terminology I'm not so sure of.'

'That is just a manner of speaking,' he said with a smile. 'I speak as a horse breeder, it's all the terminology I know.'

She sat looking at him for a moment.

'What?' he said.

'I was just wondering, do you view everyone according to what you might call their pedigree, their breeding? Do you take your work everywhere, so to speak?'

'Of course. I can even tell, with you for instance, I can even tell things about your husband from his daughters, just as I can tell something of a foal's sire, even though in both cases I have never met him.'

'Oh? Do explain.'

'Let us see. Jessica.' As he mentioned her girls so he pointed at them, one by one, as if they were standing right there in the room. 'Vibrant, beautiful Jessica, this she gets from you. Easy-going, open, this she does not get from you. Harriet, also vibrant and beautiful, in a very different way, but intense, *complicado*, tight, this she gets from her mother. Lastly the beautiful Flora, gentle, very intelligent, very passionate, very dedicated to her work, like her father, very driven – she works very hard, you know.'

'I've no doubt she does.'

'And she has a strong stomach, which is her father's, I

think. Of them all Harriet I think is the one most like her mother. Hiding her true self behind the,' he gestured down his body, '?*como se dice "carapacho"*?'

'*Carapacho*?'

'Carapace,' Carlos clicked his fingers. 'Or even,' again he struggled for the word, '*camiza de fuerza*'. He wrapped his arms around his body.

'Straitjacket.'

'This is it, straitjacket. For . . .'

'Mad people,' said Claudia, mildly.

'For restraint,' said Carlos. 'The passion – this is from the sire or the dam?' He cocked his head to one side and looked directly at her.

'Oh,' said Claudia after a moment. 'Was that a question? I have no idea. The dedication, the drive, have to be Gerald's.'

'And the passion?'

'Goodness, I really don't know.'

He continued gazing at her for a few seconds until she laughed shyly, and looked away.

'So my conclusion is,' said Carlos, 'your husband is a man with fair to mid brown hair who is open-hearted and driven and very dedicated to his work.'

'All the things I'm not, in other words,' said Claudia.

'Now, were you and I to have children, they would be elegant, and very beautiful, of course, sometimes open but sometimes,' he leant across the table towards her, '*very* closed. And *very* passionate.'

'Very passionate?'

'From *both* sides,' he said, leaning back in his chair again. He started playing with his coffee spoon.

There was a short silence.

'Well, that's interesting.'

'You don't believe a word.'

'I . . .' she shrugged.

'You don't like what I say about you, but it is true.'

'I didn't realise I was hiding inside a carapace. I always thought I was rather open and transparent, actually.'

'Who, you, Mrs Faraday? Open?' He rocked back in his chair and laughed, louder than he needed to.

She was not offended, or she felt she should not have been. He was, after all, right about most of it, except, possibly, the passion. She was not one to feel passion easily, she wasn't sure she was capable of it; it had been bred out of her, like everything else that did not conform to good manners and politeness.

'What did you mean,' she asked, 'about Flora having a strong stomach?'

'Stud farming is not a polite business, Mrs Faraday. There is no "Can I have this dance please?" or "May I have your permission to court you and I agree never to see your naked body until we are married, and even then not without your permission".'

It was Claudia who laughed now. 'What are you talking about?'

'Stud farms are about sex, Mrs Faraday. They are about the stallion coming to the mare, and the mare being restrained while he takes his pleasure. There is no foreplay no – "Would you like it this way, or do you prefer it when I do that?" It is raw, Mrs Faraday, I think you would not like to see it.'

'Why not?'

'Because they are *animals*,' he said with a snarl, for emphasis. 'It is not polite, it is not elegant, it is not even particularly sexy, to tell you the truth. It is *animalistic*.'

'Well, that's only to be expected.'

'Not many women can stand by and watch, let alone help out when things get . . . '

'Out of hand.'

'Indeed.'

Claudia cleared her throat. 'Do they, er, enjoy it? Or does the mare have to be coerced?' She looked at him rather coyly.

Carlos thought for a bit. He placed the coffee spoon back on his saucer. 'She, shall we say, tolerates it. But the stallion . . .'

'Needs no encouragement at all.'

'He needs to be held back. It can take some strong men to hold him until the time. And bearing in mind, for much of the year the stallion is doing nothing, he is waiting for the season, he is,' Carlos mimed becoming breathless, 'he is hanging around, and – and pawing the ground.'

'Just like a man.'

'Well no, not like a man. Because a man . . .'

'Doesn't have to hang around or paw the ground.'

This seemed to floor Carlos momentarily. He pretended to loosen his collar.

'Mrs Faraday, you are making me, how do you say, hot under the collar.'

'All this talk about sex,' said Claudia.

'You are emerging a little too fast . . .'

'From my carapace,' said Claudia. 'Perhaps it's about time.'

So it was that, with a tiny exchange of glances, the two of them got to their feet simultaneously, replacing their chairs with equal precision, before leaving the room and ascending the stairs to Carlos' bedroom.

33

It was the second time in Claudia's life that she had entered a room for the purpose of seduction.

With Gerald, on the first night of their honeymoon, it had been an awkward business, and far from satisfactory for a number of reasons, not the least of which was her virginal terror of sexual congress and his understandable inability to know how to handle it. It got better, in time, though if she were to be truthful it always felt more of a duty than a pleasure: a little like homework, satisfying when over, and done well, but never exactly enjoyable. But then nobody had ever suggested it could be otherwise, other than Prudence of course.

Now here she was, in another time and place, with another purpose. Instead of the terror she felt anticipation, and a kind of curiosity – not just for what might be about to happen but for how she, within her carapace, would respond to it.

As Carlos closed the door behind her Claudia went to stand in the middle of the room and looked around her. It was comfortably rather than luxuriously appointed, furnished in the old style, with panelled walls and a four-poster bed designed to appeal to travellers, especially from overseas. A fire glowed quietly in the hearth.

Carlos made for the fireplace, rubbing his hands. 'Please, sit down,' he said, indicating a chair. 'Make yourself warm.'

She did so.

'Did you know,' he said as he knelt to give the logs a hearty nudge, 'that almost all thoroughbred horses are descended from just one stallion?'

'No,' said Claudia, 'I didn't know that.'

'He was called the Darley Arabian. He was acquired by a wealthy Englishman who brought him back from the Middle East to his farm in Yorkshire in the early eighteenth century. Either Mr Darley was a clever judge or he was very lucky.' Carlos stood up. 'Unlike most stud stallions the Darley Arabian had never raced, so he was, as you might say, an unknown quantity.'

He walked over to the bed and switched on the bedside lamps, and then the standard lamp in the corner, before extinguishing the overhead light. His voice, quieter in the confines of the room, was in its sibilant Spanish way quite soothing.

'That's better,' he said, looking around. 'And the interesting thing is,' he went on, 'he did not directly sire many foals, even though he was covering mares for a long time. And yet his progeny went on to win races for generations and right down to the present day.'

He came to stand behind Claudia's chair and rested his hand lightly on her shoulder. 'Remarkable when you think about it, what that one horse could be capable of.'

'How do you know,' asked Claudia, 'what to look for in a horse?'

'Pedigree,' said Carlos. 'Lean forward, please.' She did so, thus enabling him to take hold of her jacket and ease it off her shoulders. 'The look of the horse, the length of the legs, the coat, the way it carries the head. As for the rest, good health, careful handling and a lot of luck.'

With the greatest care he folded Claudia's jacket and placed it on a chair.

'Stand up, please,' he said, and so she did.

'When you have been in the business for a while,' he said, placing his hands on her waist and gently turning her until she was facing him, 'you develop an instinct, I can only call it that. It's not a secret, in a mystical sense, although many people believe it is.'

He began to undo the buttons of her blouse. 'Of course, that is what makes it so exciting, the unpredictability. The not knowing. Not knowing is always exciting, don't you agree?'

Buttons undone, he slid her blouse from her body as he had done her jacket, so only a woollen undergarment remained – not the sort of garment Claudia would have invited anyone to see, and had she known how the day was going to turn out, well . . . Then he murmured into her ear, 'Are you still warm enough?'

She nodded, and as he took hold of the hem of her undergarment she helpfully raised her arms into the air – a bit like a child with its mother – so he could lift and pull it up and over her head, exposing her naked breasts.

'Ah yes.'

He studied her gravely for a moment with such obvious appreciation it released her, to some extent, from a sense of anxiety or embarrassment. Then he said, 'Turn please.' So she turned her back to him and she felt his hands on her naked shoulders. They were soft hands, not the hands of someone who works with horses, though that was presumably because he had someone to do the grimy work for him. Then she felt the hands go to the spot between her shoulder blades, where they paused, and felt about a bit.

'What are you doing?'

'I am looking at the withers,' said Carlos. 'The position of the withers is very important.'

'And how do I rate?'

'Rate? A little low, perhaps, but the back is beautifully proportioned. And the spine is good and straight.' She felt his fingers moving across her back and she trembled.

'Are you cold?' he asked.

'Not at all,' she said.

Both hands had moved back to her neck now and were burying themselves in her hair, in order, Claudia speculated, to test the quality of her mane. After that the hands travelled down again, past the shoulders, where they rested for a moment, across her back to her waist, where they paused. Then with a soft movement which reminded her of the way he had manoeuvred her body in the tango, so delicately she was hardly aware of being manoeuvred, he turned her around so she was once again facing him, and then his hands moved to her breasts, and over them, tracing their curves with his long, soft, exploratory fingers, at which point she felt her carapace begin to slip, and she closed her eyes.

'Excellent breastbones,' he said. 'Now for the hindquarters.'

As he knelt down and lent his attention to her skirt, he continued his commentary.

'Powerful lungs and a very strong heart,' he said.

'I beg your pardon?'

'You asked what I look for in the perfect specimen. A beautiful body and a very strong heart. And long legs, they are always useful.'

Reaching around her he undid the fastening on the waistband of her skirt and, slowly unzipping it, slid it with practised dexterity down her body to the floor, where he paused to allow her to step out of it, one foot after another. He did the same with the underskirt.

'Stamina,' said Carlos, as he unhooked Claudia's suspenders like a professional and edged her stockings, one by one, down her legs, once again pausing as she lifted her feet out of them. 'Stamina and finesse.' He folded each stocking carefully before placing it on the pile on the chair. 'Class, in other words. There is no substitute for the real thing.'

By now she was down to just her lacy underpants, resisting the urge to wrap her arms around herself for modesty, and conscious, as he attended to her, of the warmth of his skin so close to her thighs.

'And am I the real thing?' she asked him.

He did not immediately reply. With great concentration he was reaching up to divest Claudia of her final item of modesty, so she was completely naked; at which point he sat back on his heels in order to appraise her and murmured, 'Unquestionably.'

He stood up. 'You are aware, when you are with these creatures, of being in the company of royalty. It is a very special feeling.'

'I can imagine.'

'One feels very privileged.'

Then he leant forwards and kissed her softly on the mouth.

'How are you doing?' he murmured into her ear.

'Very well thank you,' she said.

'Now.' He took her hand and led her towards the bed as if he were leading her onto the dance floor, or maybe the stable.

'Please, make yourself comfortable.'

She lay back onto the wonderfully soft bed and, removing his shoes, he joined her, still fully clothed. His face was so close that with her imperfect near vision all she could see was a pale blur with two dark spots where his eyes were.

He kissed her, not on the mouth but on the breast, first one and then the other, tenderly. Then cupping a breast in his hand he began to suck it, and then he did the same with the other, flicking his tongue over her nipples and causing her to squirm.

He licked her chest and kissed it lightly, then he kissed her stomach, and her hips, and moved swiftly down her body, where he paused and looked up at her.

'Are you ready for this?' He was grinning at her, like a schoolboy about to be up to no good.

'It depends what "this" is, precisely,' said Claudia, and a moment later she gasped and thought, Oh my God, his tongue.

It was only momentary, the briefest 'hello', but it felt to Claudia as if a trap had been sprung open, and now she had to wait in suspended animation as he sat up and, again with deliberation, removed his clothing item by item, folding each one and placing it on a chair as he had done with hers, stepping off the bed to remove his braces, his trousers, socks and finally his undergarments until he stood before her quite naked.

Claudia gazed at his body without shame. He had a fine physique for a man of his age. Slender yet muscular, with smooth arms and powerful shoulders and legs, and barely a hint of a middle-aged belly. He was proud of it too, that much was obvious. So Claudia propped herself up on one elbow and allowed herself to appraise him properly before he came to kneel above her once again, leaning over her, his semi-erect penis brushing lightly against her stomach. She reached up to touch him, running her fingers across his chest, his face and his lips. He took hold of her finger between his teeth and bit it, quite sharply, so she cried out in mock pain and then, seeking revenge, with no time to think, the violated hand reached down and took hold of his naked penis.

There is no knowing who was taken most by surprise by this. Never in her life had Claudia touched a naked penis before, not even Gerald's, not even (not quite) in fantasies. It was the thing she feared above all else, this beast, this animal, as Prudence had once described it: troublemaker, governor of the male species, scourge of the female, that drove men mad and women too. And here she was, now, holding onto it and marvelling at the silkiness of it and not wanting to let it go.

He was watching her with a faint smile on his face as if waiting to see what she was planning to do with him. She had no idea, so she began stroking the monster, and squeezing àit, and when he did nothing to stop her so she began playing with it, moving it from one hand to the other, like a children's toy. This is what whores do, she'd heard it said, but professionally, dispassionately, with the aim of getting the job over and done with quickly without regard to their own pleasure. Such a shame to be so selfless, she thought, but surprising also because as she continued to play with the beast and to feel it growing between her fingers, so she felt a reciprocal physical reaction inside her, as if something were opening out, preparing for something. Then letting go of him with her hands she slid her body quickly down the bed and took him into her mouth.

She heard him gasp, and felt his body stiffen, and as he gently pushed himself into her until she was almost gagging, still she did not want to let him go as it was a kind of miracle, what the body can come up with without engaging the brain. After a moment she pulled back and took hold of him with her fingers once again and began to lick and suck on him like a lollipop, except that no lollipop was ever as big as this one.

'*Madre mia!*' he breathed.

She was aware that some boundary had been crossed, the barrier between self-control and instinct lifted. So, freed from self-consciousness and a lifetime of good manners she guided the monster towards her secret spot and rubbed it against her, and as she did so she felt the last of her inhibitions vanish, and raising her buttocks she allowed him to slide deep inside her.

He moved in and out of her slowly, watching her reaction. He was a perfect fit and it was not uncomfortable, not in the least. But just as she was beginning to get happily used to it, he withdrew.

He had not satisfied himself, that much she knew, but nonetheless she thought that was it; it was all over now. Gerald never managed more than once a night, perhaps twice in the very early days, once in the evening and again the following morning if he didn't have to go to work too early. Perhaps he'd have managed more if she'd shown more enthusiasm.

But it was not all over by any means. As Claudia lay prone, legs spread like a whore's, Carlos kissed her on the mouth and then once again moved down her body until he reached the most secret spot between her legs, where he began to lick her.

Gracious me that's bold, she thought, but only for a moment because it was also very sweet, so much so she thought it might be the sweetest thing her body had ever experienced, sweeter even than when young Gabriel Carter had first brought her to a climax with his fingers. She writhed as she felt his tongue flicking in and out of her and around that same spot, and she could feel it swell, just like the monster penis, and he did for her what she had done for him, took her in his mouth and sucked on her, this tiny thing, but oh, what pleasure it brought.

She felt her body beginning to shake, and her whole being beginning to hurtle through space at speed – towards what she neither knew nor cared; and as his tongue moved faster and faster so she felt herself accelerating until she thought she could bear it no longer, at which point, just as she reached her peak, he was back inside her and she felt herself climaxing, over and over, her insides contracting and releasing as he pumped in and out of her so hard her body began leaping all over the place like a rag doll, until at last, with a great groan and a cry, his body went into spasm and he came.

They were locked together so tightly it was as if they were one entity. Then Carlos, his arms tightly around her, lifted her bodily off the bed so she was suspended, on him, and as she felt him pushing yet deeper inside her she closed her eyes and thought, So *that's* what all the fuss is about.

34

When she woke up it was dark. Though as her eyes became accustomed to it she could just make out a faint glow through the blinds of the window and, now as she looked around her, a thin line of light from beneath the door of what she assumed was a connecting bathroom, from where she became aware of the sound of whistling.

It took her conscience longer to acclimatise than her eyes. She was a whore and an adulteress, that much was obvious. Worse, he was her daughter's father-in-law, practically family, which meant on top of it all it was virtual incest.

Claudia Faraday, what were you thinking of?

There was another thought however, altogether less proper, that winked and whispered at her, *What larks!*

Oh my. She felt exhausted, sticky, happy and glorious.

The whistling grew suddenly louder as the bathroom door opened and Carlos emerged, rubbing himself with a towel. He looked in her direction and said, 'Are you awake?'

She nodded. She was staring at the roof of the four-poster. He followed her gaze.

'What are you looking at?'

'My soul,' said Claudia. Then she looked at him in his nakedness and smiled.

'And what does your soul say?' He came to sit by her

on the bed.

'That I am an evil, wicked woman and I am going to rot in hell,' she said, sitting up and reaching over to take hold of his penis.

'This is true,' he said.

'I don't suppose I will ever forgive myself.'

'That is too bad,' said Carlos.

But there was another thing. Gracious, thought Claudia, as she stroked her lover's penis, almost absently, I'm not used to this many thoughts pounding through my head all at once. What's this one trying to say?

You do not love this person, said her conscience.

I don't really care, Claudia replied, silently. Her conscience was beginning to annoy her. There was not much further for her to fall, after all. She reminded herself to apologise to Prue.

'What are you thinking about?' said Carlos.

Animals do not particularly care for one another when they fornicate. Or at least horses don't. The stallion does not love the mare he is covering, he may not have even *seen* the mare he is covering. That of course is one of the many differences between horse and man.

Carlos' penis was starting to twitch and dance between her fingers and it was making her laugh.

'Are you doing that on purpose?' she said.

'Of course not,' he said, lifting his hands in the air to prove his innocence. 'I have no control over him, he is an autonomous object.'

'Is that what it is?' said Claudia, and she leaned over to kiss the autonomous object, which smelt of soap, fresh and rather sweet.

'When you are making love to a woman,' she said, still holding him, 'do you imagine you are a stallion?'

He raised his eyebrows. 'Why do you ask this question?'

'It's a fairly obvious one, in the circumstances.'

'I think this is a trick,' he said, and very gently he removed her hand from his penis.

'Why did you do that?'

'Because he is interfering with my thought,' said Carlos. 'What are you trying to say to me, that I was rampant, virile? Or a beast?'

'Yes, and then no.'

'I do not think of myself as a beast. Was I rough?'

She shook her head.

'Then what are you trying to say to me?'

'That you are a beautiful lover and I very much enjoyed making love with you.'

Making love. That was better, and so much *kinder* than the alternatives: copulation, fornication, sexual congress, even Prue's favourite, which she could not bring herself to articulate, not even to herself.

'I'm glad to hear that,' said Carlos, still with an anxious frown. 'But will your soul forgive me? Or perhaps I should say will your soul forgive you?'

'I doubt it,' said Claudia.

'He is troubling you because you enjoyed yourself.'

'He?'

'She, if you like. Yes. Because you enjoyed yourself so much you allowed your passion to get the better of your better nature.' He laughed. 'If you understand.'

'I do.'

'And now you have returned to your usual polite self you realise you have done something intensely improper.'

That sounded so ridiculous that she, too, laughed out loud.

'And yet, maybe this was not so wrong, after all. Maybe you discovered something in yourself you did not know was there. And nobody is harmed. Quite the opposite.' He paused for a moment. 'Is this true or is it not true?'

'Life is simpler for men,' she said.

'Life is as simple as you wish to make it.'

This was it, this was the whole point. Damn her conscience, and along with it her upbringing, her manners and her conditioning.

She reached out a finger and lightly flicked his penis, which made it dance again.

'You want more?' said Carlos.

'Do you?'

'I think so.' Carlos looked down at himself. 'On the other hand,' he shook his head and sighed, 'he is not as young as he used to be.' With which he reached towards her and gathered her naked body into his and embraced her.

'Time to return to the children I think,' he said, releasing her and standing up.

'What time is it?'

'Late.'

She leant back. 'What a shame,' she said.

'Indeed,' said Carlos.

She tried to think what it would be like if you *did* really love someone. With your body and your soul and your mind. Just imagine.

~

Later on, in the car, they discussed their alibis.

'We drove far into the country and got lost,' she offered.

'Or stuck in the snow.'

'Maybe, in which case how did we get out?'

'We dug ourselves out with our naked hands.'

'Which is why we are now all wet and covered in mud and snow and axel grease.'

'Indeed.' He thought for a bit. 'Or, we came back to the hotel for lunch and then retired to my bedroom and spent the afternoon making passionate love.'

'That's a good one, I never thought of that.'

'During which Lady Faraday took her lover's penis into the mouth in which butter would not melt and sucked it so hard her lover almost came.'

Claudia was silent for a bit.

'You are shocked?'

'I am beyond shocked,' she said. 'I feel as if I've just spent the afternoon on a different planet. And perhaps . . .' She stopped.

'That sounds promising. Perhaps . . ?'

'Perhaps things will never be quite the same again,' she said, and she gave him a sideways look and smiled.

'I'm glad to hear it,' he said.

He pulled up outside the house, stopped the car and sat there for a moment lost in thought.

'What are you thinking?' she asked.

'I am thinking,' said Carlos, 'how much I would like to turn right around and go back to the hotel and continue where we left off.'

He sighed.

'And for the moment I cannot think of a reason not to. Except that we are bound by constraints, greater than those we were bound by when we were young. Which is ironical, if you think about it.'

'What do you mean?'

'Because children are meant to be impulsive and irresponsible, and no matter how much you admonish them for their misbehaviour it was ever meant to be. Whereas a misbehaving adult . . . '

'Should in theory not be answerable to anyone,' said Claudia. 'Should in theory be able to do exactly what he or she wants to do.'

'Exactly. So,' He turned to look at her, 'when the children ask us what we've been up to . . . '

'We tell them to mind their own business,' said Claudia.

'*Precisamente*,' said Carlos.

~

'Where have you been, *Maman*, we've been worried sick!'

It was Harriet who greeted them just inside the front door, as if she'd been waiting there all afternoon.

'Why, darling? Cannot grown-ups have a day out?'

'Is that what it was?' She was watching her mother closely and her mother was smiling broadly back at her.

'Did you have a good time?' asked Jessica, coming to stand by her sister.

She was looking from her mother to Carlos and back to her mother again, and frowning slightly. She knows, thought Claudia. God knows how, but she does. And she doesn't like it. Even Jessica disapproves.

'Just in time for dinner,' said Flora, as Claudia entered the drawing room. 'We were going to send out a search party and then we decided against it.' Flora spoke blithely, and if she suspected anything she showed no sign of it.

'And after dinner,' said Jessica, 'we want to talk to you, seriously.'

'Oh dear,' said Claudia, trying not to catch Carlos' eye. 'Are you going to tell me off?'

'Tell you off for what?' said Harriet, wide-eyed.

It seemed the quarrel that had threatened breakfast had been resolved, or at least put to one side for the time being, and it took Claudia a while to realise that for the first time since she had made his acquaintance, Jonno had not dressed for dinner.

In his defence he looked distinctly uncomfortable, and when Jessica caught her mother staring at him she leant over and whispered in her ear, quite loudly, 'He hates it, actually Mama, but he did promise.'

'Promise who?'

'It was a bet,' said Jonno, nodding at Leonard. 'To see if you would notice.'

'To see if you would disapprove,' said Harriet.

'Oh, I see. I think.'

'And do you?' Jessica asked her mother.

Did she? In the circumstances Claudia did not feel in a position to disapprove of anything.

'We are sons of the revolution,' said Leonard, leaping to his feet and reaching over the table to shake hands with Jonno. 'And as with all peaceful revolutions, minds are changed as humanity marches into the future. Cheers.' With which he raised his glass to Claudia and took a swig of her best claret.

Jessica was watching her mother for her reaction but in truth, Claudia's mind was not fully focused on the (slightly puerile) proceedings being enacted in front of her.

'Are you offended, Mama?' It was Jessica again.

'Offended by what, darling?'

'I think that proves she is not,' said Leonard, once again raising his glass to his mother-in-law, and taking another long swig. 'Your mother, if I may say so,' he said to Jessica, as he resumed his seat, 'is a good deal more enlightened than many half her age.'

Claudia smiled. She was aware of feeling vaguely patronised, and it crossed her mind that it was invariably the revolutionaries who managed to consume most of other people's wine, and their food, while looking down on them from some lofty moral plinth upon which they had placed themselves; and how ironical it was, to borrow a word from Carlos, knowing what she did about Leonard and how she ought to despise him for it. But the afternoon's activities had thrown not only her body but, for the time being at least, her mind into total disarray. Whether or not she regarded herself as a fallen woman she no longer considered she had a right to draw judgement upon anyone else, which state of mind she found remarkably liberating. So she adopted what she assumed was a bland expression and carried on eating her dinner in silence.

35

After dinner the ladies retired to the drawing room, where Claudia was placed in the most comfortable armchair while her three daughters arranged themselves around her.

She leant back and tried to cross one leg over the other in an attempt to look relaxed, but the afternoon's exertions had done something to the muscles in her groin so she found herself wincing a bit, and then smiling secretly as she acknowledged the cause of the stiffness.

'We've been giving you a lot of thought, Mama,' Jessica began, as the eldest. 'And in fact we were hoping to have a discussion with you this afternoon but you didn't seem to be around.'

'No,' said Claudia.

'You know we love you very much,' said Flora. She was seated close to her mother on her right, and as she spoke so she reached over and placed a soft hand on her arm.

'Why does that sound ominous?' said Claudia.

'We wondered if you'd given much thought to the future,' continued Jessica. 'What you were planning on doing now that we're not around.'

It was all sounding rather rehearsed. Claudia looked at her three daughters in turn.

'We were thinking,' Jessica went on, 'what a shame it is

that you and papa have become so . . . '

'Estranged?' offered Claudia.

'Well, distant. He hardly ever comes over any more, so we thought, why don't you go to see him?'

So that's what it was all about.

'In Tanganyika?'

'He hasn't been in Tanganyika for months *Maman*, do keep up,' said Harriet.

'Oh dear. I should pay more attention. Where is he then?'

'He was in Egypt for a while but he's now in Palestine,' said Flora. 'And he expects to be there for some time, so now is a good opportunity.'

'I see,' said Claudia.

'We were thinking,' said Jessica, 'you don't seem to have taken a lot of interest in his work recently and, well, that's a bit of a shame.' She spoke kindly, but the point was clear.

'Hilda Petrie never leaves her husband's side,' ventured Harriet.

Claudia wondered when the name of Hilda Petrie would rear its head. 'I'm certainly not Hilda Petrie,' she said.

'I'm not saying you are.'

'You do know,' said Claudia, 'how difficult it is, out there? You do know I spent many months with your father, on his digs, before you were born?'

'That was a while ago, Mama.'

'And how he couldn't wait to get rid of me? No, that's not quite true. But I was certainly an impediment. Or if not an impediment exactly, a liability, somebody he had to worry about, and he doesn't need to worry about anything but his work.'

She thought back to those early years of their marriage, when she spent months sleeping under the stars, which sounded romantic, and was, to begin with, with nothing between her and the hard ground but a thin hessian mat; or stretched out by the entrance to some cave, guarding it against pilferers. It was all very well for someone like Hilda Petrie, who loved every minute of it and acted as her husband's assistant, working alongside him, living and travelling with him, making herself indispensable. But for an ordinary woman like Claudia it was a very different matter.

'I feel I did my bit, all those years ago,' she said. 'You have no idea how tough it is out there, and I was a lot younger then.'

The girls looked at one another. There is something they are not telling me, she thought.

'Look at it as a refresher course,' said Jessica cheerily. 'You know, like when you've passed an exam but it was an awfully long time ago and you think – I really need to brush up on things.'

Claudia stared at her eldest daughter for a moment.

'You mean it's time I brushed up on my archaeology?' she said. 'So that . . . ?'

'So that papa would appreciate it, as he would,' said Flora. 'So that it would bring you closer together.'

'Give you an interest,' said Jessica.

'Save my marriage, is that what you're trying to say?' Claudia spoke more harshly than she had intended.

Jessica frowned and Flora looked thoughtful. Harriet examined her nails.

'Harriet doesn't necessarily agree with us,' said Jessica. 'But we believe a woman's place is with her husband, which is very old-fashioned of us, I grant you.'

'We are concerned for you, above all,' said Flora. 'For the future. For all of us.'

They were honestly doing what they thought was right, Claudia realised. They had obviously discussed it, argued over it no doubt, over her, their poor, lonely, bored, unfaithful mother. Whether or not it had to do with her dalliances, if they could be so-called – of which they maybe knew something or maybe not – above all they did not want to lose their father.

'I understand what you are saying,' she told them.

'I do hope so, Mama.' She felt Flora's fingers on her arm. 'It's because we love you and because above all we want the family to stay together.'

'We thought it might be something to ponder on, before you hear the rush of tiny feet, you know.' Jessica was making little running gestures with her fingers.

'Oh! Is there something you're not telling me?'

'Not yet,' said Jessica. 'But one day, who knows, and then Mama we will be calling on you all the time.'

'I see.' Claudia nodded slowly, and then she laughed softly. 'I see.'

'Sleep on it, Mama,' said Flora, getting to her feet and kissing her mother on the forehead.

She did. Or rather she lay awake thinking about it. It had been quite a day, one way or another, and of course her initial resistance to her daughters' suggestion had been partly due to her own nagging guilt and the knowledge that they were, let's face it, absolutely right. She hadn't even paid attention to where Gerald was working now, let alone to what he was doing. His letters used to be long, and detailed, almost like diaries, and probably of huge fascination if you were someone like Hilda Petrie; but over the years they had become not only less frequent but much sketchier, token letters almost. And so what if she didn't know he was no longer working in Africa when he didn't tell her. Was she supposed to study the postmark?

Her thoughts drifted to the afternoon: had it been a dream? It felt like a century ago now, another world, another time. Remarkable really, almost life-altering. Now she knew sex was something to be enjoyed, and indulged in – rejoiced at even – what if she were to transfer her new-found skills to her relationship with her husband? Might that not awaken their dormant marriage?

This thought made her feel a whole lot better about everything. And so she turned on her pillow and for the next eight hours she slept like a newborn baby.

~

The party left the following morning and Claudia was delighted and relieved to see that Harriet and Leonard had deigned to accept a lift from Jonno and Jessica, who now appeared to be the best of friends (if it lasted the journey back to London that at least was something to be grateful for). There was much kissing and hugging and slightly tearful farewells, and what a wonderful time they had had – *And you will give our suggestion some serious thought, won't you, Mama?*

That left Flora and the two Carloses, who were travelling back to Shropshire together. Since the previous afternoon Claudia had found no opportunity to be alone with Carlos Senior, not that she had sought one especially, nor had he given the slightest indication that anything in particular had taken place between them. There were no secret smiles or covert touches on the shoulder. If anything, he was rather more formal than he'd been before, which made Claudia wonder whether he didn't do this sort of thing quite regularly.

She was not particularly put out by this; on the contrary, it was rather a relief. She had no idea how one was supposed to behave towards a clandestine lover, whether one was required to keep one's distance rather more than usual, or to lurk in dark corners for a stolen kiss, both of which might have been manageable. But to act as if nothing at all had happened was an indication perhaps that sleeping dogs should be allowed to lie.

There was a moment, a brief one, just before they left, when the two of them found themselves alone in the drawing room. 'Found themselves' being perhaps misleading as it was carefully choreographed by Carlos Senior who, having settled his passengers in his car (the chauffeur having returned from his time off), found an excuse to return to the house.

He bent over Claudia's hand, kissed it and announced, 'I have this to say. When I was first introduced to the lovely Flora I thought perhaps at long last Carlitos had as you might say landed on his feet. When I was first introduced to Flora's mother I thought, Now I know why she is who she is. From where comes her beauty and her stupendous pedigree.'

Claudia inclined her head and smiled.

'If you will forgive the expression.' He looked quite anxious. 'You will think kindly of me, I hope.'

'Of course I will.' Claudia squeezed his hand, which still held onto hers.

'However,' he went on, 'it molests me to think I am leaving you here on your own. What opportunities we could have. But I have a wife and you have a husband.'

'This is true.'

'And in a sense we are family, so we will see one another again.'

'I'm sure we will.'

'I love my wife,' he went on, almost as if he were reluctant to finish the conversation. 'She is a very good woman and a wonderful wife and mother. With the biggest will in the world I would not hurt her.'

'Of course you wouldn't.'

What was he really trying to say?

'What are you trying to tell me, Carlos?'

'I have really no idea. I do not want to leave. Knowing you will be alone.'

'I will manage, I've managed before.'

'Of course.'

He made to go and then turned back again.

'What is it now?'

'I forget why I said I needed to come back inside the house.'

'To say goodbye to your hostess perhaps?'

'I told them I had left something but I cannot now remember what it was I said I had forgotten.'

Claudia laughed, and gently edged him towards the front door.

'I'm sure you will think of something.'

Carlos patted his pockets. 'Perhaps it was small enough to fit inside a pocket, so they will not question me.'

'I don't see why they would do that anyway.'

'May I please kiss you briefly?'

'Well . . . '

So he did, softly, on her mouth.

'Now go,' she said. And he went.

And once again silence blasted through the empty house like a biting north wind.

36

In the event life took its own course.

Before she could even think of writing to Gerald she received a letter from him saying he was planning on coming over in a month's time, at the end of January. He gave no reason for his visit, which did not surprise her these days, but she presumed he was to give a lecture at some university somewhere, or to present his findings to the Royal Society or whatever venerable institution had sponsored his latest project. It was a brief letter and to the point and he did not even bother to say that he was looking forward to seeing her and catching up with the girls.

Having been relieved, if temporarily, of having to make a decision – she thought she would put it to Gerald while he was here, even perhaps suggest they travel back to wherever it was (Palestine?) together – Claudia was able to turn her attention to her next set of guests, who were due to arrive any day now, in time for New Year's Eve.

She had seen neither of them for a long time, ever since her childish falling out with Prue and her charged encounter with Dougie and The Letter.

Prue had had an affair with Dougie, years ago, so what? Why should that have mattered? More to the point she had cast aspersions on Claudia's sexuality, or on what she had described as her repulsion of the sexual act, which was the sort of thing Prue was prone to say simply in order to provoke. Besides, what could she possibly know of what Claudia got up in the bedroom? She might think of changing her tune had she any idea what took place in a certain hotel room on a certain Boxing Day afternoon. Not that that was something Claudia was planning on divulging to anyone, not even to her best friend, not now and not ever.

Dougie was another matter of course, dear Dougie. Her unintentional humiliation of her erstwhile (would-be) lover preyed badly on her conscience. True, they had spent the following day in friendly companionship: it was the least she could do to make it up to him, even though in retrospect she wondered if she should have gently pushed him out of the door right away instead of, just possibly, sending false messages to raise his hopes. But wasn't that Dougie all over? Forever on one's conscience for some reason or other, the victim of something one had or hadn't done, inadvertently or otherwise?

Anyway it was water under the bridge now, she hoped, and having the two of them here together should, apart from being enormous fun, dispel whatever grievances they had towards one another, of that she was quite sure.

They arrived together, in Rosie, who to Claudia's surprise was still roadworthy. Dougie looked distinctly shaken as he emerged from the passenger seat, breathing hard and muttering, 'Twelve pedestrians, barely missed by an inch. One stray sheep and a collection of wildlife and who knows how many birds, escaped *just*, with their lives.'

'Nonsense,' said Prue, slamming the driver's door. 'Missed by an inch missed by a mile. I have never yet caused physical damage to man or beast behind the wheel.' Then, greeting Claudia on the doorstep, she said,

'How – are – you? Darling girl, it has been a long time, are you still speaking to me?'

'Of course,' said Claudia with a laugh. Then reaching out a hand to Dougie, 'I should have warned you, you might have been safer coming by train.'

Dougie mock-staggered up the steps to the front door and gave Claudia a kiss on the cheek. 'Perhaps, but I'm here in one piece, just about. Dearest Clot, how wonderful to see you.'

It was, as Claudia had hoped and imagined, just like old times. The bad driving joke wore thin after a while and they settled down to compare notes about their respective Christmases, which for her guests had been relatively quiet – almost, in Dougie's case it seemed, non-existent. 'Can't be doing with all the fuss,' he said, which Claudia took to mean he'd had a pretty boring time of it. Prue had spent hers with an eccentric friend who had more aunts than anyone could technically lay claim to, who sat around all day doing absolutely nothing except glare at Prue with differing degrees of disapproval and dislike, none of which got in the way of her having a thoroughly grand time and drinking far too much.

'So I'm here for a rest, darling,' she said, leaning back in the sofa to illustrate her intention. 'A quiet couple of days in the country, what could be more . . .'

'Restful,' said Dougie.

'Indeed,' said Prue, and yawned.

'Perhaps you would like a nap before dinner?' Claudia asked politely. 'It is obligatory to stay up to see in the New Year you know, even in this backwater.'

'Certainly not,' said Prue, leaping to her feet for no reason whatsoever, before realising it and sitting back down again. 'I'm all go, aren't we, Dougie?'

Claudia took them for a brief stroll around the garden in the afternoon and she told them about the girls and their suggestions she go to visit Gerald.

'Why?' demanded Prue. 'Why would you want to go all that way to a country where it's as hot as hell and you get to sleep on pallets? Makes no sense to me at all, darling. Especially since he's coming here anyway, what's the point?'

Dougie made no comment.

'Because I'm his wife,' said Claudia. And though she couldn't swear to it she thought she heard Dougie snort.

Dinner was a convivial affair. Prue regaled them with her latest experiences running the gauntlet of her friend's son (not the friend she spent Christmas with), who she swore was young enough to be her own son – or grandson, mused Claudia – but who nonetheless had pursued her and flirted with her quite brazenly, in full view of his mother, who either had no idea what was going on or had chosen to turn a blind eye. All of which Prue found intensely distressing, and embarrassing, as it threatened to compromise her friendship with one of her oldest and dearest friends – *Not as old or as dear as you Claudia, of course* – and while truth to tell she had been just the *tiniest* bit tempted, though not seriously, of course not, yet she had quite enjoyed, 'between us three', stringing him along just enough.

'Enough for what?' asked Claudia.

Prue threw her friend a disgruntled look, and Claudia responded with one of her own.

Then Prudence dropped the bombshell.

'Shall I tell her or will you?' she began, looking at Dougie.

'You know you're going to anyway,' he said.

'Very well,' said Prue, and then turning to Claudia she announced, with deliberation, 'Dougie and I are moving in together.'

'I beg your pardon?'

'That's to say,' said Dougie, 'I am moving in with Prue.'

'His sister can't stand the sight of him any more, so it makes sense.'

'It's not that she can't stand the sight of me,' said Dougie. 'Not exactly. But there comes a time when, you know . . .'

There comes a time when what?

Claudia's heart went cold. She did not know why exactly. Perhaps it was the shock, perhaps it was the almost vicious way Prue had thrown it at her, to get back at her, was that what it was all about?

'Well,' she said primly. 'I am very happy for you.'

She waited for more. As in were they going to be living together or *living* together, as in sharing a bedroom, and a bed, or as lodger and landlady? Was she expected to ask them such things? As their old and intimate friend, was she not entitled to just a little more information?

'Don't be like that,' said Prue.

She wasn't going to ask her what she meant by 'that', and she never did find out any more because Dougie went on to change the subject, rather abruptly she thought, which meant to return to the topic in question would have looked even more odd.

So they saw in the New Year, raised glasses, drank toasts to the 'future', to new beginnings, to travel and adventures and other such vague ambitions, and it might have been Claudia's imaginings but as the evening went on she felt more and more like the odd one out, like the disgruntled schoolgirl who has not been invited to the party; which feeling made her deeply ashamed, so she punished herself twice over.

She was annoyed at herself for feeling upset. She was even more annoyed at what she suspected were twinges of jealousy: of her oldest friend setting up home with her old flame, the man who only weeks ago had declared his undying passion for her, Claudia. What did that say about him? That he was fickle, superficial and immature? Or simply pragmatic? How he could stand to be in the same house as Prue was beyond imagining in the first place, they'd drive one another mad within days. He never did have much time for her, he found her musings if anything more irritating than did Claudia – he said as much on many occasions. It made no sense whatsoever.

And there was something else that needed explaining – and try as she did to shift her thoughts away from it they persisted on floating back, like a piece of driftwood caught on the tide – and that was the precise layout of Prudence's flat. Claudia had not visited it since goodness knows when because, as Prue always insisted, while it was technically a two-bedroom apartment the second bedroom was strictly speaking *More of a storeroom darling, really not fit for human habitation, piled high with my stuff – where else am I supposed to keep it? So honestly while you're welcome to stay overnight, you truly wouldn't want to spend any longer here.* Which meant – and God, why am I pondering on such things? Claudia admonished herself – that she and Dougie must be sharing a bedroom, and a bed.

But to feel jealous of her friend setting up home with a man whom only weeks ago Claudia had turned down so resoundingly was frankly unreasonable. She should be happy for them, and so she was. However unlikely the combination. Good luck to them.

Those were the thoughts that accompanied Claudia that night on her tortuous road to the Land of Nod.

37

At breakfast the following morning Dougie – Prue had not yet risen – was uncharacteristically mute. Nor did he seem anxious to catch Claudia's eye, so the subject hung in the air between them for some time until she could bear it no longer.

'It's absolutely no business of mine,' Claudia began, 'but I can't help commenting.'

'Comment away,' said Dougie. He ate his toast like an old man, like Claudia's father used to, breaking it into tiny pieces and buttering and marmalading each piece in turn before consuming it; a laborious procedure and quite prim in a way too.

'Whose idea was it?'

'Was what?'

'What do you think?'

'Oh, you mean moving in together? I can't honestly remember, but I'm sure it was Prue's. Do you disapprove?'

He still wasn't looking at her.

'Disapprove? Who am I to disapprove?' She took a sip of coffee; it tasted rather bitter for some reason. 'And anyway, what is there for me to disapprove of?'

Dougie shrugged. He had finished the final fragment of toast and was dabbing at his mouth with a napkin and Claudia thought, I'd never noticed it before but some of his habits are decidedly priggish.

'Your attitude is, shall we say, disapproving.' He looked at her for the first time. 'Are you jealous?' He gave her a lopsided smile.

She was not rising to that. 'Of whom?' she said carelessly, watching him over the rim of her cup.

'Of Prue, of course.'

'Why would you think that?'

He shrugged again.

'I am surprised,' Claudia said. 'I have to admit it, I didn't think you and Prue had that much in common. If anything.'

He shrugged yet again, it was beginning to get on her nerves. 'Perhaps that's not always a bad thing.'

'Are you intending to,' now how was she going to put it, 'live in each other's pockets, so to speak?'

'I will pay my way, if that's what you mean.'

It wasn't. She tried again.

'I meant . . . ' She sighed. Why was he making it so deliberately difficult? 'Oh, never mind.'

'So,' Dougie said, leaning back in his chair, 'you're thinking of travelling to the exotic east?'

'To – oh, yes,' said Claudia. 'To see Gerald, well, maybe.' She paused for a moment. 'He's coming over here as it happens, later this month.'

Dougie nodded. 'It's been a while.'

'Yes, it has.'

'I don't suppose I will have the pleasure of catching up with him while he's here,' said Dougie, with what Claudia took to be a smirk. 'He will be far too busy for the likes of me.'

'Probably,' she said.

'A shame.'

'Or vice versa.'

'Sorry?'

'*You* will be too busy to see *him*.'

'Probably.'

He really was an odd man, quite perverse in a way, there were times when he was impossible to talk to.

'Don't look so sad, Clot,' said Dougie, with an edge. Or perhaps there was no edge, perhaps he meant it. Everything was suddenly so loaded, everything he said and did. How dare he make me suffer like this, thought Claudia.

'You should be excited,' he went on. 'At the prospect of seeing the old man again. Are you?'

'Am I what?' she said obtusely.

'Excited at the prospect of seeing the old man again, after – how long has it been? A year? Two?'

'Nine months.'

'Is that all? How long is he going to be here?'

'I've no idea.'

'No? How odd. But you'll have time to do some fun things together, I'm sure.'

'Stop this, Dougie.'

He raised his eyebrows, and then he pursed his lips as if to say, Enough, very well, I'll shut up now.

Thus they sat, two old friends, two near lovers, in silence for a whole minute, and even Claudia was grateful for the arrival of Prue.

It came as a relief, and in the circumstances a surprise, that the three of them were able to spend the rest of the day together in relative harmony. Claudia decided to be on her best behaviour; after all, it did not take Prue to point out to her – which she would have done given half a chance, which she was not – that she, Claudia, had had plenty of opportunity and that she had not once, but twice turned Dougie down. So for the time being maturity prevailed and they spent the rest of the morning and part of the afternoon in idle and harmless chitchat, going for long walks around the garden and beyond, arguing – in a friendly manner – about whether they thought they could risk a short drive in Rosie without ending up in a ditch or killing something. And finally deciding that it would be fun to drive to D for tea, as Prue and Claudia had attempted to do all that time ago, if only to prove that Prue could get them there and back safely, which she did. This gave them a topic of conversation that lasted the whole of the journey back: not the drive so much as the extraordinary quality of the scones at the teahouse in D, which were, by general agreement, pronounced the best in the entire country and well worth risking life and limb for; and, in the case of Dougie, who had gallantly offered to cram himself into the tiny back seat, there and back, the continued use of his limbs.

One can have fun without upsetting people, it was totally possible, even if the conversation were banal.

Over dinner Claudia asked Dougie how his writing was going.

'His writing!' exclaimed Prue, with a 'pah!'

'And what exactly do you mean by that?' asked Dougie politely.

'Dearest Dougie, what made you think you could be a writer?'

Claudia saw a moment of hurt, or perhaps annoyance pass across Dougie's face.

'What makes you think I can't?'

'Everyone wants to be a writer,' said Prue, spiking a sausage with her fork. 'But it seems to me the people who really have something to write *about* are very rarely the people with the skill, or the time, to write about them.'

'Such as you, you mean.'

'Perhaps.'

'Then maybe I ought to write your story rather than mine,' suggested Dougie. 'A novel rather than a memoir.'

Prue gave him a baleful look. 'That is exactly the problem,' she said. 'People simply don't believe a word I say, because fact is so often far, *far* weirder than fiction, so if anyone tried to write my stories, well . . . ' she turned her attention back to her sausage.

'They could be offered up as fantasies perhaps.' Dougie smiled, inoffensively. 'Or even,' he sniggered, 'immorality tales.'

'Laugh away,' said Prue cheerfully. 'Say what you like. Anyway, what precisely do you mean by immorality tales?'

'I'd have thought it was obvious.'

Prue leant forward in her chair and all but stabbing Dougie in the chest with her fork, she said, 'You mind what you say or you may find yourself homeless.'

Dougie pulled a face, glanced at Claudia and chuckled.

'Writing,' continued Prue, 'and books never made the slightest difference to the world.'

'I beg your pardon? How can you say such a thing?'

'Very well, give me one example of a book that made the slightest difference to the world.'

'I could mention the Bible,' said Dougie.

'Yes, and what else?'

'The Koran, and the Talmud.'

'Other than religious books.'

'The works of Dickens, and Shakespeare, John Bunyan.'

'Bunyan? Ha!'

'Dostoyevsky, Victor Hugo, Mark Twain, good God, do I really need to go on?'

'What difference,' again Prue was using her fork as an aggressive object, 'did they make to the sum of human experience, or behaviour? When did an anti-war book ever stop a war? When did a morality tale ever make anyone moral? Show me the proof.'

Dougie looked momentarily flabbergasted. 'It's not

something you can *measure*!' he said.

'I will tell you what makes a difference: actions. People doing things makes a difference.'

'You mean people fighting wars?'

'Them certainly. You can find plenty of people responsible for starting a war but not many people who were responsible for a war not happening.'

'That's absolute nonsense!'

'If the anti-warmongers had half the strength and influence of the warmongers there would be no wars.'

'The lack of something,' said Dougie – he was beginning to look quite rattled – 'is no proof that it might not have existed.'

'"The lack of something is no proof that it might not have existed".' Prue glanced at Claudia. 'May I quote you on that?'

'What do *you* think, Claudia?'

Claudia's mind was racing in a quite different direction, as in how could these two people possibly think they could live together?

'I think books do change people, in subtle ways,' she offered. 'They certainly can alter a person's way of thinking.'

'Actions speak louder than words,' said Prue.

'The pen is mightier than the sword,' said Dougie.

'This is a totally ludicrous conversation,' said Claudia.

'Yes, but it's fun, isn't it?' Prue placed her knife and fork down on her empty plate. 'We,' she reached over and jiggled Dougie's sleeve, 'are going to have a lot of fun.'

Oh my, thought Claudia.

But she felt better at the end of the day. One could enjoy one's friends, it wasn't hard; all you had to do was take them at face value, not to overthink everything a person said or did. Overthinking, Claudia was beginning to realise, was the scourge of the idle classes. Dougie and

Prue might last the course or they might not, it would be interesting, very interesting, to see.

They left together, in Rosie. Despite Dougie's experiences and Claudia's warning he seemed to think it preferable to the train, or maybe Prue had bludgeoned him into it. That was a concern. Prue was a great bludgeoner and Dougie was quite easily bludgeoned. For example he never did get to answer Claudia's question about his writing.

Pull yourself together, Claudia, she hissed, drawing herself up to her proper height and brushing down her skirt as if to rid it of the crumbs of her overworked imagination. Now, of course, there was Gerald to look forward to. Was she looking forward to seeing him? Was she excited? Should she be?

Lily certainly was. 'It will be so good to see Mr Faraday again. I'd quite thought he'd forgotten all about us!' she exclaimed, before once again thrusting a hand in front of her mouth in shock at what she'd said. Then, 'How long will he be staying, madam, and what plans do you have, do you mind my asking? I suppose you'll be going up to London to see the girls, he must be missing them. And you, of course. And you, er, you must have been missing him too madam.' Oh God, Lily's expression seemed to say, why do I ever open my big mouth?

Claudia gave her a smile by way of reassurance, both her maid's and her own.

38

She had precisely three weeks to work on some improvements. Being Gerald, attention had to be paid not so much to one's appearance – which was a pity in a way as it was so much easier, transformation could be achieved in a day – as to the mind. She needed to turn herself, as much as it was possible in the time available, into the semblance of an Interesting Woman.

She spent several mornings in the local library leafing through recent copies of *National Geographic*. She read about record-breaking journeys across continents in airships and the cultivation of goldfish in America. She pored over pictures of charabancs in Cornwall and stories of 'Weird Ceremonies Performed by an Aboriginal Tribe in the Heart of Yunnan Province, China'. She paid particular attention to articles with an archaeological bent, such as one featuring recent excavations in Yucatan, which she thought might be somewhere in America and where, rather extraordinarily, they had uncovered, among other items of interest such as temples and palaces, pyramids. She studied closely the tale of the Daring Explorer who found 20,000-year-old rock statues beneath a river in the Pyrenees. She searched for anything that had to do with the great unearthing of the tomb of Tutankhamen, perhaps the most remarkable discovery in the history of archaeology, or at least of Egyptology, even Claudia knew that. Not that Gerald had had anything to do with it, not directly, although they were all connected, archaeologists from all over the world, so Gerald used to say; connected in their ongoing quest to uncover and understand the mysteries of times past. That was why he, and others, had left Egypt, now they were no longer permitted to take the artefacts they had discovered out of their countries of origin, and quite right too, though it made the life of the archaeologist that much more complicated. Claudia took notes and wrote down facts and dates which she resolved to put to memory.

It was a strange and interesting challenge, the wooing of one's husband.

She scoured the newspapers for information on Palestine and in particular on the great British archaeologist and recently knighted Sir Flinders Petrie. She could not pretend to be anything like Sir Flinders' wife Hilda, who was an archaeologist in her own right and had worked alongside her husband for most of their married life, though of course she'd be fascinated to meet her. Perhaps they would get along, maybe even become friends, write to each other, that sort of thing. Fun. Something to ponder on.

She would give Gerald trout, with mustard sauce. The food on these digs was atrocious, so she'd make sure he caught up on his favourites, good old roast beef and Yorkshire pudding. She could see his eyes lighting up at the prospect. Perhaps there would be time for a brief run through the countryside in the car, staying at some quaint roadside inn somewhere – Devon perhaps, close to the sea. Get him away, like the old days.

As for her appearance, well here again while this would most likely go completely unnoticed, he being a man and moreover Gerald, she would do what she could to look her best because as all women are aware, one dresses mostly for one's own self-esteem, rather than for compliments expected and so rarely paid by the opposite sex.

The days went by remarkably quickly. Lily had been given time off, she needed it, and she returned to work in a state of high excitement at the impending visit.

'Shall I do your hair, madam?' she offered.

Why not? However wasted it might be on Gerald, if it made her feel that much more special it served an important purpose. Claudia felt she was getting first-night nerves, not like an actress, more like the virgin she once was, and how crazy was *that*?

She asked Lily to prepare Mr Faraday's dressing room. It had been a long time – how long exactly she couldn't, or chose not to recall – since the two of them had spent a night together; and while she didn't want to push things she fully intended to work on him and do her best to persuade him, before the end of his visit, into her room, and her bed.

She thought long and hard about what she would wear and settled eventually on a simple, pale green shift dress, with near matching earrings; the overall effect subtle, sophisticated and understated. She did not want to startle him.

Gerald arrived late. So late – by around five hours – that Claudia had convinced herself he wasn't coming at all and just hadn't bothered to telephone and explain. But he was there on the last train, on the doorstep as she was beginning to think about bedtime, looking exhausted, and a touch bedraggled (journeyworn, as he called it). He kissed her rather perfunctorily on the cheek and muttered that he was no good for anyone tonight, *Sorry old girl, catch up properly in the morning if you don't mind*, all of which of course she quite understood.

But he wasn't much more forthcoming in the morning.

Claudia kept up an incessant chatter over breakfast, filling the silence, showing off her newfound knowledge of airships in America and curious findings in Yucatan. Unfortunately when it came to hard facts and dates she found herself stumbling, but since he made no comment at all she knew he was probably not listening to anything she said; which rather than taking the wind out of her sails encouraged her to babble on, realising as she did so that she had barely paused long enough for him to get a word in edgeways. Mention of 'the great Sir Flinders Petrie' and his remarkable wife Hilda, whom Claudia would very much like to meet and get to know, did elicit a nod and a grunt, which was something at least. She tried telling herself to shut up for a moment but found herself quite unable to do so because, deep down, she did not want to allow the silence.

At last she stopped, and he heaved a sigh of what may have been relief, looked at her across the breakfast table and smiled, rather wearily.

'You look as if you've been working far too hard,' she said.

'Probably.'

'How long are you here for?'

'I don't really know.' He looked away. 'I've got a few, er, things, you know.'

'Talks? Lectures?'

'Those too,' he nodded, and lapsed into silence.

'Listen,' he said after a long moment. 'There is no easy way to say this but, old girl, the point is – I've come to ask you for a divorce.'

He looked up at her then, at last, and properly, but said nothing – as he had said nothing since he arrived – about her appearance, her hair, the care with which she had presented herself, her new self, as she thought she was. But he was not seeking to compliment her.

'Say again?' she said.

'I have met someone,' he said, with effort. 'She's been working with me, for some time now.' He rubbed his face. 'She came to work for me and . . .'

And she took such interest in his work, so much more than his wife did, she stood at his side, assisting him, looking after him, labelling his findings, like Hilda Petrie, sleeping under the stars, guarding the tunnels and caves and probably cooking for him, so knowledgeable and, of course, so *young*.

'Is she younger than me?' It was a stupid question, and it took him aback for a moment.

'I expect so,' he said, unsatisfactorily. 'That isn't the point, that's not the point at all. The point is she's interested in what I do, it's her life, as it is mine, she's . . .'

'A student?'

'Once, yes. Why?'

'No matter,' said Claudia, and stared at the tablecloth.

Time stopped. The clock ceased ticking, the birds went quiet, there was not a sound, except for Gerald's breathing, which was deafening.

'So you want to marry her?'

He seemed to think for a while before he said, 'I don't know, possibly, but I need to know at least I'm free.'

He was, she acknowledged, an honourable man, who wanted to sleep with another woman but didn't feel able to do so as a married man. Despite herself, and the situation, Claudia admired him for it. He could have just gone ahead and done it and no one would have been any the wiser, or sadder, or more humiliated. But he'd done the honourable thing.

'So that's why you came here,' she said. 'That's the reason for your visit.'

Again he thought before replying, 'Yes.'

'There were no lectures, or talks.'

He half shook his head at this, as if to say, 'Maybe, maybe not.'

Claudia knew she ought to say something, to fight back, refuse him his divorce, take control, tell him she was coming back to Palestine with him, like it or not, that he should put this ridiculous little dalliance right out of his mind – the sort of thing Prue would have said. She was his wife, he couldn't just roll up virtually out of the blue and demand a divorce, not without warning, or explanation.

'I don't know what to say,' she said.

'I'm sorry,' he said, gruffly. 'I didn't think it would come as much of a surprise to you. Let's face it, we haven't exactly seen much of one another over the years.'

And whose fault was that?

'You never seemed to show a lot of – you know – in what I was doing. I'm not blaming you for that – different paths, different, er, types. Perhaps we should never. . .'

'Don't you dare,' said Claudia.

Then Lily arrived to clear away the breakfast things and there followed minutes of such silence, such stillness, it was as if her mistress and master had been turned to stone. She looked from one to the other of them with alarm, then left the room as quickly as she could.

'I'll make sure you're all right,' Gerald continued. 'You won't ever have to worry about – that side of things.'

'That side of things.'

'Money. I'll be more than generous. Make sure you're secure.'

'Thank you.'

There was a pause.

'What if I had . . . ' she began.

'What?'

'Nothing.' Claudia laughed. 'I had been about to suggest I come back to Palestine with you.'

'What for?' He looked positively alarmed.

'Because I thought it was time. Because you are my husband and I thought, it's perfectly true, I haven't been paying you enough attention recently. It was pointed out to me by our daughters, in no uncertain terms. And of course they were right. And you were right. *Are* right.'

He stared at her.

'And what are you intending to tell them?' she went on. 'I assume you were intending to tell them. To their faces.'

'I suppose so,' he said. 'Unless you would . . . '

'Tell them on your behalf, certainly not. You will explain yourself, and your actions, to their faces. It's the very least you can do, and if you ever thought otherwise then you are . . . ' She paused. She didn't really know what she was about to call him, and anyway what was the point?

What was the point.

She had no fight in her. She slumped in her seat as if her skeleton had collapsed.

'Very well,' said Gerald. And then, 'Do you want me to go right away, or could I hang around for a day or so?'

Hang around? What was he thinking of?

'Of course you can,' she told him, not really knowing why. Not because she thought she could change his mind, more because some kind of pretence of normality, if only for a day or so, would help her over this particular hurdle. One step at a time sort of thing.

So he did. He stayed on for two more days, during which he took himself for long walks, and chatted to the gardener about this and that, and to Lily, who looked increasingly wide-eyed and bewildered, as well she might. At night-times he took to his own room, early, where he sat into the small hours reading, or so Claudia assumed. She could see his light on but she did not think to disturb him.

There existed a kind of unspoken atmosphere of affection, even regret, between the two of them. Without saying much of consequence, and never touching, it was for a brief time as if life could continue as it was, surrounded by the predictable comforts of a home they had built between them, a home that he was brought up in but seemed prepared to let go, for there was never any question that she should be turned out of it. It is ironic that at the point when a couple are on the point of separating, they learn perhaps for the first time what it was that brought them together in the first place. Which maybe was only time, and shared experiences, children, memories, nothing more.

She felt surprisingly little rancour, but she did feel a sense of profound sadness, and not the sadness of a woman who only appreciates someone they've lost. Neither was it sadness for herself necessarily, for the future, the empty future – to be truthful it wasn't going to make a huge difference to her daily life, which is why she thought the whole divorce thing wasn't really necessary. It was sadness for a life, for a family, even a dispersed one such as theirs. For a life that was never going to be the same again.

He left after three days, catching the train to London to see the girls. He gave her a long hug and she thought she might have seen spots of tears in his eyes, though they may have been for the family home rather than for her. He said he had made an appointment to see a solicitor, who would be in touch with her soon to do whatever it was deemed necessary to do. Then he went, and she watched him trudging towards the car, with just the suitcase he had arrived with, eyes trained on the ground as usual, clambering into the vehicle, waving briefly, and driving off.

39

There were things she could have said, she thought about them after he'd gone; in fact she did little other than think about them.

The business of taking an interest, it cuts both ways, she'd have said. 'Not once have you asked me about myself, or the girls, we do have lives you know, not as interesting as yours maybe but all the same.' She could have quite lost her temper with him about this ludicrous affair with a younger woman, possibly young enough to be his daughter. Did he really want to throw away thirty years of marriage for that? She could have, she could have, she could have – and she didn't. It was pointless, his mind was made up. But it might have done something for her self esteem.

In the event the girls did it for her.

'I told him it was shoddy. Frankly shoddy.' Coming from Harriet that was quite a surprise. 'I asked him how old she was and he said – do you know what he said?'

'I've no idea.'

'"What has that got to do with anything?" I ask you!'

'Well, I don't suppose it has.' Claudia smiled wanly. It was a topic she didn't particularly want to discuss.

'I told him you'd stood by us all these years, you'd loved us, nurtured us, devoted your life to us, and all for this!'

'His timing was atrocious,' said Jessica, 'we told him as much. Right now, when we've all fled the nest and you're all alone down here and so forth.'

Claudia nodded.

'It was as if it hadn't occurred to him. I asked him if he'd noticed any change in you.' Jessica gestured at her mother. 'In your appearance, you know, your clothes, your hair and everything. He said he thought you were looking well.'

'What's wrong with that?'

'Oh, Mama!' Jessica sighed. 'It's a paltry response, honestly. After everything you've done. I wanted to say, I really wanted to say, "Look at her! Just take a look and see what you're throwing away!" Truly, it made my blood boil!'

'Throwing away?' Claudia laughed gently. 'You gave him a very hard time by the sound of it.'

They'd travelled down to Claudia's together, the three of them, right after their father had made his announcement to them in London. The joint onslaught, which is what it felt like to Claudia, gave the whole sorry business the air of an emergency. A bit of her was deeply moved by her daughters' angry loyalty but another bit of her thought their reaction, understandable though it was, threatened to turn it into a bigger crisis than it was. A large bit of her rather wanted to be left alone.

'He was crying, Mama,' said Flora. 'He was trying terribly hard not to. I've never seen him cry before.'

'You're not defending him, are you!' exclaimed Harriet.

'Not really.' Flora smiled at her sisters but they did not smile back. 'I'm only trying to point out how difficult it was for him too. To be truthful I'm not sure he quite understands himself, and you know how bad he is at expressing his feelings. I think he was tremendously moved.'

'Well, bully for him.' Harriet got up abruptly and started pacing the room.

'I also think we should calm down, just a little. We don't want to lose him, do we?'

Harriet stopped in her tracks and shrugged, and Jessica stared at the floor.

'Of course we don't.' Flora looked at her mother and reached over to take her hand. 'He was crying not for himself but for us, Mama. It's the nearest he could come to telling us he loved us, I do believe that.'

'A funny way to show it,' growled Harriet.

Claudia nodded and smiled at her daughters in turn. She didn't want to say anything because she thought she was quite close to breaking down herself. It had been all right until they arrived. She'd managed to keep things together, more or less, but this tidal wave of sympathy threatened to overwhelm her.

'These things happen,' she said after a moment, rather lamely.

'I don't know why you're being so darn reasonable, *Maman*,' muttered Harriet.

'There's little point in being otherwise, darling.' She was trying not to sound defeatist. She did feel reasonable, and almost slightly noble, both of which were preferable to feeling sorry for herself. After what she'd been up to over the past few months she thought it was really no more than she deserved, so self-pity was out of the question.

Somewhere, in the midst of the irony of her marriage crumbling just as she had resolved to try to salvage it, she sensed there was a message, if she could just work out what it was.

'It is very important,' she said eventually, 'that you don't lose touch with your father. Whatever you think he's done, people have done worse. And as you told me yourselves I am as much to blame . . . ' She faltered for a moment. 'There it is.'

There was a short reflective silence during which all three daughters looked with love and sympathy upon their mother, and their mother looked blankly and unblinkingly at the fireplace.

'Meanwhile,' said Jessica, perking up, 'let's think of the future. What *I* think you should do Mama is go to Italy. With Dougie.'

It came so out of the blue it rendered Claudia mute. Before she could regain her speech Jessica had told her all about this perfect little fishing village on the Med, a simple family-run hotel, quiet and very pretty, especially out of season, just the place to forget the troubles of the world. Claudia nodded quietly and went on saying nothing until her eldest daughter threatened to call up right there and then to make the arrangements if she liked, at which point Claudia regained her powers of speech sufficiently to explain that Dougie was otherwise engaged.

'What does that mean?'

'Just that's he's – busy elsewhere.'

'Oh? In what way?'

'I'm not sure, Jessica, it's really not my business.'

She didn't want to discuss it, not even with Jessica.

She hadn't been in touch with either Prue or Dougie since Gerald dropped his bombshell. She didn't want to have to listen to Prue telling her how much better off she was without him and Dougie saying he told her so.

'Whatever it is, it won't last,' said Jessica, and for a moment Claudia wondered if she knew. 'Just you wait and see. Dougie'll be on your doorstep the moment he hears the news.'

That precisely is what Claudia did not want. Or she thought she did not want.

~

She spent the next few weeks in a fog. It was February, the drabbest month of the year, the endless winter dragging on, the days still dark, the trees stark against a leaden sky. She ate little, did little, spoke little and slept a lot. Sleep was the only thing that made sense – it was a form of hibernation. And then like an animal, along with the first daffodils, come March she gradually awoke and decided it was time to pop her head out of the slough of her despond and look around a bit.

Perhaps, she thought mildly, her life was over. She'd been the gay young thing, laughing and flirting and partying her life away, settled down to the wife thing and then the mother thing and now . . . The unexpected reappearance in her life of sex and the discovery of new possibilities had given her a thrilling new lease of life, for which she was profoundly grateful, but it didn't seem to have led anywhere. She was an actress who had reached the peak of her powers only to have her role snatched away from her. She had cast off her carapace, as Carlos called it, and exposed herself in all her naked vulnerability only to find the audience had all gone home.

These were the thoughts that preoccupied Claudia as she watched, from a detached distance, the gradual lengthening of the days and the subtle brightening of the spring skies.

Prue had once said to her, 'You live your life in a mist, darling, not really connecting. It's time you came down from your cloud and joined the world.'

The slightly mixed metaphor hadn't meant much at the time. A person is who she is, Claudia had always believed. Besides, there was nothing like living behind a smokescreen to create an air of mystery. But that was all very well when one was young and beautiful and people paid attention without one having to do very much. It had, Claudia realised rather late in life, turned her into a *reactor*, and while there was nothing to react to, it meant one was pretty well stuck. Perhaps it was this very passivity, this acceptance, that had so infuriated her elder daughters. Perhaps it was time for the actress to seize the role and demand the audience return to their seats.

Then Prue rang. Surprisingly, she hadn't heard the news about Gerald; but she had plenty of her own.

'He broke one of my best Spodes the other night,' she said.

'Who, Dougie? How come?'

'I threw it at him.'

'*You* threw it at *him*?'

'He made me. He said I was illiterate, just because I'd never heard of Edward Gibson.'

'Who?'

'What has the decline of the Roman Empire to do with the here and now, tell me that?'

'I think you mean . . .'

'So I said to him, "name me the most famous artist of the Renaissance who nobody has ever heard of", so he said, "if nobody has ever heard of him why should I have the faintest idea?" And so I said if ever there was an assumption that was it, and her name was Maria Piazzarola.'

'Who?'

'Made her up on the spur of the moment, darling, but it did the trick, made the point.'

'But it didn't mend the Spode.'

'Who cares, it's only a thing. So, when are you going to come and see us?'

'Perhaps when things have calmed down a bit up there,' said Claudia.

'That'll be never, darling. Have you been to visit Gerald?'

'Not yet.'

'Then come now.'

'I can't. I'm going away.'

'Oh? Where? And who with?'

'Italy. With nobody.'

'On your own? What an adventure. I hope there's not something you aren't telling me, Claudie.'

Claudia was about to ask to speak to Dougie but changed her mind. She realised in a blinding flash she'd been wrong all along: Prue was a better match for Dougie all round. She was exactly what he needed, someone to kick against (metaphorically speaking), to enjoy plate-smashing sessions with, to bring the kind of vibrancy to his life that Claudia could never provide. It was the differences between them that would bind them together, it seemed obvious now.

'I'm glad things are going so well for the two of you,' she told her friend down the phone.

'I'm not sure about that,' said Prue. 'But somebody had to get his mind off you.'

With which, having extracted a promise from Claudia to visit on her return from Italy and *to tell all*, Prue said goodbye and put the telephone down.

40

It was everything Jess had said it would be. In April, out of season, there were very few people about, it was not too hot, the sky was cloudless and the light so clear it almost hurt the eyes. She had a room with a view of the Mediterranean, which was more intensely blue than anyone would dare to paint, and behind the hotel was a little garden which was such a profusion of colours and scents it took one's breath away. She tried to make sketches to take back home and show to Sellors to see if he could identify what was what, but her drawing was hopeless and she soon gave up.

The trip had sprung out of the top of her head as an excuse not to visit Prue and Dougie, but the more Claudia thought about a few weeks in Italy the more she had warmed to the idea. So she was on the telephone to Jess the following day and four weeks later, here she was.

For the first two days she was in paradise. She spent the mornings on a deck chair on the beach, in the shade, just her, no one else around, reading and dozing and occasionally dipping a toe into the water, which was surprisingly cold. Afternoons she took herself for little strolls around the village, then perhaps another snooze before dinner and an early night.

But after a while a sense of melancholy came over her, and loneliness dropped on her like a shroud. At least at home there were people to talk to – Lily, or Sellors, with whom she'd developed quite a rapport, thanks to the great oak – and there was always someone, daughters or friends, on the end of the telephone. Here there was simply no one and, since her Italian was non-existent, she couldn't even spark up a casual conversation with people in the village, or fellow guests – who were, to her slight surprise, almost exclusively Italian. Not that she was used to initiating conversations with strangers in the first place. So what use was perfection without someone she loved to share it with?

Someone she loved? Who might that be?

She wasn't sure, now she put her mind to it, what the word meant. Love for one's children, obviously, that was instinctive; even, in another sense, for one's friends, although that was not the kind of love she was thinking of. Try as she might she could not define it, though she thought perhaps it was like a painting, come upon unexpectedly, and perfect, in a way that was impossible to explain, but gracious me you knew it when you saw it.

Did she love Dougie? Had she ever loved him? No, actually, she didn't think she ever had. That, actually, was the reason she had turned him down in the first place: not because he had pushed himself on her, and not because of Gerald – if she'd really loved him none of that would have mattered. That was why she continued to turn him down. She may not have known what love was, but she recognised the absence of it.

And Gerald, what of him? It was such a long time ago, she couldn't precisely remember. She must have loved him once, though it had never been a remarkable thing, not like being struck by a thunderbolt, as happened in novels. Yet if she still loved him now she would, as Dougie pointed out, be missing him, surely, she'd be taking more interest in him.

It was all too hard.

She thought of Prue, and her ability to make friends wherever she went. It was something Claudia had never been able to do. For some reason she'd found strangers threatening, certainly the strangers who tried to get into conversation with her. That was why people found her standoffish, and perhaps they were right. Standoffish and judgemental, that's the sort of person I have become, she realised with alarm. She could learn something from Prue; after all it was those very qualities, her friendliness and openness, that had attracted Claudia to her in the first place, and it paid to be reminded of it.

It was because these were the thoughts that were swilling around in Claudia's head that, when on the evening of the third day, just as dinner was ending, the head waiter made a beeline for her table and sat down without so much as a by-your-leave, instead of inwardly panicking and making a hasty exit as she would normally have done, she stayed put. She even, when he introduced himself, in English, as Giovanni, managed a smile.

He began by telling Claudia how much he loved her country. He had worked in London, he said, a while ago, for a year, in a small restaurant in Soho, and his great ambition was to go back as soon as possible. He brought with him a carafe of wine from which he filled Claudia's glass (ignoring her faint protests) while apologising for intruding on her but explaining that he really wanted to improve his English, and besides, he feared she might need protection from Signor Petrucco.

'Who?'

Giovanni indicated with a jerk of his head the tubby, middle-aged man sitting on the far side of the dining room, who, he said, had been making 'sheep's eyes' – *occhi de pecora* – at Claudia ever since he sat down. Claudia laughed. She'd had no idea, she said, but she told

Giovanni she was grateful indeed.

She was quite happy too to sit there and listen as he talked about himself, as men are so good at doing and Italian men in particular: where he came from, why he ended up doing what he did, stories of his huge family, anecdotes about other hotel guests. It let her off the hook, knowing that nothing was expected of her other than that she sit there, nodding occasionally and laughing where appropriate.

It was the same on other evenings; it became almost a ritual. He spoke rapidly and repetitively and with passion on all manner of subjects, from food – about which, he said with great deprecation, the English could learn a thing or two if she didn't mind his saying so – to people, whom he found mysterious and hilarious equally, in particular his own family who he believed came from a planet far away where they spoke a different language and lived to rules only they understood; from the ludicrous nature of Italian politics to the effect that climate has on a population, which partly accounted for the fact that British people were so *sensible* and hardworking and did not, like their Italian counterparts, lounge around all day snoozing in the sun. It was his mission, he declared, to educate the English on all things to do with food and in particular on the miracles of pasta which, he swore, would one day be as popular in England as it was in Italy.

Claudia didn't mind it a bit. She even began to look forward to these interludes; they stemmed the loneliness and took her mind off herself. Once she realised Giovanni was completely harmless and possibly rather lonely himself – why else would he spend time with an English lady of certain years? – she began to relax and enjoy his company and even to rib him occasionally, though gently, especially when his passion carried him away.

Then without warning the enchanted April came to an

end. It was her final evening, warm enough to sit outside. She was drinking coffee and watching the reflected moon and the stars dancing in the water like fireflies. Giovanni came to join her, clutching a bottle of something he called firewater. He poured her a measure into a tiny glass, she took a sip and completely lost all sensation in her mouth. 'By the third glass you will be singing to the moon,' he said, topping her up.

Out of the blue she asked Giovanni if he was married – in the course of all their conversations he had never mentioned a wife – and he said, 'No.' When she asked him why not, he said, 'I haven't met her yet.' Italian women were vulgar, he explained, partly and expressively in mime – too much hip and bosom and especially too much talk. He preferred Englishwomen, 'refined, and reserved.' He had plans, later that year, once the holiday season was over, to return to London, where he would get a job at the Café de Paris and then, 'I will write you and you will come and have lunch in the house.'

'On the house.'

'On the house.' In London, he went on, he would meet a lovely English girl, maybe she'd be working at the same place, blonde hair, freckles, small, delicate and very sweet. They would get married and set up home in Soho Square and have babies, and she, Claudia, would be godmother to the first, who would be a boy.

She laughed. 'You seem very sure of it all,' she said.

'Of course,' he said. 'Because it is my dream, I make sure of it.' Once he had a bit of money in his pocket – what could possibly go wrong?

'And what is your dream?' he asked her.

She looked at him in surprise. She was on her third thimble of firewater by now, not quite so reticent as half an hour ago, but she didn't quite seem to understand what he had asked her.

'Me?' she said, dumbly. 'Oh, I'm too old for that sort of thing.'

'*No!*' He spoke so sharply she jumped. 'Never too old! This is bad talk, this is lazy. Dreams are for everyone, dreams are what you get up for, you must never not have a dream. No matter if it is impossible, all the better, then when you have decided what is your dream, then you make it happen.'

'Just like that?'

'No, not just like that.' He was almost shouting now. 'Nothing is "just like that", you have to make it work. Me, I don't sit here and wait for the Café de Paris to say, "come and work for us", I go. I go there and I' – he mimed – 'bang on the door, I say "give me a job" over and over until they say "yes". No matter if it takes a month, a year. I make it happen.'

He paused, and looked out to sea for a moment.

'And then,' he continued, with renewed emphasis, 'I look around for my wife and when I find her,' he gestured, 'it may take a day, it may take a year. Dreams take time.' He banged his fist on the table. 'Sorry,' he said, when the glasses and the bottle threatened to jump onto the floor and shatter.

'So now,' said Giovanni, raising his glass, 'when you have decided what is your dream – take your time, no hurry – we drink to it. You do not tell me what it is, and you do not wish for your dream to come true, because you know that is not what happens. You say to yourself, "my dream is . . . " and later you work out how to make it come true.'

He sat there, glass raised, for some time, while Claudia smiled, at first slightly patronisingly, and as he continued to sit there, unmoving and gradually starting to glare at her, so she began to put her mind to the proposition, seriously.

'No matter how impossible,' said Giovanni. 'Your dream. Decide.'

And so, eventually, she did. And the thought that came into her head surprised her.

41

It was another hotel in another continent in another climate altogether. She was grateful for the fans.

She had sent Gerald a telegram shortly before leaving home, giving him very little time, if any, to object. She'd worded it in the form of a statement rather than a request, as in: *Arriving Jerusalem Weds 3 June, staying at the Three Palms Hotel.* If it were inconvenient for him, which she thought it might well be, that was just too bad.

She'd booked two rooms, one for herself and one for Gerald, and finding the heat outside oppressive she spent the time awaiting his arrival in the fan-cooled hotel foyer, or reading in her bedroom. She expected a long wait, perhaps two days, but he was there on the hotel doorstep the evening of her first full day, flushed and slightly awkward in his working clothes of shorts and shirt and shabby hat; but looking, thought Claudia, considerably younger, and healthier, than when she had last seen him in the gloom of an English January day. What is more, he did not seem as displeased as she had been anticipating.

She reached out a hand to him, which he took, not to shake but to hold, as one might a close friend's, before leaning in to kiss her on the cheek. 'Forgive the appearance,' he said. 'I've come straight from the site.' He stood back then and looked at her, which was another surprise, and then he said, 'Good journey?'

'Not too bad, in the circumstances. You?'

'Not too bad, in the circumstances.'

There was a slight pause. She smiled at him, with some apprehension. He was unshaven and tanned a deep brown by the sun, and his face shone with sweat, but despite all this, or maybe because of it, she found herself thinking how handsome he looked in his working clothes: rugged and unwashed, yet somehow right. By contrast, although she fitted the surroundings of the smart, colonial hotel in which they stood rather better than he did, she felt decidedly out of place in her formal and obviously English outfit and the neat little hat that was obviously not intended for the sun. But never mind all that, he was here.

'I think I'd better have a wash and brush-up, if that's all right by you,' he said.

'Of course,' said Claudia.

'Shall we meet in the bar at say,' he looked at his watch, 'seven?'

'Perfect.'

~

She changed into her cornflower-blue number, a more casual affair than the stern two-piece in which she had arrived, and rather more suitable, she thought, with its light, flowing skirt, for the place and the circumstances they were in. He turned up wearing a pair of immaculate linen trousers and jacket, and Claudia's first thought was, Where did that all come from, and who is helping him buy his clothes? His work was one thing – quite beyond her, naturally, as it would be to most people – but domestic detail, that was something she could understand.

They ordered gins, his with tonic, hers with 'It', and she began by asking him how his work was going. He responded in that kind of noncommittal way people do when they know the person they're talking to has no real understanding of the subject-matter and is merely enquiring out of politeness. Claudia knew she only had to ask him one informed question and the whole conversation would take off. But she couldn't think of a single one, which was annoying, and shaming too. Is there really too much ground to cover? she thought. Could I ever, ever catch up?

Having exhausted that topic in ten minutes flat they moved on to dinner. The dining room was cool and elegant and overlooked a courtyard of palms, olives and fruit trees which was fringed with neo-Moorish arches, in an attempt to give the place a feel of historical authenticity; even though the hotel, like much of this part of the city, was virtually brand new.

One could imagine oneself on holiday here, without a care in the world, thought Claudia. Under British mandate the city felt familiar yet wildly exotic, so ancient it made little old England seem like an upstart. And this was now her husband's – or should that be her ex-husband's – home; more home, in his eyes, than Hallywell, the one he had left all those years ago and now rarely visited.

Over a first course of *meze* Claudia told Gerald that Harriet had finally laid down the law with Leonard and he had gone into what she hoped was a temporary sulk as a result.

'What are you talking about?' Gerald asked.

'Ah, she didn't tell you. Well . . . ' Claudia toyed with her fork. Of course she didn't. 'Leonard can be a little – wayward, shall we say.'

'In what way?'

'Shall we say he – looks around.'

'Looks around? At what? Other women?'

'That too.'

Gerald looked taken aback. 'You never told me this.'

'Perhaps you didn't ask.' She placed her fork on her plate and looked at him and he shrugged in acknowledgment.

'Anyway, it's all cleared up now, is it?'

'Let's hope so.' She sat there looking at him for a moment. 'Did you discuss their lives, at all, when you went to see them?' she asked.

'Who, the girls? Not really. Well, yes, in a way.' He shifted in his seat. 'There were other things.' He was addressing the open air.

'Are you completely uninterested in your daughters, Gerald?'

'Of course not!' He drank from his glass of wine. 'I ... ' He waved a hand in the air.

'You had other things to think about, obviously.' Claudia gave a sigh, which was more of a *harrumph,* and then, placing both hands flat on the table and leaning right across it she said, 'You know Gerald, sometimes you are the absolute end!'

'Oh I say.' Gerald gave an embarrassed laugh and placed his glass back down on the table. 'What have I done now?'

'It's what you haven't done!' said Claudia, in a hiss. She was aware of other diners taking an interest. She sat there unmoving for a moment, hands still clutching the table. She opened her mouth to deliver the next salvo when ...

'Are you finished, madam?' The waiter, at her shoulder, head inclined deferentially.

'I am, yes, thank you,' she said.

She sat back, arms crossed, biting her lip, while plates were removed and replaced by the main course, which Gerald studied with great interest. She sensed a waft of lamb cooked in spices and sniffed deeply. Oh, for an appetite.

'Do you mind if I ... ?' Gerald indicated his plate.

'Go ahead.' Then, calming slightly, she turned to face

him directly and said, 'Shall I tell you a funny story?'

'Go on.' He was tucking into his food with some relish.

'There was this woman,' said Claudia, 'of a certain age, whose daughters were concerned for her because they had all left home and got married and she was on her own, as her husband worked overseas.' She paused to take a sip of wine before continuing.

'The couple had, needless to say, drifted apart. He was absorbed in his work and she with her daughters, and with the house, and everyday domestic duties and other such fascinating pastimes. So it was that her daughters summoned their mother to a meeting and gave her what might be termed a mild ticking-off.'

'Did they indeed?' Gerald's eyebrows lifted.

'To the effect that she was not paying sufficient attention to her absentee husband and to his work.'

'And what did this woman say?'

'She said, "You may well be right, darling daughters, but it cuts both ways. It could be said he pays about the same amount of attention to my preoccupations as I do to his, which is not very much."'

'Hmm.' Gerald stopped eating for a moment, and then recommenced.

'The woman of course acknowledged there was some truth in her daughters' comments and resolved to act upon them. She spent some time reading up on her husband's work and . . . '

'Did you really?' He looked up at her, fork halfway to his mouth.

'Yes. And she started to make plans in her head to visit him and to spend more time with him. Unfortunately, before she had the chance to put these plans into practice her husband told her he wanted a divorce in order to marry some other woman of unknown age or who knows what.'

She paused. He was looking at her intently, food temporarily deprioritised.

'I thought you said it was a funny story,' he said.

'I haven't got to that yet.'

'Right.'

'Meanwhile, the woman had briefly rekindled a liaison with . . . ' Where were the right words when you needed them?

'An old flame.' He smiled at her.

'How did you know?'

He shrugged. 'Pretty obvious, from what you were trying to say. Dougie, evidently.'

Her lips tried to form a word and stopped. She looked at him quizzically. 'Did you guess?'

'Perceveral came through the other day,' said Gerald. 'He said he'd seen you.'

'Perceveral?'

'You remember him? Big chap, loud voice. Said you'd invited him to dinner and this man had his hands all over you. I asked him the name of the man and he said it was Dougie.'

'Perceveral.' Claudia sighed. 'Well, God bless Perceveral.'

'Never the most discreet of chaps, to say the least.'

'Perceveral. ' Claudia frowned. 'Remind me, exactly, who he is.'

Gerald stared at her. 'He was a colleague of mine. You met him years ago, in London. He was head over heels in love with you, along with everyone else.'

'Perceveral?'

'Are you going to keep on repeating his name?'

She couldn't help herself.

'What's so funny?'

'I'm sorry.' She was struggling to get the words out. 'He rang me, out of the blue, seemed to know who I was and so I invited him for dinner that same evening, off the top of my head. And I still couldn't remember who he was, right till the end, couldn't place him at all. Perceveral.' The whole of her body was shaking with laughter. 'I'm so sorry.'

'He wouldn't like that, old Perceveral,' said Gerald. 'Wouldn't like it at all, not to be remembered by someone like you.' And to Claudia's amazement his shoulders started to heave as well.

'He was awfully pompous,' she spluttered. 'All he wanted to talk about was sport.'

'He's an ass,' said Gerald. He pronounced the word with a long "a". 'Forgive the word, there's no other one for it.'

'He was, an absolute ass. And to think . . . ' She stopped abruptly.

'What?'

She looked at her husband for a moment before continuing. What harm could it do now?

'I had a dream about him, Perceveral Lightfoot. I dreamt we were swimming naked, in the pond, at my old place, years ago. He and I.' She lowered her head and looked at Gerald coquettishly through her eyelashes.

'Good God!' he exclaimed. 'Couldn't you do better than that?'

'But that was before. Before he came to dinner, when I was fantasising about who he might be. I certainly wouldn't have had that dream once I'd met him.' She giggled, and took another sip of wine.

'And Dougie?' It came rather suddenly, and Gerald wasn't laughing any more.

'Dougie. I was coming to that.'

She thought about touching her husband's arm – he was still technically her husband after all – as it rested on the table inches from hers. 'You may not want to hear it now, it may no longer interest you.'

'It interests me.'

'I met up with Dougie a few times. He'd been living overseas with his wife, and she had died, and so he'd come back to live in England, and . . . he looked me up.'

Gerald was starting to scowl.

'Don't worry,' she said. 'It is a funny story, remember? We had dinner together, and he came to Hallywell and, yes, he did . . . '

'Make love to you.'

'No, not at all. He touched me, yes, and I won't pretend I didn't like it. I won't pretend I didn't want him to make love to me, I almost considered we might . . . ' she bit her lip.

'Might what?'

'Have an affair.'

There was a long pause.

'Is that the joke bit?' said Gerald.

'Partly, yes.'

'Not sure I get it.'

She reached across the table and placed her hand firmly on his. 'He told me he was still in love with me, and since you were – elsewhere – and I was on my own, I was tempted. I thought, for a moment, it made sense, after all these years.'

'Still waiting for the joke.'

'The joke is that having decided that to enter into a relationship with Dougie would be, not to put too fine a word on it, disastrous, you arrived and . . . '

'Why disastrous?'

'Oh Gerald.' She was stroking his arm now. 'For the same reason I thought so all those years ago. Because he's demanding, and highly emotional, and because I wasn't in love with him, neither then nor now.'

'Right,' said Gerald. He was looking at her sorrowfully,

like a disappointed dog. So that's where Harriet gets it from, thought Claudia.

'Whereas I *am* in love with you, Gerald.'

There was a long silence.

'That,' she went on, gently, 'is the joke.' She removed her hand from his arm and placed it on her lap.

Gerald cleared his throat. 'Dearest girl,' he said.

'Anyway,' she said, 'enough of that. End of funny story. My food must be as cold as anything. What was it like, did you enjoy it?'

He didn't reply. His knife and fork lay at an unfinished angle on his plate and he was looking into the distance like someone who's had a blow to the head and doesn't quite know where he is.

'Now you can tell me all about your intended – if you want to, of course. Though I have to say I was surprised I haven't heard from your solicitor so I was wondering what was going on, if anything. That's really why I'm here.'

She took a mouthful of food and swallowed. For some reason it didn't seem to taste of very much at all.

'Gerald,' she said when he remained silent. 'Speak to me.'

'I don't know, old girl,' he said at last. 'Yes, I did want the divorce but when it came to it . . . '

'You've changed your mind?'

'It's not that.'

'Then what exactly are we talking about?'

He seemed to give this some thought. 'She was kind to me. When I was ill.'

'You were ill? You never told me!'

'It was nothing,' he made a dismissive gesture. 'A bit of a fever, only lasted a few days. But she was kind, and, and she, er, she looked up to me, even idolised, in a fashion. Appreciated. Yes.'

There was a pause.

'Go on,' said Claudia gently.

Gerald cleared his throat again. 'So I got a bit carried away, I suppose. It had been a long time.'

She waited, then, 'What's her name, this girl?'

'Juliette. More of a woman really.'

'Juliet. How romantic. Tell me more about her.'

'Juliette. Well, she, um – why?' He looked at Claudia with an expression that reminded her now of a wounded puppy.

'The divorce. It would be useful to know.'

'To tell the truth she was a bit alarmed when I mentioned it.'

'Oh?'

'Called me fond and foolish.' He looked down at his unfinished plate.

'Oh Gerald.' Claudia felt an irresistible urge to laugh. 'Why didn't you just have a fling with her?'

'A fling?' Gerald looked shocked. 'No no no, that would have been quite wrong. Not fair on her, or on you. Not at all.'

'You are so damned honourable, Gerald.'

'Honourable? Nobody ever accused me of that before!' He gave a brief guffaw.

'Do you still want to?' she asked him.

He did not reply.

'Because . . .' She took hold of his hand again and turned it so it was palm upwards. It was a large hand, and heavy, a true worker's hand, unlike other hands that had only recently touched her. 'I am not going to stand in your way, Gerald. If you're sure,' she went on. 'I won't stand in your way and I won't make things difficult. All I ask is that you stay in better contact with the girls, because they love you, and they need you too, and quite frankly it's time you came back and spent a bit of time in London and got to understand them. And their lives. Especially Harriet's.'

She placed his hand carefully down on the table and leant back.

Gerald smiled ruefully. 'God, it's little wonder a man buries himself in his work.'

Claudia watched him and said nothing.

'Why did you marry me, Gerald?' she asked, after a long moment.

'Why did I marry you? Why wouldn't I? Why wouldn't anyone? You were – perfect. Beautiful, sophisticated, poised, everything a man could ask for. I couldn't believe my luck as a matter of fact.'

'So,' she smiled, 'you married me because you thought you ought to?'

'Yes, in a way. Couldn't pass the opportunity up, you could say.'

'Gerald, you are such a romantic.' She toyed with her wedding ring.

'Yes, well. I was in awe of you. Terribly so. Afraid, even.'

'Afraid of me? Whatever for?'

'Because you were the most beautiful woman I'd ever met and I didn't know what to do with you. In any sense.'

'What do you mean?'

'The – sex. I really didn't . . .' He took a deep breath, like someone coming up for air. 'God Claudia, you know what I'm trying to say.'

'Do I?'

'You didn't like it, and I didn't know how to handle you not liking it. I didn't know if it was me or . . . I never did. It weighed on me, God how it weighed on me.'

'You never said.'

'What the hell was I supposed to say? Sorry.' He calmed down, but his fingers were drumming on the table now, so she clamped them with her hand and held it there.

'It's not the sort of thing a person discussed, in those days.' He smiled faintly. 'It wasn't proper, and we were extremely proper.'

'Was that the reason you went cold on me? Because I didn't like sex?'

'I didn't go cold on you, dear girl, we produced three beautiful children.'

'You know what I mean.'

'I did *not* go cold on you. I just put the whole sex thing out of my mind and got on with my work. And then Juliette came along and, well . . . ' He shrugged.

Claudia waited.

'She was right, of course, I did get a bit carried away. As I said, it's been a long time. Then she told me – it turns out there was someone else, all along. Fond and foolish, yes. You can say that again.'

He thought for a moment.

'Then who turns up but Perceveral Lightfoot! I mean I ask you, what kind of a name is that? Wouldn't a man want to change it, first opportunity? Out of the blue. Passing through, he said, though he didn't say where to. The ass.' He paused. 'Told me about you, not that I asked, but he told me anyway and I thought, Well, there we go, we've come full circle. It's where we should have been all those years ago. You and Dougie and me and . . . ' He waved a hand in the air. 'You're not saying anything.'

'No,' said Claudia.

'For the life of me I'll never understand why you chose me over Dougie.'

'Nobody does,' she said.

'Except you.' He looked straight at her, then away.

'Not even me, as a matter of fact. No, I tell a lie. I do know. It's because you are, above all else, a decent man. You are honest, and honourable, and accomplished, and terribly good at your job. And because beneath your ridiculously gruff exterior you are kind, even loving, though you try not to be. Don't interrupt. That's why I fell in love with you all those years ago, even though you were hopeless in bed.'

'I beg your pardon?'

'I'm not talking about your sexual prowess, I'm referring to your handling of women, if you'll excuse the expression.'

'Explain yourself, please!'

'Sometimes . . . ' She leant across the table and lowered her voice. 'A bit of sweet-talking is not a bad thing, Gerald. I know you hate it, and God knows you were always useless at it. Unlike Dougie, who is a master.'

'Thank you for reminding me.'

'All those years ago when you thought I didn't like it, the sex, you were right. But I could have been talked round, you see. Or perhaps that should be "coaxed". I was very, very green, as you know, I needed reassurance. Do you get me?'

'If you say so.'

'People – well, Prue – used to tell me it was fun, but I didn't think it was fun at all. I was more concerned with what the chambermaid might think when she came to make the bed in the morning.' She pulled a face. 'As if I were the first and only young woman who'd been ravished on her wedding night.' She smiled at him, fondly. 'I've spent most of my life worrying about that imaginary chambermaid, in one sense or another. Until recently.'

'Until recently.' He was gazing at her intensely now.

'Yes.'

There were things she was not going to tell him.

'That's it really,' she concluded. 'That's all I have to say. I'm going to go to bed now.'

She didn't move.

'Good idea,' said Gerald, but he didn't move either.

She yawned, and waited.

'May I,' he hesitated, 'come with you?'

'If you wish. If you think you could risk it.'

'I could have a go at the sweet-talk, if you think it would help.'

'That would be nice,' she said.

He stood up then, and as Claudia placed her napkin on the table and reached for her handbag he went to help her up from her chair.

'What else?' he asked, as she linked her arm through his and, nodding at the waiters, they exited the room together. 'You tell me and I'll do my best.'

'I'll think of something,' she said.

They walked slowly across the hotel foyer towards the lift.

'What about the chambermaid?'

She did not immediately answer. She pressed the bell for the lift, and as they stood there together waiting and watching the lift indicator descend to ground level, she said, 'To hell with the chambermaid.'

Acknowledgements

I owe huge thanks to Joan Deitch for her immaculate and incisive editing, and for her enthusiasm and encouragement.

§

If you enjoyed this book it would be delightful if you could post a review on the retail platform you bought it from. Thank you.

Author biography

Patsy Trench lives a quiet and largely respectable life in north London. Claudia's story shows a side of her normally shy and reserved nature that is little known, even to her friends and acquaintances. Her previous books, about her family's history in Australia, are informal yet informative accounts of that country's early colonial beginnings. In a previous life she was an actress, scriptwriter, playscout, founder of *The Children's Musical Theatre of London* and lyricist. When not writing books she emerges from her shell to teach theatre and organise theatre trips for overseas students. She is the grateful mother of two grown-up children and, as of 30 March 2021, a grandma.

Social media

Website: https://patsytrench.com/
Substack: https://substack.com/@patsytrenchauthor
Facebook:
    https://www.facebook.com/PatsyTrenchWriting
Twitter/X: Patsy Trench (@PatsyTrench) / X
Instagram:
    https://www.instagram.com/claudiafaraday1920